FIRE 1
WEST

Submarine WWII Series
Book Five

Charles Whiting
writing as
Leo Kessler

SAPERE
BOOKS

FIRE IN THE WEST

Published by Sapere Books.

24 Trafalgar Road, Ilkley, LS29 8HH

saperebooks.com

ISBN: 978-0-85495-139-0

PREFACE

On a hot July day in the summer of 1942, large incendiary balloons started to drift in from the Pacific over the western coast of the United States. Some continued to drift and vanished into the barren interior, never to be seen again. A few, however, burst on impact when they collided with the huge redwoods of Oregon. Here and there they caused the tinder-dry underbrush to burn and started isolated forest fires which were quickly put out by the forest rangers. Nothing was ever mentioned of these mysterious balloons till long after World War Two.

President Roosevelt acted wisely. For in that first summer of the war for the United States, the inhabitants of the west coast were in a state of panic. Daily they expected a 'Japanese invasion,' now that the Pacific was virtually a 'Jap lake'. It would not have helped public morale there to learn that it was the Japanese who had floated the balloons over the thousands of miles from their Pacific bases to take the war to the American homeland.

This rather amateurish balloon attack was the only recorded assault on the United States of America throughout World War Two. For four long years, from 1941 to 1945, America, or so it seemed, was safe from attack behind the two great oceans which protected it. *But was it the only assault ever made on the USA?*

Of course, there were rumours. One is even recorded in the official US history of the war, namely that in March 1945, all available ships were alerted in the North Atlantic to prevent a last-ditch, suicidal U-boat attack on the American eastern seaboard. But what form this attack was going to take is not recorded. The official historian in Washington deliberately played coy. *Why?*

Because he was writing when our present-day missile launching nuclear submarine was one of America's greatest secrets, still on the planners' drawing boards, fussed over by the 'father of the US nuclear submarine,' Admiral Rickover, like a broody old mother hen. The potential enemy, Soviet Russia, could not be given even the faintest clue to what was to come — and, *what had already happened, back in 1944*!

For on that Black Christmas, when the US Army in Europe was fighting desperately for its life in the Belgian Ardennes, in what became known as the 'Battle of the Bulge,' the German High Command — at the orders of Hitler himself — had decided to carry the war to the homeland of what they called 'the American air gangsters.' That Christmas, the German U-200, commanded by one of the Reich's greatest U-boat aces, *Kapitänleutnant* Christian Jungblut, was to assault no lesser a place than New York City itself!

Now, nearly half a century later, ex-Captain Christian Jungblut has broken his long, self-imposed silence to reveal the bizarre story of how, on that Christmas Eve so long ago, he attacked the great American city and came within a fraction of changing the history of World War Two. But the strangest irony of all in this tale from the war in shadows fought that winter is that the brave men who gave their lives to save the 'Big Apple' came from the same nation which two centuries before had launched the last attack on New York — *they were British*!

Leo Kessler, Wittlich, West Germany, Spring 1986

PRELUDE: A BEACON IS PLACED IN POSITION

'*Stop both!*' the U-boat commander whispered into the tube. Below, the throb of the diesels died away and the long black sub wallowed in the swell, the only sound the soft hiss of the night breeze and the slither of the dinghy being dragged across the wet deck.

The skipper focused his glasses. Next to him a sailor muffled in an ankle-length oilskin waited tensely, as if what the U-boat commander would say next was very important to him. Below the four saboteurs had lowered their dinghy into the swell and were beginning to load their equipment into it. Their boastful chatter of an hour ago had died away. Now they concentrated on their task in the grim, dogged silence, as if they had already realized they were condemned men.

The skipper lowered his binoculars slowly, although he knew just how exposed he was here, only two kilometres from the enemy coast, riding on the surface, an easy target for their Catalina flying boats. 'Long Island,' he announced. 'Amagansett Point!'

The four saboteurs looked up, faces pale blobs in the darkness, but the sailor in the ankle-length oilskin could sense their fear. He could almost smell it. He grinned maliciously to himself. Let 'em sweat, he told himself. They'd had a damned good time of it back in the Reich these last six months, playing around with invisible ink and explosives, filling their guts with booze, screwing the paid whores every night, while he'd been—

'Cast away dinghy!' The youthful skipper's command cut into his reverie. He tensed expectantly, ready to move immediately, his hard lean body flexed underneath the cover of the oilskin.

Below, the grizzled *Obermaat* in charge untied the final knot that held the bobbing dinghy to the side of the sub. 'Stick one in for me, comrades,' he whispered throatily. 'I've got so much ink in my fountain-pen, I don't know who to write to first,' he chuckled hoarsely.

There was no answering laugh from the four saboteurs; they were too scared. Like the dumb animals they were, they prepared for the slaughter to come. Their leader placed his paddle against the slick, dripping side of the submarine and pushed hard. The dinghy broke loose and started to bob up and down on the swell. The others began to paddle.

The young skipper licked his salt-caked lips and tugged hard at his battered white cap, the gold insignia long tarnished and turned green by the salt air. 'Give 'em five minutes?' he asked.

The man in the oilskin nodded and began fumbling with the buttons. 'Five minutes should about do it, *Herr Kapitänleutnant,*' he agreed. Now he had dropped the tone of deference which he had adopted for the long voyage across the Atlantic. Now there was authority in his voice.

The skipper bent his mouth to the conning tower's speaking tube once more. For a moment he hesitated, a sorely troubled man. But back in Kiel his orders from the 'Big Lion' had been specific. There was no turning back now, although he hated to do what he was going to do now. 'Gun crew,' he said, 'topside... *At the double!*'

Now the dinghy with the four saboteurs was beginning slowly to disappear into the soft grey mist which curled in around the coast, the sound of their paddles muffled and muted by the damp fog. The man in the oilskin ripped at his last button, nodding his approval, as if he welcomed the sudden mist.

A clatter of heavy, nailed sea-boots and the first of the gunners started to push his way by him and clamber down the ladder attached to the side of the conning tower. Already the Dönitzgrizzled *Obermaat*, who had cast off the dinghy, was waiting by the deck gun.

Swiftly, expertly, the man in the oilskin slipped into the heavy diving gear, telling himself as he did so that he would use pure oxygen on this one. But he'd have to be careful with the depth. If he went below six metres, he'd chance oxygen poisoning; the usual twitching of the extremities, the feeling of apprehension and vertigo — and hallucinations. And on this particular winter's night hallucinations were the last thing he needed.

'Stand to!' the *Obermaat* snapped softly below and reported in the prescribed fashion to the tall skinny submarine commander standing on the conning tower. 'Gun party fallen in, sir... All present and correct!'

'Thank you, Hansen,' the commander answered. 'All right, load a star shell.'

'Star shell it is, sir,' the *Obermaat* replied dutifully, though he must have been as puzzled as the rest of the gun crew. What in three devils' names, he must be asking himself, were they doing loading a star shell a couple of kilometres off the Yankee coast? The man in the oilskin grinned softly. Let him wonder, he told himself. Let them all wonder. He would be safer that way. He picked up his heavy bundle, wrapped in an oilskin, and dropped it over the side of the conning tower on to the deck. With a grunt he tugged on his flippers.

The U-boat skipper watched him, his face a mixture of bewilderment and distaste. The man in the oilskin ignored the

U-boat skipper's look. What concern was the morality of the whole business to him? He had his orders from the Führer personally. Ever since the Yankee air gangsters had commenced their terror bombing of the Reich, morality had been thrown out of the window. Soon, if *his* mission succeeded, the Americans would get a taste of their own rotten medicine. His harshly handsome face cracked into a wintry smile at the thought. What a surprise it would be for those fat complacent Jewish cats over there beyond the horizon, so sure that nothing could happen to them, five thousand kilometres away from the battlefront!

'Ready?' the skipper queried.

He tapped the oxygen bottles strapped to his back and rasped, 'Ready, *Kapitänleutnant.*'

The young skipper hesitated. He held out his hand and then thought better of it. Instead he said, 'Good luck... *Hals und Beinbruch.*'

'*Danke,*' the man in the oilskin answered, oblivious to the withdrawn hand.

'Have a safe voyage back to the Homeland.'

'Thank you,' the U-boat skipper replied tonelessly. The man in the oilskin could see that the naval officer would be glad to be rid of him.

'Give me,' he looked at the green-glowing dial of his wristwatch, 'till exactly zero two hundred hours and then you can —' He left the rest of his sentence unfinished. The U-boat skipper knew what he had to do. Why waste precious time? Awkwardly he began to clamber down the conning tower ladder, the unhappy skipper virtually forgotten already, as he concentrated on what was to come. He picked up his bundle and dropped it over the side, but still hanging on to the rope which was attached to it.

The crew mustered at the 88mm cannon stared at him in numb bewilderment. He knew what they were thinking. Why the four saboteurs and then this strange chap, disguised as one of the crew for the whole long voyage across? Why was he going in separately and unknown to the other four, somewhere out in the fog bank around the coast? What was going on out here this dark winter's night?

Again the diver's face cracked into a hard grin. Probably they would have slapped him on the back as a hero or given him three rousing cheers if they had known. But if the great surprise to come were to be achieved there had to be absolute secrecy.

'Stand by to fire, *Obermaat*!' the skipper above rapped.

'Stand by number one!' the petty officer barked and clapped his horny old hand down hard on the aimer's shoulder. The man tensed and pressed his right eye against the rubber suction pad of the sight.

The man in the oilskin thrust the tube into his mouth and took a deep breath. Quite calmly he counted to three. Next to him that long menacing barrel pointed towards the coast, the gunners immobile, as if they had been frozen into the firing position for all eternity. He took one last look at them and wondered when he would see Germans again, and then quite deliberately he allowed himself to fall backwards over the side of the submarine into the water. Next moment he had begun to swim, trailing his bundle behind him, like some sinister human shark seeking his prey.

Kapitänleutnant von Cramm watched him go, a little flurry of white water marking his passing, a few pearly bubbles from the air trapped in the man's suit exploding on the surface, and then he was gone, disappeared into the grey gloom. Von Cramm flashed a look at the dial of his watch. Nearly time. He raised his right arm and ordered '*Feuer frei!*'

The *Obermaat* tensed. This was it!

The skipper looked at his watch again. Exactly zero two hundred. He let his arm fall.

'*Feuer!*' the *Obermaat* yelled.

A sharp crack. A hollow boom. The whiplash of explosive dust. Automatically the skipper on the tower opened his mouth to prevent his eardrums from bursting. The shell shrieked towards the shore. Mentally the skipper counted off the seconds. A sudden tearing noise and, in a burst of blinding white flame, the shell exploded. In an instant, all was thrown into glowing harsh white-and-black relief. The smudge of coastline, the squat outline of Amagansett coastguard station, the bobbing dinghy, the dark figures paddling no more, just squatting there in petrified amazement staring at that glowing white light which had betrayed them.

A searchlight clicked on with startling suddenness. There was the harsh metallic crackle of a loud-hailer, followed an instant later by the slow rattle of a machine-gun like the chatter of an irate woodpecker. Glowing golf balls of angry light started to stream out to sea. Tracer! A sudden roar. Motorboat engines burst into pulsating life — and still the four saboteurs sat there in absolute, total bewilderment…

'*A… L… LARM!*' the skipper shrieked with frantic urgency, as the first motorboat curved into the bay, an angry white bone at its teeth.

The siren shrilled. The gun crew slid down the dripping ladder to collapse in a wet, confused heap on the deck below. The skipper took one last look at the men he had betrayed and then he, too, was sliding frantically down the ladder, as the hatch closed and U-202 crash-dived…

Ten minutes later the four saboteurs raised their hands gingerly in surrender as the patrol boat came to a halt in a wild sweep of water which set their frail craft bobbing and ducking crazily. Next instant the spotlight clicked on and blinded them, the harsh voice from the bridge crying, 'Okay, you jerks, I want you to keep just like that, with your mitts frozen in the air...! Gunner's mate, keep 'em covered. Plug the first one of the Kraut bastards that makes a wrong move!'

'Ay, ay, sir,' the gunner answered gleefully, as the boathooks began to reach out to drag the dinghy aboard the patrol vessel. 'I ain't shot me no kraut so far, sir. An' I've had an itchy trigger finger ever since Pearl Harbor.'

Five hundred metres away, protected by the surrounding darkness, the lone swimmer surfaced. He removed the tube from his mouth, breathed in the cold damp sea air gratefully, treading water easily. Intently he stared at the little scene taking place in that circle of hard white glowing light; the jubilant Yankee coastguards, the scared apprehensive would-be saboteurs waiting to be taken aboard, the bobbing little grey coastguard boat with its two guns trained on the Germans.

Slowly his harsh face relaxed a little. For now he knew he was safe — at least for the time being. He could make land without difficulty. The coastguards would be too busy with their captives to worry about the possibility of a second attempt at infiltration this cold November night. The decoy plan worked out so carefully in the Reich had succeeded. What had the Big Lion snapped? 'You can't make an omelette without cracking eggs!' the admiral had barked, in that curt unfeeling manner of his, his bitter tight mouth working as if on steel springs, 'Someone has to be sacrificed. Even if they die, they do so for Folk, Fatherland and Führer. *Heil Hitler!*'

Now those four unhappy Germans clambering into the Yankee patrol boat would surely die. It would be the electric chair for them, undoubtedly.

The lone swimmer's grin changed into a look of utter contempt, for he was a man who did not understand human weaknesses or fear. 'So long, *suckers*!' he called out softly in that perfect Bronx accent of his. Then he was gone, swimming effortlessly and purposefully for the American shore and the task ahead…

BOOK ONE: A MISSION IS PROPOSED

CHAPTER 1

Kapitänleutnant Christian Jungblut ran his fingers through his cropped blond hair, fiddled with the gleaming medal of the Knight's Cross at his throat, and then gazed in bored frustration through the tall window of the court at the grey expanse of Kiel's dockland. Next to him, the president of the court-martial, a bluff cruiser captain with a ruddy sea-going face, looked decidedly embarrassed by the whole business; while at his side, the ensign from the E-boats, with that pasty sick face they all had from the constant buffeting of their stomachs at sea, stared fixedly at his papers, as if he were trying to ignore the trial.

But if the panel was bored, embarrassed, and indifferent, *Marinerichter* Dr Hans Pfeiffer was decidedly interested. Licking those thick red sensualist lips of his yet again, he peered hard through his pince-nez and barked, 'Accused, you must realize that this is a very serious charge, contrary to paragraph 175 of the Civilian Code of Law and paragraph 50 of the Naval Legal Code.' He stared threateningly at the poor little frightened female naval auxiliary. 'There is also the ethical side to be considered, too. Hasn't our beloved Führer Adolf Hitler decreed that the act of sexual intercourse is to take place solely for the furtherance of the German race?' The judge looked at the dingy ceiling, as if he half-expected the Führer to be floating up there, staring down at him benevolently.

Christian Jungblut groaned, while the other accused, the fat gross corporal cook, with a suspicion of a moustache, looking with her enormous breasts like a tethered barrage balloon, chuckled. But the poor little 'grey mouse' clinging to the dock as if her frail little body might be blown away at any moment, quailed, face ashen with fear.

Marinerichter Dr Pfeiffer licked his bright red lips yet once again. Christian, bored as he was, could see he was really enjoying this. 'Now, Accused,' he continued, 'I am going to ask you a few simple questions and I want — no, *I demand*' — he raised his right forefinger dramatically — 'simple answers. *Verstanden?*'

The skinny young 'grey mouse' nodded urgently.

'So let us begin. When did this disgraceful business really start?'

The grey mouse flashed a look of appeal at the corporal cook, but the latter just shrugged carelessly, her breasts rippling like puddings under her blouse. She knew already what was going to happen to them. They would be sentenced to a military prison and then they would be offered the chance of serving their sentence or being sent to the front. She, for her part, would elect to stay in prison. There would be plenty of her kind in there and she'd survive the war that way. The pompous prick of a navy judge was really doing her a favour, though he didn't know it.

'We were sitting in the barracks one afternoon,' the accused began hesitantly.

'Speak up!' Pfeiffer barked.

'And she said that I had nice — er — legs.'

Christian groaned to himself. What in three devils' names was he doing here, a U-boat commander, listening to the sordid little love affair of two lesbians? '*What are you doing here, shipmate?*' a little voice at the back of his mind sneered. '*I'll tell yer. It's 'cos you're on the shore, mate, 'cos you ain't got a ship. At this particular moment, you're lower than a whale's arse!*'

'Did she play with you, love you, fondle you in any way?' Pfeiffer was demanding, little beads of sweat now glazing his high forehead, eyes sparkling behind the pince-nez. 'Come on now, what did she want to do with you?'

The fat corporal cook raised one massive haunch and farted contemptuously.

The naval judge pretended not to notice. His whole attention was now concentrated on the poor miserable little grey mouse. Cynically Christian told himself the man was going to have an orgasm any moment now.

The accused lowered her gaze demurely, 'She pulled up my skirt, sir —'

'— *Then what?*' Pfeiffer rapped hoarsely, as if he were suddenly very short of breath.

'She started kissing me and then she took off me — me knickers,' the accused gulped and Christian thought she might burst into tears soon.

But Pfeiffer showed no mercy. 'Then what did she do to you… after she had taken off your — er — *knickers?*' he asked, face flushed with excitement.

'My privates, she touched my privates,' the grey mouse whispered miserably.

'*Great crap on the Christmas tree!*' the president blurted out and slapped his hand to his forehead like a man sorely tried. 'How much —'

'— With her finger?' Pfeiffer gulped, head twisted to one side, as if he were being strangled, face flushed a brick red, eyes glittering. 'Your privates, did she touch them only … *with her finger?*'

The grey mouse shook her head.

'What with, then?' Pfeiffer's voice was choked with barely suppressed excitement. A dark blue vein was ticking frighteningly at his temple, as if he might have a stroke.

In spite of his boredom, Christian grinned. This encounter with the poor little lesbian was probably the high point of his sexual experience. He'd be talking about it in an awed whisper to his cronies of his local inn for years to come.

'Come on, woman, out with it!' Pfeiffer demanded, hands shaking as he pointed a menacing forefinger at the grey mouse, 'or it will be the worse for you. With what else did she touch you?'

'She started kissing my privates, sir,' the accused blurted out suddenly. 'Is that what you want?'

Marinerichter Dr Pfeiffer's mouth dropped open incredulously. 'I beg your pardon,' he stuttered, while the big cook tittered. 'Do you mean to say that … the other accused — inserted her tongue into your privates?'

'Yessir,' and in that instant as the first dread wail of the air raid sirens began to drift across Kiel from the east, the little grey mouse added with a show of sudden defiance. 'And I liked it as well. *So there*!'

The fat cook raised her massive haunch once again and farted in triumph.

Now all was controlled confusion. High above Kiel the sky filled with ugly red and black smears as the gargantuan rumble of massed engines came closer and closer. Down below, helmeted wardens rushed back and forth, shrilling on their whistles, whirling their rattles furiously. Dispatch riders hurtled to and fro, skidding round corners in a screech of protesting rubber. Fire engines, sirens shrieking, rushed to take up their positions. For now the terror gangsters were almost there.

'*Port!*' the president of the court yelled above the thunder of the flak, the staccato crack and snap of the shells. 'There they are — *the Amis!*'

Christian shielded his eyes against the glare of the exploding shells, which had transformed the grey sky into a sea of dazzling motes. A great silver arrow, trailing brilliant white vapour behind it, was ploughing its way towards them majestically, as if that lethal storm of sudden death concerned it not one little bit. 'Flying Fortresses, Captain,' he exclaimed. '*Himmelherrje*, there must be hundreds of them — and not one single German fighter in sight,' he added bitterly.

The captain shrugged his shoulders expressively. 'This is 1944, young man. The great days are over. We have to face up to reality and realize —' He stopped short. The bomb doors of the leading wing had opened as one. Almost immediately, the sky seemed to fill with a silver shower of bombs, which heralded their approach with an awesome keening. 'HE and incendiary — *mixed!*' the captain yelled through cupped hands. 'They're going to try for a fire storm. Come on, young man, I think we'll have to go into the cellar with Doctor Pfeiffer and his damned lesbians. *Los*, let's make a run for it!'

Next instant the two of them were running across the barrack square for their very lives, as that cyclone of death descended upon Kiel; and as he ran, Christian Jungblut was animated, not only by overwhelming fear of what was soon going to happen, but also by burning rage and hatred. Could nothing be done to make those damned Ami air gangsters pay for what they were doing to Germany's ruined cities? When would they be able to strike back at the murdering Yankee swine? *When…?*ö

On that same November afternoon that the Americans reduced Kiel to ashes and *Kapitänleutnant* Christian Jungblut wished fervently that there might be some means of striking back at the '*Ami* air gangsters', Admiral Karl Dönitz finally received the signal for which he had been waiting so long.

On the face of it, the decoded message from the other side of the North Atlantic seemed of little importance. But on that grey afternoon at Mürwik, staring down at the three-word message, Dönitz, known to his U-boat crews as 'Big Lion,' felt the same sort of thrill he had experienced in the great days when his wolf packs had signalled the sinking of hundreds of thousands of tons of enemy shipping.

'BEACON IN POSITION'

Silently he read the three words over to himself once more, his hatchet face set and tense, his pale blue eyes glittering fervently.

'*Beacon in position.*'

His personal adjutant, tall, elegant and sleek, waited. He knew only a little of the great secret, in spite of his position; but he did know that the Big Lion must now have reached some decisive stage in the top secret planning which had been going on these last weeks, ever since he had been summoned to meet the Führer so urgently back in September. Then, when all had seemed lost, with the enemy armies pressing hard on both Germany's frontiers, the Big Lion had returned to Mrwik with the light of new hope in his eyes. Why, his very first words had been a triumphant, 'We will achieve final victory after all, Neurath...! The Führer, in his infinite wisdom, has decided on one great decisive stroke which will send the western allies reeling. And we of the *Kriegsmarine* must do our utmost to help.'

Now Neurath waited expectantly for the Big Lion's next move. But apparently his chief was not his usual dynamic self, always in a hurry, always a bundle of thrusting, urgent energy. Instead of snapping out a series of orders, as was his custom, he remarked in an almost conversational tone, '*Kapitänleutnant* Jungblut is on the beach, I believe, Neurath?'

'*Jawohl, Herr Grossadmiral*,' Neurath snapped, knowing that the Big Lion savoured his title of 'Grand Admiral.' 'Since his last boat was sunk in September, you have not given him another command.'

Dönitz nodded. 'And do you know why?'

Neurath shook his head.

'Because I do not altogether trust Herr Jungblut, that is why,' the Big Lion answered his own question, puffing out his skinny cheeks thoughtfully. 'Admittedly he is one of my few remaining aces — he has been in this business since the sinking of the *Royal Oak* back in 'thirty-nine. He is brave enough. That he has proved often enough in the past. But has he got sufficient National Socialist fervour, that elemental drive which can overcome mountains? For the mission I have in mind, I must have a skipper who is one hundred per cent committed to our holy National Socialist cause. Is *Kapitänleutnant* Jungblut that man?' The Big Lion stared up at Neurath almost angrily.

The suave, elegant aide moved back a pace, as if physically struck by the force of those cold, pale, fanatical eyes. '*Herr Grossadmiral*, if I may be so bold —'

'— Please be so bold, Neurath.'

'Well, sir, *Herr Kapitänleutnant* Jungblut is the last of our old hares. The rest have vanished. What we have left is a bunch of greenbeaks. I don't think one could safely entrust any vital mission to one of them and hope for success…' His voice trailed away to nothing, for he saw that the Big Lion was no longer listening. His eyes were set on some distant horizon known only to himself. *Grossadmiral* Dönitz was listening to those inner voices of his once more. Neurath waited.

Finally the Big Lion made his decision. 'You are right, Jungblut is the only U-boat skipper we have left capable of carrying out the mission I have in mind for him…' Dönitz hesitated momentarily and Neurath, looking down at that pale cruel face, could almost sense his brain working. 'But I do not know if we can trust him one hundred per cent, Neurath.' Dönitz's voice was suddenly very urgent. 'I want an officer to accompany Herr Jungblut — an officer, who in a moment of failure could —' Instead of completing his sentence he made a gesture with his claw of a hand as if he were pulling a trigger.

Neurath paled. The Big Lion was planning a murder…

CHAPTER 2

Christian shook his head — and wished next moment he hadn't. A skewer of burning hot pain bored its agonizing way into the back of his skull. Slowly he repeated the movement and things swung into focus once more. In their full devastating horror…

Marinerichter Dr Pfeiffer lay sprawled out in the smoking debris of the air-raid shelter, scarlet blood jetting out of the shattered glass of his pince-nez. Christian had seen enough men killed in action in these last terrible five years to know there was no hope for the judge; he was either dead already or would be in that state very soon. He staggered across the room, with smoke pouring in through the great jagged hole in the roof, to where the two accused women fearfully clasped each other. '*Los!*' he commanded thickly, 'we've got to get out of here — *quick*! There's fire somewhere.' He tugged at the grey mouse's arm urgently and she toppled forward. He gasped. The back of her head was missing! It was as if someone had thrown a handful of strawberry jam at her head.

He peered down at the fat one. But her days of seducing lonely little eighteen-year-olds were over. She was dead, too. A great gleaming silver wedge of shrapnel had penetrated to her heart. Blindly he let her fall back against the shattered wall.

Numbly Christian staggered over the bodies of the other members of the tribunal, and reeled outside, already feeling tremendous heat buffeting his face, his ears assailed by the frenzied screaming of those in the street. It was a kind that he had never experienced before. In spite of the heat, he shivered violently.

A woman ran by him, completely naked, her hair on fire, screaming, screaming, screaming. Another woman lay in the gutter, a dead baby beside her, writhing in agony as the flames consumed her. 'Phosphorus!' she gasped weakly, looking up at him with dying eyes. She saw the pistol at his belt and whispered, 'Shoot me ... shoot me, *please*!'

Christian fled.

Now those who had been hit by the phosphorus pellets that the enemy incendiaries carried were fighting and screaming, jostling and tearing at each other frantically to find a place in the water of the fjord. Behind them more and more of these hapless souls, shrieking and trailing smoke, dashed madly for the saving water. As the terrible, flesh-consuming flames mounted steadily higher, men, women and children ran hysterically, stumbling and falling, rolling over and staggering on, knowing that only the water could save them. The water cut off the oxygen the phosphorus needed in order to burn.

Sickened and revolted, a helpless, impotent Christian watched the victims with phosphorus on the face and head thrash wildly in the water, screaming in absolute agony and madness. For there was no way out for them. They met a slow and pain-wracked death as, choking and spluttering, unable to keep their burning faces long enough under the water to put out the flames, they alternately burned alive and drowned. Unable to watch any longer, Christian turned and blundered blindly through the burning streets, as the great fire storm thundered to its orgiastic climax, the houses on both sides shuddering like stage backdrops, with occasionally a wall sliding down in a cascade of bricks and stones.

Blindly he struggled on and on as the world all around him fell apart. '*Why does God allow all this?*' a woman wailed piteously, surveying the flaming ruin of what had been once her home.

'It is nothing to do with God,' the old man next to her growled. 'This is man's work…'

On and on, not knowing where he was wandering. Motivated solely by the desire to get away from this crazy doomed place where dead women clasped dead children, untouched by flame or shrapnel, but killed by heat prostration and fused together for eternity. A team of horses, wild-eyed and terrified, their manes on fire, dragging a cart with a headless driver on the seat. Naked babies blown into a skeletal tree, trapped in the black branches like grotesque white fruit. Charred pygmies that had once been men, the skin burst everywhere by the effort of contraction, oozing a purple juice like the syrup of an overripe fig. Heat radiation sucking away the lives of the trapped victims, mindless now and unmoving, their eyes bulging and bulging until they finally burst out of the sockets. *Horror upon horror…*

In a state of demented despair from this horror, Christian was abruptly confronted by the trapped American. He hung there from the guttering of a smouldering building, his shroud-lines trapped in the shattered roof. His face was black with dirt and so covered with grease that he appeared to be sweating profusely as he writhed and twisted in his attempt to free himself before the building burst into flames. One of his legs had been ripped to shreds.

His struggles ceased suddenly as he glimpsed the hard-faced naval officer below, his skinny chest covered with decorations for bravery. For what seemed an age the two young men stared at each other. There was no fear on the American flier's face, just a calculated awareness of how close he was to death. If the flames didn't get him, the Kraut would. Christian could read his every thought, as if the *Ami* had spoken them out loud.

'Well, what are ya gonna do?' the American broke the heavy brooding silence. 'Are ya gonna let me fry up here? Then you might as well shoot me here and now and put me out of my misery. My leg is sure all shot to hell an' all. If you're not, then, fella, see if you can cut me down.'

Christian didn't answer. His mind was in a turmoil. He thought of the skinny grey mouse with the back of her head staved in, the wretched victims of the phosphorus, their hair burning above the surface of the water even as they drowned, the dead mother and her baby... *He* had been through Hell and *survived*. Surely he had a duty — a debt — to pay to those who had perished so horribly?

He stared up at the *Ami*. The American stared back boldly, almost as if challenging him. There was no sound now, save the crackle of flames, the muted cries of the dying, the soft drip-drip of the blood from the flier's shattered leg. Christian's rage increased. If he let the *Ami* go, it would be the cage for him, nice and comfortable, where he would get fat on Red Cross parcels, do correspondence courses, take part in amateur theatricals — *and survive*! Then the damned Yankee swine would never pay for what he had helped to do this grey November day in 1944. He would return to his fat, rich country to forget what he had done to Europe and live to die — *in bed*!

Slowly, very slowly, not taking his eyes off the trapped *Ami* for one moment, Christian reached down for his pistol holster. The American watched him fascinated. With nerveless fingers, Christian fumbled with the catch and pulled out his pistol. The American's eyes flashed alarm for a fleeting second; then his blackened face again showed no emotion.

For an instant, Christian recognized his courage. Trapped and badly wounded, the *Ami* knew there was no hope for him, but he would not break down and plead for mercy. He was accepting his fate bravely, without a murmur.

Christian clicked off the 'safety' and raised the little service pistol. Somewhere behind him there was the sound of a racing engine, but the young U-boat commander did not seem to notice. Slowly, seeing himself carry out the action from afar, almost as if he were part of a dream, he raised the pistol. The *Ami's* face filled the sight. Carefully he began to take first pressure. Up above, the dangling flier saw the whitening of the young German officer's knuckles and knew that the end was near. He swallowed hard, his Adam's apple racing up and down his skinny neck. But it was the only sign that any kind of emotion — fear, anger, remorse, whatever — animated him. It seemed as if he had accepted the inevitable.

There was the screech of protesting rubber, as if a car were taking a corner at high speed. Christian did not appear to notice. His whole being was concentrated on the *Ami* up there, who he was now going to kill in cold blood. He would be the scapegoat for all those arrogant young men who hailed death on harmless civilians from their great silver birds at ten thousand metres, totally unaware of the horror they wrought.

Tyres screeched to a halt. The mesmerized American took his eyes off his murderer for the first time. Christian's gaze, however, did not waver. '*One*!' he whispered to himself, feeling himself consumed by a blood-red blinding rage now at the thought of all those who had been slaughtered by the Americans this day. '*Two*!'

'*Kapitänleutnant* Jungblut!' a well-remembered voice cut into his blinding rage. '*Kapitänleutnant* — N-E-I-N!'

Christian started, wavered, but he still kept his finger pressed on the trigger of his pistol.

There was a knock on the jeep. 'Sir,' that familiar voice pleaded urgently, 'don't do it… Sir, it would be cold-blooded murder!'

Christian shook his head, as if attempting to waken from a heavy sleep.

'Sir, it's me, Frenssen, sir… *Obermaat* Frenssen!' The voice had nearly reached breaking point now.

Slowly, very slowly, Christian began to turn his head. Above him, the American gasped. He let his own head drop, as if someone had opened an invisible tap and all courage had abruptly drained out of him.

It was Frenssen all right, sitting behind the wheel of the Volkswagen jeep, helmet perched on his shaven skull like a child's toy, brick-red face full of concern as he gazed at the little scene. He clambered out and strode over to the officer with whom he had sailed into action ever since 1939. Towering above Christian, he saluted with unusual formality for him and said softly, 'Sir, I think we'd better cut the *Ami* down. He's bleeding to death.'

Christian hesitated as his rage still flickered.

Frenssen saw the struggle that was going on within his old commander and said urgently, 'Sir, were we any better in the old days? When we sank all those old Tommy tubs? Did you think we gave them Tommy seamen much of a chance? Sure, we allowed them to get to their boats, before we slipped the last tin fish up the old tub's arse, but did we care what happened to them afterwards? *No!*' he snorted with forced indignation, 'course, we frigging well didn't! Whether they snuffed it or not *then* didn't matter one frigging little bit, did it?… *Did it, sir*?' Frenssen's voice bored into the numb young officer.

Christian nodded. Slowly he lowered the pistol. Above them the American flier sighed softly. He knew he was saved.

'Right then, sir,' Frenssen said, voice full of relief. 'Let's get that *Ami* shitehawk down before he goes and dies on us — with that leg of his. Too many poor sods have snuffed it already today. Come on, sir, gimme a hand…'

It was only after they had fought their way through the pathetic mob of wounded civilians who besieged the Kiel Naval Hospital, pleading, begging for assistance, and delivered their prisoner to the medics that Frenssen remembered the reason for his hasty journey from Mürwik.

He said to Christian, slumped in the other seat, obviously drained of energy, eyeing the refugees streaming out of a shattered Kiel, dragging their pathetic bits and pieces with them on anything which had wheels, 'Message from the Big Lion hissen, sir.'

'A boat?' Christian queried, a new light of hope dawning in his bloodshot eyes. 'Are they taking us off the bloody beach at long last?' Even the rigours of a patrol in the North Atlantic seemed attractive after what he had seen this day. He knew he couldn't stand this terrible bombing of Germany's cities and their defenceless men, women and children much longer. He'd go crazy like he had done this afternoon with the *Ami* flier. 'Come on, you big horned ox, *spit it out*!'

Frenssen changed down hastily and swung round the heap of what looked like charred legs in the middle of the debris-littered road. Christian looked away hurriedly. They were a pile of children's bodies, fused together by the tremendous heat of the fire storm.

'I don't know about that, sir,' he said, not looking at the dead bodies. 'All I know is what the Big Lion's adjutant — Neurath—'

'— *Kapitänleutnant* Neurath to you, remember,' Christian warned, trying to forget what he had just seen.

'*Kapitänleutnant*-frigging-Neurath then,' Frenssen growled and put his big foot down on the accelerator, in a hurry to get away from this place of death. 'Do you know he uses Chanel and wears frilly silk knickers —'

'— Get on with it!' Christian snarled.

'Well, sir, the dear delightful *Kapitänleutnant* ordered me to take you to Goslar —'

'— But that's in the Harz mountains, damnit,' Christian exclaimed, the dying city suddenly forgotten. 'What in three devils' names is a sailor supposed to do in the Harz mountains?'

'Search me, sir,' Frenssen answered. 'All I know is, sir, that we are supposed to meet *Obersturmbannführer* Skorzeny there at the Three Moors Hotel — *Obersturmbannführer* Otto Skorzeny,' he emphasised the Christian name significantly.

Christian whistled softly, catching Frenssen's eye in the driving mirror. 'You mean *that* Skorzeny?' he said, a little shaken.

'Exactly *that* Skorzeny,' Frenssen echoed.

Christian slumped back in the hard seat of the Volkswagen, suddenly deflated. What had he, a mere U-boat commander, to do with Germany's foremost commando? *What indeed?*

Next to him, now they had finally cleared the outskirts of the great port, Frenssen put his foot down hard on the accelerator, while at his side Christian Jungblut seemed lost in thought. His brain was racing at the prospects this strange meeting in the remote mountains might open for him. But already he knew one thing. Whatever Skorzeny offered him, if that was what the meeting was for, then he'd grab it with both hands. Even if it were a date with the devil himself, he'd accept it. Anything to get back to sea and away from a dying Third Reich…

CHAPTER 3

Now the rickety old Volkswagen jeep was labouring up the steep winding road in third gear, its air-cooled engine so loud that conversation was virtually impossible. Not that Christian minded. His brain was too full of other things.

Their progress across the flat North German plain from Kiel had been very slow. In spite of the danger from Allied bombers, there were long columns of vehicles and troops everywhere, with officious road marshals, mostly field-grade officers, backed up by squads of 'chain dogs' carrying sub-machine-guns, clearing the roads to let them through. There were infantry packed into open trucks; ponderous slow convoys of tank transports laden with brand-new Tigers and Panthers straight from the factories; column after column of artillery, mostly drawn by horses. It had been no better in the small towns through which they had passed on their long journey. The railway sidings were packed with troops and tanks, and time and time again they had been forced to halt at railway crossings to allow long heavy trains of ammunition and equipment to rumble by.

Even an undemonstrative man such as *Obermaat* Frenssen, who always claimed he had seen everything — 'and then some' — had been impressed. 'Holy strawsack!' he had exclaimed once, after a train-load of brand-new 88mm cannon had rumbled past ponderously, the passenger coaches packed with bright-faced eighteen-year-olds straight from the depot, 'where the fuck are we getting it all from, sir? I haven't seen so much equipment since we marched into France in 'forty. I thought those soldier boys of ours were about finished?' He had pushed his helmet to the back of his big head and scratched his shaven skull with a hand like a small steam shovel in bewilderment.

An equally puzzled Christian had nodded his agreement and had breathed, almost as if he were talking to himself, 'Perhaps it's not a question of where they come from, but where they are *going*, Frenssen?'

But when the *Obermaat* had queried, 'How was that, sir?', Christian had remained obstinately silent, as if he had not heard the question.

Now the trains and convoys had been left behind as they advanced deeper into the remote countryside, where the half-timbered villages seemed empty and the ski resorts that had provided the region with its main source of income before the war had an air of run-down failure about them. Here the war seemed as remote as the moon. Again Christian wondered why they had been ordered here. What could this seemingly deserted place have to do with the U-boat service?

The air was becoming appreciably colder as they climbed higher and higher. Here and there were patches of new snow among the firs which lined both sides of the winding road and covered the steep slopes like ranks of spike-helmeted Prussian guardsmen.

Happily Christian took a deep breath of the icy air and exclaimed, 'Get a snoutful of that air, Frenssen. After the smoke and dust and the stink of explosives in the cities, it's like wine!' He breathed in again, sucking in the air gratefully. 'Great God, I'd forgotten what good clean air damn well smelled like!'

Frenssen was unimpressed. Expertly he whipped a large opaque dew-drop from the end of his big nose and out of the open window, and grunted. 'Gimme the big smoke any day, sir. Bombs or no bombs, the women are randier when there's a bit o' danger about.' His eyes sparkled suddenly. 'D'yer know, sir, ever since the *Amis* have been dropping their square eggs on Kiel, there ain't been a night when I haven't dipped my wick in the old honeypot at least twice? When them sirens go' — he wiped a pig paw across his mouth, licking his lips in memory of the pleasures of the last week — 'the women just about tear the pants of'n a poor ole sailor man. That's all they can think about then — *the two-backed beast and the mattress polka!*'

Christian grinned. Frenssen was running true to form. 'Can't you think of anything else but the — er — honeypot, *Obermaat?*'

Frenssen shot him a hard look in the driving mirror. 'The way we live now, sir, what else is there to think —' He stopped abruptly and hit the brakes hard.

Hastily Christian grabbed for support, as the Volkswagen jeep slithered to a stop, with Frenssen fighting the wheel desperately to prevent the little vehicle from skidding over into the deep drainage ditch at the left side of the road. 'What in three devils' —' he began and then he saw the reason for Frenssen's abrupt action.

Five burly figures in field grey had suddenly appeared from the trees, their bodies hung with stick grenades and extra ammunition, and all of them pointing their weapons directly at the wildly swaying jeep. And there was no doubt about it, they wouldn't hesitate one moment in using them.

Angrily Christian raised himself above the windscreen of the open jeep. 'What the hell do you mean just jumping out on us like that?' he cried. 'You could have got us all killed, man!' The scar-faced *Oberscharführer* in charge of the little group of SS men was not impressed. Almost casually, he came to attention and raised his gloved hand to his helmet. 'Restricted area, *Herr Kapitänleutnant,*' he said by way of explanation. 'Have to be very careful about who comes in — and who goes out,' he added darkly. Only later would Christian become aware of the significance of those last words, but at this moment he was too angry to note them. He stared back at the SS man's evil face and barked, 'Damn you, we have full passes to enter this area, signed by *Grossadmiral* Dönitz himself. Besides what's the fuss? Who in his right mind would want to penetrate this arsehole of the world?'

The SS *Scharführer* did not seem to hear. With barely concealed contempt, he said, 'Would the *Herr Kapitänleutnant* do me the great favour of allowing me to see his pass and that of his chappie, *bitteschön*?'

Frenssen's broad face flushed scarlet at that 'chappie'. He clenched his right fist threateningly and growled through gritted teeth. 'Matey, you're about to lose a set o' teeth in zero-comma-nothing-seconds, if you're not careful.' He half rose in the seat as if to fling himself at the SS man to carry out that terrible threat. Hastily Christian forced him down in his seat again and handed over both their passes to the waiting NCO, while the others grouped themselves to rear and front of the Volkswagen, their Schmeissers cocked, ready, and aimed.

Carefully, very carefully, the NCO examined the papers, checking the photographs with their faces, holding up the paper to inspect the Navy watermark and finally comparing Dönitz's brittle, scrawled signature with a copy he had obviously obtained somewhere or other.

Finally he was satisfied. Ungraciously he handed the passes back to Christian and grunted, 'There's been a change in plan, *Herr Kapitänleutnant.*'

'*A change in plan?*' Christian echoed.

'*Jawohl*, you're not to go to Goslar after all. *Obersturmbannführer* Skorzeny is to meet you here.' He whipped a map out of his sleeve like a magician producing a rabbit out of a top-hat to the surprise of a bunch of snotty-nosed children. 'I've marked the grid reference for you. I don't suppose it'll be too hard for you to find, even though you do belong to the Navy.' He grinned at Christian in his scar-faced evil way.

Now it was Christian's turn to flush angrily. 'What in heaven's name is going on?' he demanded angrily. 'What's all this damned secrecy? Security checks on country roads! Changes of plans!' He shot an angry look at the grid reference. 'Meetings in the middle of goddamn nowhere! *What's the goddamn game*?'

The big *Scharführer* was unimpressed by Christian's outburst. 'Nothing to do with me, sir. Just carrying out orders, like.' He winked at the others and they grinned at the officer's discomfiture. 'For some reason *Obersturmbannführer* Skorzeny ain't taken me into his confidence.' He guffawed carelessly and the others did the same. It was obvious to a fuming Christian that his naval rank did not impress these burly toughs one bit.

'Oh, come on, Frenssen, hit the juice! Let's get away from these SS morons.'

Frenssen glowered and for a moment it appeared he might refuse Christian's order. Then he rammed home first gear angrily and let out the clutch. With a jerk, the little vehicle moved on once more, turning left on to an even narrower forest road, leaving the SS laughing softly behind them, as the first soft flakes of snow began to trickle gently down…

They came upon them, puffing silently at their cigarettes, collars raised against the snow, five giants with stick grenades and weapons, as the others had been. But these were

37

all officers and there was no mistaking their commander, who towered head and shoulders even above these huge men.

Frenssen slowed down and whispered out of the side of his mouth, 'His nibs, sir. The big 'un with the shoulders like a wardrobe. That's him all right. Can't mistake him, even with his back turned towards us, sir. That's Otto Skorzeny all right.'

Christian nodded his agreement. It was the legendary head of the SS's own commando unit; the man who had rescued Mussolini, the Italian dictator, from his mountain fastness prison; who had kidnapped the son of the Hungarian dictator to keep that country in the war on Germany's side, the bold hero of half-a-dozen dashing exploits. Christian frowned. Why did such a man want to meet him at this lonely crossroad in the middle of a snow-bound forest? It was strange, very strange indeed.

Suddenly the waiting officers became aware of the jeep coming up the trail towards them. As one they turned, hands flashing to their weapons, cigarettes already spat out and spluttering in the new snow. Then they recognized the naval uniforms and relaxed, as Frenssen brought the jeep to a halt.

Immediately *Obersturmbannführer* Skorzeny detached himself from the rest, as Christian dropped hastily to the ground and clicked to the position of attention, hand raised stiffly to the peak of his cap.

Skorzeny, his sallow face dominated by a pair of restless dark eyes, his face terribly scarred from his student-duelling days, mustered the young sailor for a few moments and was obviously pleased by what he saw, for he said in his lilting Viennese accent, '*Grü Gott, Herr Kapitänleutnant.*'

Christian must have shown his surprise at the greeting instead of the usual harsh 'Heil Hitler' favoured by the SS, for Skorzeny grinned and said, 'We of the SS are not all barbarians, you know, my dear Jungblut. We too appreciate civilian niceties, *mein Lieber.*' He beamed down at Christian and then took his arm as if they were old friends, and said in that easy *gemütlich* Austrian manner of his, 'But it is too cold to stand around here. Let me introduce you — *swiftly* — to my officers and then we must be on our way.' With a nod he indicated the big camouflaged Mercedes hidden in the trees, next to a half-track filled with hard-faced, helmeted SS men. Numbly, Christian allowed himself to be propelled forward, followed, at a respectful distance, by Frenssen.

One by one the SS giants were introduced, all of them bemedaled, sporting the campaign decorations from half-a-dozen fronts, each one clicking to attention, throwing up his right hand and bellowing at the top of his voice 'Heil Hitler' as if they were back at the SS depot.

'And this, my dear Jungblut,' Skorzeny said, as he came to the last of his staff, 'is *Hauptsturm* von Arco, who has been with me ever since Italy —' He stopped short and stared down at Christian, who was gazing at the last of the SS officers as if he had just seen a ghost. Then he turned back to von Arco, whose arrogant, affected face revealed nothing, his eyes fixed on some distant horizon known only to himself.

Numbly Christian stared at that face which had suddenly come back from the dead to haunt him, while behind Frenssen gasped, 'Christ on a friggin' crutch — *it's him*! *But* he snuffed it…' He did not finish the sentence, as if he could not find the words to express the strength of his shock.

Skorzeny's smile vanished. 'Do you know this officer, *Kapitänleutnant*?' he snapped, iron in his voice now.

'I once knew an officer … of that name, sir,' Christian stuttered, unable to take his gaze off *Hauptsturm* von Arco's face, 'but he committed sui —' He caught himself in the nick of time — 'I mean, he suffered a fatal accident back in nineteen forty-two …' Now Skorzeny flashed a glance at von Arco. 'Do you know anything about this, *Hauptsturm*?' he demanded.

Von Arco gave his chief that cunning, malicious smile Christian remembered so well from the old days before *it* had happened. 'My brother, *Obersturm*,' he said easily, the eyes cold and knowing. 'I believe he once sailed with *Kapitänleutnant* Jungblut here. I recall him talking about you a lot on leave —' He stared pointedly at Christian, as if challenging him to say more — 'before he met with his — er — fatal accident.'

'Excellent, excellent,' Skorzeny said, seemingly relieved. 'Good, the two of you will be able to reminisce about old times. But enough talk. My outside plumbing is freezing up in this damned cold. God knows how you Prussians can stand it. Driver!' he bellowed, 'bring up the car and let us be on our way. There is a lot to be done before this day is over.'

There was a throaty growl and the Mercedes started up, flooding the grove with blue smoke. Next instant the half-track followed suit. Numbly Christian allowed himself to be led to the big staff car, von Arco smirking at his side.

Frenssen watched them go, the snow falling softly on his big shoulders. 'Heaven, arse and cloudburst,' he cursed softly to himself, 'what frigging next?' Then he turned, too, and began to stamp his way through the snow back to the jeep…

CHAPTER 4

That day back in 1941 when Christian had had his final showdown with *Kapitänleutnant* von Arco, the elegant staff officer who had tormented him for so long had broken down completely. Feeling absolutely confident and sure of himself, Christian had faced the court of inquiry into the sinking of the U-69 and snapped to Dönitz, the president, 'Sir, I accuse *Kapitänleutnant* von Arco of cowardice in the face of the enemy, grave dereliction of duty and an absolute and complete breakdown of moral courage and conduct in the presence of subordinate officers and men!' He had cast a scornful glance at von Arco, a cowering broken man, shoulders slumped in defeat. 'I contend, sir,' he had continued harshly, 'that *Kapitänleutnant* von Arco is not fit to hold a commission in the U-boat arm. That is all, sir.' Thereupon he had sat down, noting that he was not even breathing very hard.

Next to him Frenssen had whispered gleefully out of the side of his mouth, 'Now that sonofabitch couldn't even run a third-class knocking shop without getting his dick in the wringer.' Then he had tensed for the storm to come, for it was well-known throughout the U-boat service just how much the Big Lion relied upon *Kapitänleutnant* von Arco.

But the expected storm had not come. Von Arco had broken down completely. His face had turned ashen and his hands had begun to tremble. Suddenly he had seemed to shrink, his elegant blue uniform becoming too big for him. 'It is true,' he had quavered to Dönitz, voice barely audible. 'I just ... broke down completely ... I couldn't help it ...' Two large tears had begun to trickle down his wan face and at that moment, three years before, young Christian had known

that he could not hate von Arco any more. He was too pathetic to hate. Indeed, he had felt the first stirrings of pity for this broken man, who had once terrorized and betrayed him so wilfully.

Then the court had left, not one of them venturing a glance at the broken man standing there in the middle of the room, looking so absurd now in his trappings of glory — the elegant uniform, the silver sword and bright bauble of the Knight's Cross.

If Admiral Dönitz had said something to the broken man that afternoon, Christian never found out. All he knew was that as he had slumped on his bunk exhausted, the afternoon calm of the officers' quarters at Mürwik naval barracks had been disturbed by the sharp, dry crack of a single pistol shot. Supposedly Dönitz had commented to one of his aides later, 'At least he had the common decency to take the officer's way out.' And that had been the end of *Kapitänleutnant* von Arco…

Now as the big staff car fought its way ever higher through the blinding snow, Christian had the uncanny feeling that von Arco had come back to haunt him from his suicide's grave. *HauptsturmFührer* von Arco, sitting next to the driver in the front of the Mercedes, could well have been the dead man's twin, not just his brother. He sat there in that same brooding hunched way that Christian had often noticed when he had caught the dead man off guard during some dangerous underwater patrol, as if he was tensing his body against some threat known only to him.

Christian knew, too, that the SS officer knew all about him and his relationship with his dead brother. More than once he had caught von Arco looking at him in the driving mirror and every time his pale eyes had been filled with sheer naked hate...

At his side, Skorzeny prattled on in that easy-going manner of the Viennese, his conversation ranging from the famed Vienna New Year's Ball to his experiences as a young student in the fencing ring, the latter in jargon incomprehensible to Christian. Yet while Skorzeny chatted, obviously attempting to set his guest at ease, Christian noted that he flung searching, anxious glances to left and right, as if trying to reassure himself about something or other. Once Skorzeny caught Christian looking at him as he did so and the scar faced giant had said easily, 'Just checking security, my dear *Kapitänleutnant*, that's all. We can't be too careful up here, can we, what?'

And when Christian asked, 'But where is — *here?*' *Obersturmbannführer* Otto Skorzeny had appeared not to hear the naval officer's question. Now they had virtually reached the top of the Harz. The firs had thinned out and the view might well have been spectacular from this height, if the driving snowstorm had not cut down visibility to a mere twenty metres. The cold was intense, in spite of the Mercedes's heater going all out. Even the SS officers, who prided themselves on their hardiness, noticed it, and huddled into their greatcoats with collars drawn up about their ears and gloved hands dug deeply into pockets.

Suddenly Skorzeny leaned forward, the casual look vanished from his face, the dark eyes hard. Christian saw the man's determination. Now, for the first time, he realized that he was really sitting at the side of the bold plotter who had released Mussolini from his mountain fastness and had rolled Horthy's son in a carpet and smuggled him out of that Budapest castle. 'Listen, Jungblut,' he said urgently. 'Soon we will be arriving at the castle — '

Christian opened his mouth to ask a question, but Skorzeny held up his hand for silence.

'— there you will be told many things, many top secret things. These officers you see all around you are loyal and trustworthy, but one never knows. Therefore, I must warn you — *on pain of death!*' — his dark eyes bored into Christian's face — 'not to breathe a word about what you will hear up there, even to them. Nobody is to be trusted, do you understand?'

Christian nodded his head hurriedly and asked, 'But where's the fire, sir?'

'The fire?' Skorzeny echoed the word and laughed, but his eyes did not light up. They remained cold and very wary. 'Why, *mein Lieber*, the fire — it is in the West …' And then he relapsed into silence, as the Mercedes turned a bend in the trail and started to grind its way up a long drive to the stark Gothic outline of a medieval castle.

But Christian had no eyes for their destination. His mind raced electrically, mulling over what Skorzeny had just told him. Now things were beginning to fall into place. The 'fire in the West' — that was some kind of new offensive on the Western front against the Anglo-Americans. It explained the great movement of troops and equipment that had delayed their drive from Kiel to this remote castle. They had all been moving in a north-east to south-westerly direction. It didn't take a crystal ball to figure out why. *They were heading for the front facing the Western Allies!*

That much was clear. But what did the Reich's chief commando have to do with a conventional land attack? That was not his style at all. Ever since Skorzeny had hit the headlines with his liberation of the *Duce* and had come into national prominence, he had been engaged in unconventional, covert operations. What role could he possibly play in a set-piece land battle? But more importantly, Christian told himself, his forehead suddenly furrowing in a puzzled frown, what the hell had a ground offensive got to do with one of Dönitz's 'Lords'? Had he been transferred to the damned infantry or something? But the presence of von Arco's brother in Skorzeny's entourage told him that the role of a hairy-arsed stubble hopper was not the one *he* was going to be playing in whatever was to come…

Five minutes later, the car skidded to a halt outside *Schloss Hartmannstein* and the guards sprang down from their half-track to kneel aggressively in the snow, their weapons already levelled as if this were the Führer come to visit, instead of a very bewildered naval officer. *Obermaat* Frenssen, his face purple with cold as he braked behind the big Mercedes, summed it up in his own inimitable way, 'Frenssen, old horse, *I think you and the boss have gonna and landed yersens right up to yer hooters in shit once again!*'

Next moment, an ugly faced SS man, with a black patch over his right eye, had poked his head through the cab and snarled, 'All right, sailor boy, paddle yer frigging canoe round the back door. This entrance is for officers and gents only.'

Angrily Frenssen thrust up a big thumb like a hairy pork sausage and growled, 'Try that one on for frigging size, matey!'

The one-eyed SS man guffawed coarsely and rumbled without rancour, 'Sorry, comrade, got a frigging two-decker bus up there already. Just ain't no more room. All right then, comedian, *move it!*'

Frenssen mumbled something under his breath, then he crashed into gear and began to reverse, slithering and skidding in the wet snow. Darkness drifted down from the snow-heavy peaks like some great silent bird. The remote castle's crenellated battlements began to vanish, wrapped in its black wings. And still the snow continued to beat down with relentless fury…

Up above on the naked outcrop, where even the snow had not been able to settle, the lone watcher decided there was no use hanging on. Besides, soon it would be *Appell* and the SS were getting ever more thorough with the body count since the great project had commenced. He blew on his frozen, skinny claws, the finger ends still scabbed and crusty with black blood where they had ripped off his nails, and began to write with his stub of pencil. Paper was scarce (he had stolen this piece from the SS latrine that very morning — the prisoners were forced to use anything they could find to wipe themselves, grass, shavings, their own hands) and wrote in a tight crabbed handwriting, abbreviating as much as was possible. '*S. + N. Off. arrive*,' he wrote, his right hand racked with pain. '*U-boat man. Suggest tie-in with Project N.Y.? Will observe further & report.*'

Now the light was almost gone and he could no longer see his own writing. He breathed out hard, his breath a grey fog around his emaciated face, and wondered if *they* would understand what he meant. For an instant, he considered whether they ever received his messages at all, in spite of what the Luxembourger always said when he came for them. Then he dismissed that horrifying thought immediately. God, what else would he have to live for, if it was not for this — the belief that by somehow reporting on 'Project N.Y.', as the SS called it so mysteriously, he was helping to bring about the downfall of this monstrous '1000 Year Reich'?

He told himself he would coach the Luxembourger the best he could. The courier didn't speak a word of English, but he'd make him learn the English off by heart so that he could repeat it parrot fashion to whomever *his* contact was in the long mysterious chain of agents and couriers that led back to London.

For a moment he indulged himself at the thought of London. Fog and fish-and-chips and all those shabby bookshops by the British Museum. What a romantic place it had been in those days! How he had loved it, although as a newly created *Doktor der Philosophie* he had been annoyed and surprised that he had been unable to understand a word of English the natives had spoken. Their argot had been too much for him.

Beneath his striped rags, he felt the faint disgusting stirrings of the lice with which his body was infested. Idly he scratched the spot. At least the cold kept the damned things dormant for a while, he told himself gratefully. Once back in the heat of that 'Satanic Mill', as he always called that place of horror to himself in English, they would begin to feed off his emaciated body once more, tormenting and torturing him.

Suddenly the thought of the lice reminded him of *Appell*. Soon those of the poor wretches, from half the countries of Occupied Europe, who were his fellow slaves, and who had survived this day would be dragging their skinny bodies back to the barracks. There they would be counted, fed the nauseating pig-swill the SS called food, and then packed three into a wooden bunk, shelf after shelf of them reaching right up to the roof, so that they could sleep and be ready for yet another day of unremitting labour in that 'Satanic Mill'.

He tugged his *Kapo* badge straight and tried to overlook the pink triangle, which was as much a badge of shame as the yellow star of David the Jews were forced to wear, at least in the eyes of those SS brutes. It branded him as a homosexual, or 'a warm brother' as the guards called his kind scornfully, usually accompanying their sneers with a hard kick to his skinny backside. He must be getting back to wait with the other *Kapos*, most of them communist and all of them German, for the poor wretches and organize their brief respite from that harsh unremitting labour which killed them all in the end.

With fingers stiff with cold, he unfastened his flies and took out his organ. Awkwardly he furled back his foreskin, wondering yet again as he did so how important that absurd piece of skin had become since the Nazis had taken over power. How many times had he seen it happen in the many camps he had been in these last terrible years! The scared bunch of new arrivals, the swaggering guards with their whips and ferocious, half-wild dogs, and then the brutal command, '*Pants down!*' Then some burly, suspicious *ScharFührer* going from prisoner to prisoner, whipping up his shirt-front with his stick and eyeing his genitals to cry in triumph, 'Here's one — circumcised. *Dick docked by the rabbi!* Haw, Haw! Come here, *Jew boy!*' And yet another Jew would be given that mark of death — the star of David. Now he inserted the tiny tube of paper with its precious message beneath the skin and rolled it back, shivering in the icy cold. There, at least, no one would search during one of the spot checks the SS carried out all the time. There it would be safe until the time came to hand it over to the Luxembourger.

The little homosexual took one last look at the castle, a squat black shape outlined against the white of the snow, spat angrily (for it was there that those sadists who ran the 'Satanic Mill' lived) and then began to trudge back to the camp, heart full of hate …

CHAPTER 5

Skorzeny yawned and threw another log on the big crackling fire, slumping back once more into his chair with a lazy sigh.

Dinner was over half an hour ago. A strange affair with the SS officers loud and boisterous, drinking prodigious quantities of wine and champagne and indulging hugely in the excellent food; while at the other end of the long table, the middle-aged civilians, mostly clad in white coats, engaged in hushed whispered conversations among themselves, occasionally throwing frightened glances at the red-faced giants.

Again Christian had asked himself what he was going to do here in this remote place. What conceivable project brought together Skorzeny's commandos and these frightened, middle-aged civvies, who looked as if they could be scientists or technicians, or something of that kind?

The big commando leader seemed to read Christian's thoughts, for he put down the glass of kirsch and said in his lilting Viennese sing-song which contrasted so sharply with his tough, brutally scarred face, 'I think, my dear chap, the time has come to tell you something of what we intend — why we had you brought here, to what most of my fellows regard as the arsehole of the world.' He chuckled, his face hollowed out to a red death's head by the flickering flames of the log fire.

Christian put down his glass, too, suddenly tense. 'I would appreciate it, *Obersturmbannführer*,' he said, realizing that Skorzeny had dismissed his staff after dinner specifically so that he could talk to him alone here in the study, its walls covered with dusty hunting trophies and yellowing photographs of bearded nineteenth-century worthies posing in front of their massed kills.

'As I am sure you have already guessed, clever young man that you are,' Skorzeny continued, as the clock in the hall ticked away the seconds of their life with grave metallic inexorability, 'there is going to be new action in the West. Soon the balloon is about to go up.' He flashed a glance at the heavy oaken door, deep in the shadows, as if he half-suspected that someone might be listening there. But there was no one. 'You are right, Jungblut. Our Führer has decided to launch a massive counter-attack against the Americans along a ninety kilometre front in Belgium.' He beamed at a surprised Christian. 'Yes, one quarter of a million troops, fresh, fully armed, supported by massive armour, are soon to give the Americans the biggest surprise of their life. With luck we shall drive them back to the sea.' He shrugged eloquently in his un-German manner (on leaves in Vienna Christian had seen waiters make exactly the same careless gesture) and said, 'Who knows, we might even be fortunate enough to Dunkirk them, as we did the Tommies back in May nineteen forty.'

He took a delicate sip of his kirsch, lingering over it, unlike his officers who gulped down their drinks in one fierce swill in the approved SS manner, while Christian absorbed the information which he had just been given.

'Now you are perhaps wondering, Jungblut, what the *SS Jagdkommando* has got to do with a land operation planned for the stubble-hoppers?' he chuckled at the Army expression for infantrymen.

Christian nodded and took a drink from the glass of excellent whisky Skorzeny had offered him before they had settled down in the study.

'Well, our immediate task is to spread alarm, uncertainty and confusion behind enemy lines once the offensive has started. How shall we do it?' His massive chest swelled out with pride as he answered his own question. 'Currently I have three thousand, yes *three thousand*, English-speaking volunteers from every arm of the *Wehrmacht*, undergoing training in Bavaria. There they are learning to play at being Americans.'

'*Americans?*' Christian echoed in surprise.

Skorzeny beamed, pleased that he had been able to surprise the younger officer. 'Yes, we are teaching them how to talk, walk, even think as Americans. God, what a job we had to make them lounge with their hands in the pockets, chewing gum all the time like your *Ami* does! I'm afraid your old Prussianism is very deeply engrained in the average German soldier.'

Christian let the gentle dig pass. Like all southern Germans and Austrians, Skorzeny, the Viennese, obviously had a thing about the 'sow-Prussians', as they called them among themselves. Instead he asked, 'And are these the men who are to cause the confusion behind the American lines?'

'*Genau!*' Skorzeny replied excitedly. 'They will infiltrate behind the crumbling American line once the attack has started, in jeep teams of three and four English-speakers, in order to misdirect enemy traffic, change signposts, sabotage bridges and railheads and generally cause the maximum amount of confusion behind the American lines.' He beamed hugely at Christian, obviously very pleased with his plans.

'But we are going to go further than that,' Skorzeny continued, 'We are to drop assassination squads by parachute far behind the front, perhaps even over Paris, in order to take out the Supreme Commander Eisenhower himself. In Holland, too, at Eindhoven where the Englishman Montgomery has his headquarters. The Führer has given this part of the plan his full approval. Chop off the head, he maintains, and the body, however vast, is dead…'

Christian whistled softly. He hadn't realized that the Reich had so much power left at its disposal. He saw now that he had been wearing blinkers for this last year or so. He had concentrated too much on the failure of the U-boat campaign in the North Atlantic and the disastrous losses the 'Lords' had suffered there, plus the horrific destruction of Germany's cities at the hands of Anglo-American 'air gangsters'. Suddenly he realized that Germany was still an immensely powerful country, able to strike back at its enemies in this massive manner.

'Of course, we intend to spread this disruption and general confusion even further afield,' Skorzeny was saying, dark eyes flashing excitedly, carried away by the heady excitement of the great plan. 'There will be a breakout from Lorient. From the Channel Islands, our hard-pressed garrison will launch a commando attack on the French coast, perhaps even on some small English port — Poole, Weymouth or the like. In the north of England we aim to raise the inmates of the Tommy POW camps. With luck they will be able to break out in a mass escape and capture the port of Hull. If they do, we can easily supply them with arms.' He shrugged, big chest gasping from the effort of talking so much. 'Even if they don't, and that scheme as well as all the others fails, can you imagine the effect it will have on the civilian populations behind the enemy lines? Why, it will be mass panic.' He slammed one great fist into the palm of his other hand. '*Himmelherrje, it will be nineteen forty all over again!*'

Christian Jungblut felt his whole body tingle with excitement, that old heady feeling of the great days when every new dawn heralded a fresh German victory. Was it possible? After month after month of defeat upon defeat, could Germany still pull victory out of the hat? *Could it?*

Outside in the corridor, he could hear the sound of unsteady boots and officers calling good night to each other in slurred tones. Skorzeny's staff was going to bed, and by the sound of it, most of his officers had had more than their fair share of drink. For a moment or two Skorzeny was silent, obviously waiting for his officers to go to their beds. Someone said outside, 'Well, Johann, *tonight?*'

'Von Arco,' Skorzeny commented softly. 'Johann von Arco.'

Christian nodded his understanding and wondered why the scar-faced giant had pointed his old enemy's brother out, but he said nothing.

'Why not?' von Arco replied casually. 'They've all got to for the first time somewhere along the line.'

The other officer laughed. 'You old dog, you. Well, good night.'

'Good night,' von Arco replied and then there was silence, with only the muted hush of the snowstorm outside.

'Now then, Jungblut,' Skorzeny went on, 'what has all this got to do with you — an officer in the U-boat service? This is the question which has tormented you ever since you arrived here, what?'

'Yes, it has, sir. I know nothing about land warfare. My war has been spent mostly eighty metres below the surface of the ocean.'

'Exactly.' Now Christian realized that Skorzeny had even more ambitious plans than the ones he had already detailed. 'What you have just heard covers France, the Low Countries and England. But none of these countries is our real enemies. In nineteen forty-four England's power has waned. The United

States of America is undoubtedly the supreme power in the West, the dynamo of the Western Coalition against us. Yet of all the countries engaged in this war, it has never once been touched. No single bomb has dropped anywhere in that vast country. No shell has ever landed. Not one single American civilian has been killed or injured ever since America entered the war in December 'forty-one. What a fortunate people they are these Americans, don't you think, Jungblut.' He smiled softly, but there was no answering smile in those dark eyes. Abruptly Christian shivered involuntarily. Skorzeny was up to no good. Outside a sudden wind rattled the shutters. Christian shuddered again. There was something definitely uncanny about this evening, with the storm outside, the dying fire and this giant sitting opposite him, dreaming up monstrous plans — to do *what*?

'Imagine what the American civilian reaction would be,' Skorzeny continued softly, lowering his glass and stroking the rim with his middle finger, 'if by some chance' — he hesitated momentarily — 'the war was abruptly brought to their own back-yard? What a tremendous shock that would be! Suddenly they would realize they, too, were vulnerable, that their cities could be destroyed, as ours have been so cruelly destroyed … that their men, women and children, innocent or guilty, it matters not one iota, could be slaughtered indiscriminately, by the hundred, the thousand, the hundred thousand —' Skorzeny's voice rose and for a moment it was out of control; then he calmed himself swiftly and stared challengingly at the other man.

Christian remembered Kiel and felt a burning enthusiastic excitement sweep through his lithe young body, just as presumably a similar excitement had just animated Skorzeny. 'Why, *Obersturmbannführer*,' he cried, 'it would be a tremendous propaganda victory for us. It would put new heart into our long-suffering people to realize that the *Amis* were getting back as good as they give —'

'— And think of the effect on their troops three — four thousand kilometres away here in Europe,' Skorzeny cut in triumphantly. 'What do you think *they* would feel if they knew their own people were being slaughtered, just as our people are currently being slaughtered? How good do you think their fighting morale would be then?'

'But *Obersturmbannführer*,' Christian cried almost desperately, 'what has all this … this daydreaming got to do with me?'

'It is no longer daydreaming, *Kapitänleutnant*' Skorzeny replied, his terribly scarred face now glazed with an excited sweat. 'Project N.Y. can be realized at last and you, *Kapitänleutnant* Christian Jungblut, are to be the man who will take the war to the United States of America.' He raised his glass as if in toast, drank its contents down in one fierce gulp, and with an air of savage finality threw the glass against the fireplace. As the glass shattered, he cried, 'Report to me at zero eight hundred hours tomorrow morning, *Kapitänleutnant*, there is no further time to be lost.' And even before a startled Christian could rise to his feet, *Obersturmbannführer* Otto Skorzeny had staggered out, leaving the young naval officer to stare at the dying embers in complete and utter bewilderment as the wind howled outside.

Three floors above the brooding young officer, *Obermaat* Frenssen stirred uneasily, the old wooden bed creaking under his weight as he turned. At supper the teenage Russian maids had fed him in the kitchen in between serving the officers taking their dinner. He had eaten at least a litre and a half of good thick 'fart soup' — pea-soup to a civilian — and followed it by two litres of the strong local beer. With his stomach swollen as if he were pregnant, he had staggered off to his bed in the maids' quarters and had fallen into a deep sleep immediately.

Now something had awakened him. For a moment or two he lay there, thinking it might be the wind howling around the turret outside. Then he heard whispered voices and he knew he was wrong. There was a man next door, in the room of little Tanya, the pretty little fifteen-year-old Russian maid! Frenssen sat up abruptly.

'*Nyet*,' he heard her terrified whisper. '*Nyet*!' followed in broken German, as she pleaded with an unknown man. 'No, please sir, no. I am innocent…'

'Don't be a damned little fool!' the man hissed. There was no mistaking that voice, slurred as it was with drink. It could have been the same arrogant voice of that swine who had been dead these three years. It was von Arco's pig of a brother. Frenssen's broad honest face flushed angrily as he heard the little maid cry out in pain as von Arco struck her. He flung back the heavy cover and naked as he was save for his underpants, he rushed to the door, down the corridor and wrenched open Tanya's door.

There by the flickering yellow light of the candle, he saw them, Tanya cowering in the corner, her nightdress ripped open to the waist to reveal her small budding breasts with their pink-tipped nipples, and von Arco towering drunkenly above, his face flushed with desire, fumbling awkwardly with the flies of his riding breeches.

'*Sir*!' Frenssen bellowed in a voice that would have awakened the dead, fists clenched angrily. 'You've got to stop that — *now*!' Von Arco swung round, eyes crazed with drink, sex and rage. 'Get the hell out of here, you great oaf!' he hissed menacingly, 'or it will be the worse for you.'

The little Russian maid, trying frantically to hide her breasts, looked pleading at the sailor. Frenssen stood his ground. He knew his von Arcos. 'I'm going to count three, sir,' his voice was cold and bitter, 'then if you haven't gone, I'm off to fetch the duty officer, *sir*!'

Von Arco looked at him incredulously. 'But the little bitch is only a frigging Ivan,' he snorted. 'What does it matter — a frigging Ivan, I said!'

'*One*,' Frenssen intoned icily.

Von Arco flashed a wild glance from Frenssen's hard cold face to the maid cowering in the corner, her delightful virginal body all too visible in the shabby thin nightdress. What a delicious morsel she would make. He had been savouring the thought of ravishing her innocence all day.

'*Two*!' Frenssen said threateningly.

'Be reasonable, man!' von Arco pleaded. 'You can't blame a man for wanting to have a little bit of fun —' He stopped short. Frenssen had opened his mouth again. 'All right, all right,' he cried, holding up his hands, as if attempting to push the grim giant of a sailor away physically. 'I'm going … I'm going, man!'

Drunkenly he brushed by Frenssen and staggered off into the gloom of the corridor, still fumbling with his flies.

Frenssen heaved a sigh of relief. In the corner the little Russian maid had begun to weep softly, her face a mixture of joy and shocked relief, plus a great deal of surprise, as if she couldn't believe that the Germans who had dragged her so cruelly from her homeland could also be kind.

Frenssen forced a smile though he knew now that he had made a deadly enemy in the SS officer. The von Arcos had always borne a grudge. '*Davai*,' he said softly in Russian. 'Off you go … into bed.' He tucked his hands under his head, as if he were asleep. 'That swine won't bother you anymore. *Ponimayu?*'

'*Da, da*,' she said happily through her tears. Suddenly she dashed forward and placed a wet kiss on Frenssen's big face. A moment later a surprised *Obermaat* Frenssen was staggering barefoot down the corridor to his own bedroom telling himself he'd be helping old grannies across the road next…

CHAPTER 6

The big Mercedes halted in the snow. The long column of prisoners in their ragged striped pyjama suits stumbled on, the guards cracking their whips, the half-wild police dogs snapping angrily at the ankles of the laggards. Christian frowned. The prisoners were obviously on their last legs; it was only fear that kept these walking skeletons going.

Skorzeny noticed Christian's look and said easily, 'Feel no pity for them, my dear chap. They are all communists, pimps, perverts, anti-social types, trash of that kind! Honest labour on simple food can be only to their advantage.'

To their front one of the shaven-headed wretches stumbled and went down on one skinny knee in the snow. Almost immediately one of the giant guards began belabouring him with his whip, crying angrily, 'Keep moving, you red swine … *keep moving!*' Blood seeping through his striped pyjamas in a dozen spots, the unfortunate prisoner staggered on somehow through the wooden arch bearing the mocking legend, '*WORK MAKES FREE*'.

Now the driver thrust home first gear and slowly they began to follow the long stinking column inside, as the *Kapos*, supervised by the guards, rapped out orders to the individual work parties. He indicated a skinny bespectacled *Kapo*, who looked more like a former schoolteacher or professor to Christian. 'Communists, most of them, and all of them *German*! They know how to give — and take — orders. They keep the rest of this rabble under control.'

'I see,' Christian said grimly, as one of the *Kapos* began kicking a wretched prisoner who was obviously too slow for him. 'But what do they do?'

Skorzeny smiled. 'Be patient, my friend. Be patient. Soon all will be revealed.'

With the driver hooting his horn to clear the prisoners out of the way, they drove slowly across the slushy compound, their progress followed carefully by machine-gunners positioned high above the wire in stork-legged guard towers. Abruptly the air outside was full of floating ash, which danced lightly on the wind, from a tall brick chimney to their right. Christian looked at the ash curiously, wondering what it could come from, but Skorzeny did not enlighten him. Instead he kept his gaze on the way ahead. Von Arco, sitting next to the driver, sniggered and muttered, 'Up the chimney, that's the surest way out of here.' Christian frowned and asked himself what the devil von Arco meant?

Now for the first time Christian was able to see the huge entrance in the sheer rock wall which formed the fourth wall of the labour camp. Bright lights burned on both sides of the entrance and guards with rifles over their shoulders plodded up and down in the slushy snow, suspiciously surveying the long column of prisoners entering the place. 'Shadow factory,' Skorzeny explained, as the guards clicked to attention and presented arms. '*Reichsminister* Speer began to establish them in remote spots such as this once the Allied bombing started to become so intense in forty three. They are all over the place. But the Harz has proved particularly good because of these huge natural caves.' He indicated the glistening dripping sides of the great hole they were now entering. 'All his people needed to do was to put in a road system and electric lighting and we were in business immediately.'

Christian looked suitably impressed. Even if the Allied air gangsters found the place, there was little their bombs could do. Even their biggest bomb would be unable to penetrate the hundreds of metres of solid rock above his head.

The car stopped. Skorzeny edged his huge bulk out to be greeted by a pompous, professorial man in a white coat, who held his check-board as if it were very precious.

Finally Skorzeny stepped to one side and swept out his big hand like a Viennese head waiter inviting an honoured guest to enter his restaurant. '*Herr Professor* Dietrich may I introduce you to *Herr Kapitänleutnant* Jungblut who will be the officer who carries out the mission.'

The professor peered at Christian over the top of his pince-nez and extended his plump soft hand. Christian took it, noting with disgust that it was slightly damp, his mind racing. What had Skorzeny meant by the 'mission'?

'Well, then,' Skorzeny said genially, 'shall we have a look-see, Herr Professor?'

'Yes, of course, of course,' the professor answered in that fussy manner of his, repeating himself, as Christian would discover, all the time, as if he suspected that people did not understand him the first time. 'Let us take the lift, the lift, eh?' Turning, he waddled to the lift shaft, while Skorzeny grinned and winked conspiratorially at Christian behind his back. Then they followed...

A minute or two later Christian found himself inside a cave within a cave, perhaps some hundred metres beneath the one on the upper level. Everywhere under the glaring white light the emaciated prisoners bustled back and forth in their ill-fitting wooden clogs, urged on whenever they appeared to be slacking by the blows, hoarse cries and curses of the guards.

Modern machinery of the kind Christian well-remembered from the refitting dry-docks — oxyacetylene burners, derricks, cranes, the special cradles used for transporting engines — was piled everywhere. But it was not the machinery which caught his attention, nor the now-familiar shape of the V-ls, the new revenge weapon which had been terrorizing London since the summer. It was the long sleek cross-section of wood, painted to look like metal, with a strange contraption on its top, which drew his gaze immediately.

The professor caught his look and burbled, 'Prototype X for the —'

'— Project N.Y., Professor,' Skorzeny interrupted him sharply.

'Yes, yes, Project N.Y.,' the bumbling professor corrected himself, 'Project N.Y.'

'But it looks like the cross-section of the hull of a U-boat,'

Christian burst out in surprise. 'What in God's name is the hull of a sub doing down here, deep beneath the Harz mountains?'

Skorzeny held up his huge paw for silence. 'Please, *mein Lieber*, just have a little more patience. All will be explained in due course, won't it, Professor?'

'Yes, yes … in due course, in due course,' the civilian fussed, as they picked their way across the rubber-sheathed electric cables which were everywhere, the prisoners springing out of their path as if the hulking SS giants might strike them at any moment.

They halted and stared upwards. Now Christian could see the intricate electrical and hydraulic apparatus which linked the interior of the cross-section with the strange, awkward-looking device attached to its hull. But for the life of him he could not fathom out what it was supposed to represent. Could it be a new way of launching an aircraft from a submarine? There had been some experiments of that kind before the war. Was it an attempt to furnish a submarine with additional fire-power? Were the boffins trying to fix recently introduced electrically operated multiple mortars which the *Wehrmacht* was now using with some considerable success, on to a U-boat's deck to back up the 88mm deck gun? Christian frowned. What in three devils' names was the damned thing?

The professor cleared his throat self-importantly and burbled, 'It was a very difficult task, decidedly difficult indeed, indeed.'

'*Indeed!*' Skorzeny echoed maliciously.

But the ironic remark was wasted on the middle-aged scientist, for he continued without pause, 'At the start we thought we would be able to launch them from beneath the water, yes, beneath the water. We spent many wearisome and unprofitable months on that kind of research. But it simply did not work out … hm, work out.'

Christian's frown deepened. *What* had they tried to launch from beneath the surface, he asked himself. A torpedo perhaps?

'In the end, we concluded,' the professor went on, 'that the craft would have to surface in order to fire. Well aware of the dangers to the craft, of course, as we were, we decided this way was the only solution — er — the only solution.' Suddenly, with surprising briskness, he clapped his hands.

The guards barked orders. A group of skinny prisoners, gasping and sweating under the weight, stumbled forward bearing a large object adorned with two stubby wings and a miniature tailplane. Christian gasped. It was a wooden replica of the V-l, the feared revenge weapon!

He flashed a look at Skorzeny and the scar-faced giant smiled back at him happily. He nodded his head slowly, 'Yes, that is what they have been working upon here for the last six months or more. A V-l to be fired from a submarine!'

Christian whistled softly through his teeth. So that was what all the secrecy was about. He was impressed.

Grunting and groaning and forced on by the guards' curses and blows, the prisoners placed the awkward object into the firing cradle, swiftly attached the various electrical leads and hydraulic pipes to it and stepped back gasping.

The professor waddled forward, and like the university teacher he had once been, began to explain the technical details of firing aV-1 missile from the deck of a submarine. 'In essence, we have solved all the basic problems,' he concluded. 'The deck of one of our larger U-boats such as the model here is big enough for the launching ramp. Efficient and well-trained operatives can have the missile operational and ready to fire in five minutes, thus cutting down the length of time the U-boat must remain on the surface, exposed to the danger of enemy attack. And if the U-boat can sail to within a few kilometres of the enemy coast, the problem of accuracy can be reduced considerably.' Ponderously, panting a little with the effort, he clambered up on to the deck of the mock-up and clapped the wooden model lovingly like a fond father. '*Meine Herren*,' he bumbled, gazing down at them proudly. 'I think I can safely say that we here are as ready as we will ever be. Project N.Y. is feasible ... yes, yes, definitely very feasible.'

He stopped short, almost as if he expected a round of applause for his effort.

'Thank you, Professor,' Skorzeny said politely. 'You have worked well. The Führer will hear of it.' Then he dismissed the academic with a casual wave of his hand and turned to an impressed Christian. 'Well, my dear fellow, what do you think of it?'

Christian hesitated. 'So this is the way you intend to take the war to the United —'

Urgently Skorzeny held his finger to his lips and snapped. 'Yes, this is the way. Please, no names, Jungblut.'

He indicated with a gesture that the slave workers should be led away, thus leaving him alone with Christian and the mock-up of the missile-firing submarine. He waited impatiently until this was done, then he snapped, very urgent and impatient now, 'I shall not discuss targets with you now, *Kapitänleutnant*' he barked, his normal Viennese casualness abruptly vanished. 'But can I ask you this — is it possible to take a large U-boat, fitted with a snorkel, to within firing distance of the American coast, hampered as the craft will be by the firing ramp for the missile? What do you think?'

Christian hesitated only momentarily, excited by the challenge. 'It would be difficult. Indeed it is difficult *even* to get a sub out of one of our bases these days — the *Amis* and the Tommies have pretty well got our exits into the Atlantic sewn up. But it can be done. I should imagine, too, with good weather, a careful speed, and a sizable portion of good luck, a skilled skipper could get his craft into position off the American coast.'

'Excellent, excellent!' Skorzeny cried in delight. 'So it can be done?'

'Yes, but remember this, *Obersturmbannführer*, the *Amis* have been at war for three years now and their eastern seaboard is very well guarded with patrol boats, aircraft, and naturally their highly developed radar shield. Any unwary skipper hanging around for any length of time off that coast is not going to live long.'

'But you heard the professor say that skilled gunners could have the missile ready and fired within five minutes. That still gives you a fighting chance of survival, doesn't it?'

Christian did not answer. Instead he asked a question of his own. 'How many missiles would I be expected to fire on this — er — mission, *Obersturmbann-führer*?'

Skorzeny hesitated, as if he did not much like answering that particular question. Finally he said somewhat lamely, 'We have three missiles planned for one target.'

'So we are now talking in terms of fifteen minutes plus the time needed to reset the firing device for a new target. I don't know how long that takes, but for the sake of discussion, let us say we are talking of thirty minutes — and that is a devilishly long time to remain on the surface off the coast of the United States, especially as the first explosion will undoubtedly alert the enemy's defences.' He frowned and looked at Skorzeny significantly.

'But are you prepared all the same to attempt this mission, *mein Lieber*?' Skorzeny asked urgently.

Christian thought of ruined Kiel and all the other cities in Germany, Berlin, Cologne, Frankfurt, Munich and the like, that had been destroyed by those arrogant silver birds over these last terrible months and felt the hate well up inside him once again. 'Yes, I am prepared to make the attempt,' he said slowly.

Skorzeny clapped him enthusiastically on the shoulder and nearly knocked him off his feet. '*Groβartig ... groβartig, mein Lieber.* I knew from the very start that you wouldn't let me down!' He stopped suddenly. He could see that Christian wasn't really listening to him. 'Well, my dear fellow,' he said, 'spit it out. What's the problem?'

'This. You can understand that a U-boat skipper wants to stay below the sea as much as he can when the enemy is near.

Now I am prepared to accept thirty very long minutes on the surface while the gunners fire their missiles, *but*, can you assure me that the risk to my boat and my crew is worth taking?'

'How do you mean, Jungblut?'

'From what I have read, the missiles fired at London only managed to find their target because the launching ramps in Holland and Northern France were so designed that they would automatically reach and strike the English capital. But how can one do this from a sub, which is moving constantly and is at the whim of the waves and current, *Obersturmbannführer*?' Christian said urgently. 'Might not all the effort and all the risk be for nothing, with our missiles landing' — he shrugged hastily — 'in the middle of a swamp for all I know?'

Skorzeny smiled. 'Do not let that worry you, Jungblut. That problem has already been taken care of. As you perhaps know, the gyro-steering mechanism of the missile must be set before it is fired. Thereafter we cannot alter its course, except marginally to avoid high-standing obstacles in its path. Therefore, it is vital that the gyro-steering mechanism be set accurately before launching.'

'But how can one do that, sir,' Christian objected, thinking Skorzeny had not really understood his point, 'if you do not have an accurate bearing for it to steer?'

'But we *will* have an accurate bearing, Jungblut,' Skorzeny answered patiently.

'*You will?*'

'Yes, you see we already have an agent in place in the — er-target area over there. Once the operation has commenced and our boat is within striking distance of the target, that agent will begin broadcasting the bearings required. It will then be only a matter of moments for the gunners to set the missiles' steering.' He smiled benevolently down at an impressed Christian. 'Believe you me, my dear Jungblut, on this Christmas Eve of nineteen forty-four, those fat rich arrogant Americans over there are going to receive a Christmas present, the like of which they have never known before…'

CHAPTER 7

'*Hauptbahnhof Danzig… Hauptbahnhof Danzig… Der Zug endet hier … alles aussteigen … alles aussteigen!*' As the harsh metallic voice of the train guard began to die away over the tannoy and the long troop train started to slow down, Christian caught a glimpse of the flat grey expanse of the Baltic, which ran parallel with the railway line now. He felt once again the old thrill of the sea. Soon, once he was out there, he would again be the master of his own fate. Suddenly he felt as excited as he had been as a young, callow ensign back in 1939 setting off on his first combat patrol, in what now seemed another age.

Next to him, Frenssen took a last swig at his flat-man, from which he had been drinking ever since they had left bomb-shattered Berlin, and tossed it on the seat. 'Another dead soldier,' he commented a little gloomily, in no way sharing Christian's excitement at what was to come. 'What do you think, sir… I mean about the new mission?' It was the first time the big *Obermaat* had talked about the coming patrol, ever since they had picked up the new draft in the capital.

Christian took his eyes off the first houses, immaculate, white-painted, and with not one single bomb-shattered window. He had completely forgotten what a city looked like without bomb damage. But then Danzig was fortunate; the port was out of the range of the Allied air gangsters. 'What do I think?' he echoed. 'Well, old horse, it's not going to be exactly a bed of roses. We've got just two weeks to shake down a scratch crew, most of them without any combat experience whatsoever.'

Frenssen clenched his massive fist significantly. 'Don't worry about that bunch o' wet-tails, sir,' he grunted. 'I'll crack their asses for 'em!'

Christian grinned. 'I'm sure you will, you big rogue. Then we've got to get out of the Baltic narrows, between Denmark and the Reich, with the exit patrolled day and night by the Tommy planes and destroyers. There'll be mines, too. They plant fresh buggers every night so we can never be sure where they are!'

Frenssen nodded his agreement, as the train continued to slow down.

'Finally, if we can manage that tricky little job, we have to cross five thousand kilometres of the North Atlantic, with every man's hand against us. Not exactly a pleasure cruise, I suppose,' he mused, almost as if he were talking to himself.

'Ar, we'll do it, sir!' Frenssen said encouragingly and rose to pull his duffle bag from the rack. 'And we're in Danzig, aren't we? No sign of war here. Plenty of good Polack women and vodka, I'll be bound. After all, them blonde maidens up north, I fancy a bit o' yer Polack stuff. They say they're dead hot on the mattress.'

Christian grinned again. The big noncom was irrepressible. Now he rose, too, and taking the precious briefcase, which contained the initial details of 'Project N.Y.,' he began a little self-consciously to chain it to his left wrist.

This time it was Frenssen's turn to grin, as with a clatter of steel wheels and a flurry of smoke, the big troop train came to a halt. 'You could lose a hand like that, sir,' he said. 'Cut yer flipper right off at the wrist and make a run for it, case, hand and all.'

'You've got a bizarre imagination, *Obermaat*,' Christian said. 'Come on, let's round up our reluctant heroes…'

Danzig main station was full of the usual hustle and bustle of such places in wartime. Keen-eyed chain-dogs in pairs, with carbines slung over their shoulders, waited at the barriers on the look-out for deserters. Self-important transport officers strode back and forth, check-boards in their hands. The local prostitutes idled in the shadows, lips pouted in professional concupiscence, waiting for customers. Here and there were ragged Polish civilians, the women barefoot or wearing wooden clogs in spite of the freezing cold, begging, crying in a pitiful chant, '*Kleba* .... bread ... *kleba* ... bread for the love of God...!' But the sailors, who were everywhere, passed them by as if they did not exist. The poor defeated Poles were the invisible men of Occupied Europe.

Frenssen drew himself up to his full height in front of the skinny young greenhorns who would make up the new crew of the U-200. 'All right, you asparagus Tarzans, I'm gonna march yer through the streets to the docks, and I want bags o' swank. No slouching, throw yer chests out, swing yer arms and open yer legs. Don't worry. If anything falls out, dear old *Obermaat* Frenssen'll pick 'em up for yer!'

Someone groaned from rear rank, 'I'll catch me death, marching in this freezing weather.'

'And if yer don't hold yer frigging water sharpish,' Frenssen threatened, 'yer'll missing a set o' front teeth! Now then, parade — parade *attenshun*!'

As the new draft clicked sloppily to attention, Frenssen swung a grinning Christian a tremendous salute. 'Permission to wheel 'em away, sir?' he thundered, making startled passengers swing round and stare.

Christian touched his hand to his battered white cap, the mark of a combat skipper in the U-boat arm, 'Permission to wheel 'em away, *Obermaat*,' he replied dutifully.

Hurriedly the two chain-dogs opened the barrier wider and then Frenssen was marching them off, yelling the cadence as if he were back at the depot, leaving Christian to make his own way to the docks, unaware that once again he was being watched. A young Polish woman, whose face was not marked by oppression and poverty as were those of the men and women begging for bread all about her, was carefully noting everything that could be of interest for the Polish Underground intelligence service; the white cap, which told her this officer was probably going to leave Danzig on a combat patrol; the Knight's Cross at his throat that obviously meant he was a veteran, probably an ace to have won such a

high honour; and, most of all, the chained briefcase at his wrist. What else could that be but the German's secret orders? The question was — *what were those orders*? As Christian left the station he acknowledged the salutes of the sailors who were everywhere, savouring the cold clean sea air, nodding to the pretty women who thronged the main street. For there seemed an almost pre-war air about Danzig. The place was alive with fresh-faced, rested civilians, who obviously lived well. There were none of those ashen-faced, hunched creatures who seemed to inhabit the Reich's great cities to the west, always apprehensive, constantly casting glances up to the sky, living in permanent fear of the next raid.

Abruptly Christian felt that the mission was worth carrying out. There was still hope for Germany. Perhaps one day, if he and others like him had faith and carried out their orders successfully, *all* Germans would look like these happy, open-faced citizens of Danzig. Nothing was inevitable, irreversible…

Ten minutes later he was picking his way through the naval dockyard, trying to find the U-200. Everywhere there was noise and bustle. The crash of steel hawsers, the discordant rattle of the derricks and cranes, the insane, nerve-wracking chatter of the riveters' guns as the dockers and shipyard workers hurried back and forth, carrying out their myriad tasks. And again the sight of such industry and purpose reinforced Christian's feeling of hope, that Germany could still win this terrible war.

A moment later he caught sight of his new command. He stopped short, taken aback by what he saw. The U-200 looked as if it had just been salvaged from the bottom of the sea! Everywhere it was specked with red rust, the camouflage paint on the conning tower almost peeled away completely. All that was lacking were the barnacles and the dripping seaweed.

'Never fear, *Kapitänleutnant* Jungblut, she looks worse than she is. She has just returned from Japan as an underwater blockade breaker — four months under way — that is why she looks like that.'

Christian spun round startled. 'What in three devils' names…' The words died on his lips, as *Hauptsturmbannführer* von Arco detached himself from the shadows cast by the nearby warehouse and touched his hand to the battered civilian cap he was now wearing in ironic salute. 'Welcome to Danzig,' the SS man said, barely able to conceal the sneer in his voice.

Christian looked at him hard. 'What are you doing here, and in civvies, too?' He indicated von Arco's rough tweed suit, with a jerk of his head.

'Security, my dear Jungblut,' the other man answered easily. 'Like all ports, where there are foreigners employed, like the Polacks we use here, there is always danger of spies and sabotage. It is my task to ensure that nothing happens to our — er — project.'

'By whose authority?' Christian rapped coldly.

'You can see my papers, if you wish. They are signed by the highest authority -*Reichsführer* SS Himmler himself! But I am personally, directly responsible to *Obersturmbannführer* Skorzeny himself, of course.'

'Of course,' Christian said, but irony was wasted on the arrogant SS man, whose thick skin matched his dead brother's, Christian realized.

'The launching ramp and the — er — torpedoes will be arriving after black-out time tonight, Jungblut,' von Arco went on. 'Ensure, please, that the guard is on duty ready and waiting. Now I must be off.' And with that he was gone, leaving Christian frowning and telling himself that one von Arco in his life had been quite enough…

The next forty-eight hours passed speedily, as Frenssen chased the greenhorns back and forth, cleaning up the U-200, chipping away rust, swabbing decks, coating her with a fresh layer of green camouflage paint. At the same time, the small team of artillerymen, under the command of a runny-nosed second lieutenant who wore thick-lensed spectacles, busied themselves erecting the metal launching ramps and stowing their one-ton missiles. But busy as he was readying the ship and the missiles, and briefing his new officers, all of them without any combat experience but eager and very keen to sail on a fighting patrol at last, Christian could not overlook von Arco's presence on the dockyard. He turned up at all hours of the day and night; and a couple of times Christian had caught him whispering furtively to a middle-aged civilian who had a brown felt hat pulled low over his eyes and was dressed in an ankle-length leather coat. The civilian had Gestapo written all over him, and Christian guessed that von Arco was not alone in his attempt to maintain security for the U-200.

On the third day after his arrival in Danzig, Christian briefed his new officers on what to expect once they tried to clear the Baltic. 'Gentlemen,' he said seriously, looking around their eager young faces in the wardroom, while on the deck above them Frenssen's crew still chipped away at the rust as usual, 'once we are at sea, we and the enemy are like blind men who grope in the darkness for each other's throat — *in order to kill*.'

The sombre statement had its effect. Their smiles vanished. Now they were very attentive.

'We both employ charts, graphs, radios, radar, asdic — oh, a score or more of different gadgets — and all have one aim; to make that damned *ping* which can be the signal of death for some poor swine of a submariner!'

'Unfortunately they know most of *our* old tricks by now. So we let out some old oil from the bilges and fire out some clothes through the torpedo tubes to make out they have sunk us. What do they do? Why, they counter with the "oil thief", a piece of apparatus which tells them if the oil is the real thing and that we have been really sunk. We try to hit them with the acoustic torpedo and they fire off a special buoy which makes more noise than their ship's engine and the damned tin fish homes in on the buoy instead of the real target.

'We develop the *pillenwerfer*, which is an underwater gun that throws out a chemical that simulates the ping of a radar contact way away from the sub. What do they do? Why, they invent another apparatus which detects that it is not a true ping—'

He broke off for breath and looked at his officers hard. But none of their young faces showed any trace of fear at this litany of woe. They were as eager and as steadfast as ever. Greenbeaks that they were, he knew he could rely on them.

'And so it goes on and on, relentlessly, *meine Herren*,' he continued. '*But*, mark this. Whatever measures and countermeasures are introduced, skilled U-boat skippers still do get through to carry out their missions. And I am going to ensure — with your willing help — *that the U-200 will be one of those boats that survives*!' His voice was suddenly harsh and incisive. 'Is that clear, gentlemen?'

'*Klar, Herr Kap-loh*!' they cried as one.

Christian beamed at them and relaxed a little. 'All right, gentlemen, so much for the pep talk, as prescribed by the Big Lion himself. Let's get down to the nuts and bolts now. We have just over a week now before the usual piss-up and official send-off. No less a person than the Big Lion himself is coming to see us off.'

They were impressed and there was an outburst of excited whispering before Christian held up his hand for silence. 'But before that there are many things to be done still. There won't be enough hours in the day for everything we have to do. But these are our priorities. Engineer Officer, you will ensure — ' Swiftly Christian, the 'old hare', veteran of a score of combat patrols, began to rap out his orders, while the officers scribbled furiously on their pads, working madly to the tune of the chipping hammers above them pounding on the deck.

'Now then,' he concluded, 'there is still the question of the supercargo. The — er — weapons which the army jobs have already loaded will mean a reduction in the number of torpedoes we can carry. You will work that one out, Bremer,' he nodded to the baby-faced ensign in charge of the boat's armaments. 'Then there is a question of accommodation for these army types. Number One,' he looked at his second-in-command, a large hairy Bavarian, who was already being called behind his back 'Mountain Goat' on account of his hairiness and general randiness, 'you'll arrange for the ordinary soldiers to be fixed up among the crew. You'll have to hot bunk them, I suppose.'

Bremer laughed cheekily, 'I'm sure Number One will have no problem with that, sir. They say he's a bit of an expert in hot bunking.' Mountain Goat tugged at his beard. 'For a young 'un, you're risking a big lip, aren't you?' he said in that slow ponderous Bavarian manner of his. 'Don't begrudge a poor old seafaring man his simple pleasures.' He winked at Christian.

Christian winked back and said, 'On the night of the piss-up, there will be the usual girls provided.'

'Hurrah!' they cheered.

'But till then, there will be no more shore leave. The strictest security is absolutely essential. There'll be a court-martial,' Christian's face grew very sombre, 'or *worse*, for anyone who lets slip anything about our mission. Is that clear?'

They nodded their understanding, their faces sombre too, and not a little puzzled.

Christian waited expectantly — and it came as he had guessed it would, from Bremer, the 'Moses' of the officer corps and the most uninhibited of his officers. 'But what exactly *is* our mission, sir? I mean why are we taking these army types with us — and their weapons…' He broke off and stared at Christian.

Christian hesitated and told himself he didn't really know himself what their *exact* mission was. 'Well, I'll say this,' he said slowly. 'Within the framework of a great new land

offensive we have been selected by the Big Lion, and indirectly by the Führer himself, to carry the war to the enemy's homeland.'

They looked suitably impressed, but it wasn't enough for Bremer. 'To England, sir?' he persisted.

Christian shook his head.

Bremer's eyes flashed fire. 'To … *America*, sir?' he gasped, face flushing.

Christian licked his lips, which were suddenly dry. 'I think I can safely tell you that our mission will be off the east coast of the United States,' he answered, trying deliberately to keep it soft key.

Bremer whistled softly and the others stared at each other significantly. 'So if we are to carry out a mission off the *Ami* coast, sir,' Bremer reasoned, suddenly very thoughtful, 'and we are carrying — hm — special weapons which those army types loaded, then I don't think it takes a crystal ball to work out that—'

'— Then *nothing*, Ensign!' Christian cut the excited young officer off sharply. 'I think the discussion has gone far enough. Remember what I said about security, please?'

'Yessir. Of course, sir,' Bremer agreed hurriedly, his eyes sparkling excitedly. 'But think of it, sir. A mission against America, the first carried out by the *Wehrmacht* in the whole course of the war! Why, sir,' he exclaimed, '*we're gonna make history!*'

But Ensign Bremer was not fated to make history. He would be dead before the year was out, shot by his fellow countrymen, disgraced and dishonoured, and thrown carelessly into an unmarked grave…

CHAPTER 8

'Well, if you don't believe me,' von Arco snorted, his arrogant, affected face flushed with rage, 'just look at the damned thing yourself.' He threw the letter on to Christian's desk, while the Gestapo man looked on impassively, rolling a stub of unlit cigar from one corner of his mouth to the other. He had seen it all before; he would probably see it again. Nothing moved him anymore. Strictly nothing.

Hastily Christian adjusted the shaded desk light and looked at the little letter written in a flowery immature scrawl. 'Dearest Marianne,' he read, 'guess what? Not only am I to set out on my first combat patrol with one of our top aces *Kapitänleutnant* Jungblut (he's already got a whole chest full of "tin"), but I am also going to be honoured by taking the war to the enemy's homeland. For the first time we're going to give those air gangsters a taste of their own medicine.' Christian stopped reading.

Von Arco continued to glare at him. 'Well?' he snapped. 'What do you think now? The soft little shit has gone and given the game away!'

Christian took his time. The young fool had obviously been trying to show off to this unknown girlfriend of his back in the Reich and naturally, if the letter had landed in the hands of an enemy agent, he could have made a reasonable guess as to the U-200's real mission. For that Bremer certainly deserved punishing. A reprimand, a black mark on his conduct sheet, perhaps even open arrest during the patrol. But *not* the Gestapo. Bremer didn't deserve that fate. 'I can see Ensign

Bremer has made a grave mistake,' he said, phrasing his words carefully. '*Aber Ende gut, alles gut?* Eh, *Haupsturm?* You did intercept the letter, after all, long before it reached its recipient.'

But von Arco was not to be reasoned with. 'That is not the point,' he declared, 'not at all! The man cannot be relied upon. He almost effectively sabotaged our whole mission.'

In that instant Christian did not note that 'our'. He was too concerned about the young fool Ensign Bremer. 'Where did you find the letter?' he demanded hotly, feeling himself flushing.

'That is beside the point!' von Arco cried.

'Gentlemen,' the Gestapo man broke in, 'please. He was found handing it over to one of our people who ply the bumboats back and forth between the U-200 and the shore.'

'Your people!' Christian cried. 'Then, by God, it was almost a … a provocation!'

The Gestapo man remained unmoved. He simply chomped his cigar from one side of his mobile mouth to the other. What did the fate of the stupid kid concern him? He'd be dead one way or other. All these cocky wild U-boat kids were doomed anyway. How many of them had he seen leave Danzig in these last few years, all full of piss and vinegar, never to return?

'We had to be sure,' von Arco retorted equally hotly. 'If you can't trust an officer on land, how much can you trust him at sea under combat conditions?' He glared at Christian aggressively.

Christian calmed himself with difficulty. He knew he was fighting for young Bremer's life. He had no illusions about what would happen to him now that he had fallen into the hands of the Gestapo. Why these days they were executing people simply for having listened to the BBC.

'All right, all right, so the fool is guilty and has to be punished. But punish him later. I have need of an armament officer. Once we have come back from this mission, then you can deal with him.' Christian looked up at von Arco, hoping he would buy this suggestion. If the mission were successful, it would be glory and decorations all around; then the authorities might deal with Bremer's 'crime' more leniently.

Von Arco was unimpressed. 'Impossible!' he said stonily.

'What do you damn well mean - *impossible*?' Christian flared up once again. 'Where am I going to get another officer to replace him in time?'

Von Arco did not answer for a moment. Then he reached inside the shabby tweed jacket he was wearing and brought out an old yellowing photograph. Wordlessly he handed it over to a surprised Christian.

The latter took it and stared down at the photograph. It showed a 'crew' dressed in the traditional whites of a fatigue detail, their feet bare, posed with the customary buckets and brooms. A group of awkwardly grinning young naval cadets with the legend written in white pencil below. 'Crew 1932. Cruiser *Breslau*.'

For a moment Christian was completely bewildered. 'What has this photograph got to do with the Bremer business?' he demanded.

'Look at the front row,' von Arco commanded, 'third and sixth from the right.'

Numbly Christian did as he was ordered — and gasped. There at place number three his old enemy von Arco gazed at him and at number six, there was no mistaking it — *Johann von Arco*! 'Why,' he gasped, 'it's … *you*.'

'Exactly.'

'But I don't understand,' Christian stuttered.

'It is very simple,' von Arco replied, relishing the surprise he had sprung on the other man. 'I trained with my brother and graduated with the "crew" of 'thirty-two. But I found promotion too slow in the *Kriegsmarine*. When the late *Gruppenführer* Heydrich went to Berlin, he invited me to leave the Navy and join him in the SS there. We had been friends in the old days while he had still been in the *Kriegsmarine* himself.' He shrugged easily. 'Promotion was quicker in the SS, so I accepted the offer.'

'Do you mean you are … a trained naval officer?'

'Yes, torpedo specialist. *In submarines*! Prior to nineteen thirty-nine I did two years as a number one in the old U-16. *Kapitänleutnant* Prien was my skipper.'

Christian looked at von Arco hard. There was no mistaking the look of triumph on his arrogant face. 'You mean,' he said very slowly, as if he were formulating his words with difficulty, 'that you think you can replace young Bremer?'

'Not *think*, *know*!' von Arco tapped his pocket significantly. 'The authorization from Grand Admiral Dönitz was telegraphed through half an hour ago as soon as Naval Intelligence learned of Bremer's crime. The Admiral has granted me the temporary rank of lieutenant-commander, the same as your own. It's rather senior for an armaments officer, I suppose, but I know that should not cause problems between us. After all, you are the skipper — *still!*' He emphasized the word for reasons known only to himself and smirked.

Christian looked from von Arco's face to that of the heavyset Gestapo man, but the latter chewed on his cold cigar stump and looked away, as if he already had guessed what the naval officer was going to say and wanted no part of what was to come. He was simply a cop. He had been a cop under the Kaiser and a cop during the republic. Now he was a cop under

Hitler. Probably when the commies took over, which they would one day, he'd still be a cop, as long as he kept his nose clean. What did all this death and glory crap mean to him? All he wanted was his old woman, the odd glass of schnapps, his cigars, and a nice fat pension at the end of the day. Let the glory boys get on with it. He continued to study the ceiling.

'This is a put-up job, isn't it, von Arco?' Christian said deliberately, knowing now that the SS man was just like his dead brother. He was out for the medals he might collect during this vital mission and the promotion and advancement that went with them. 'You could have saved that young fool if you had wanted to. But you *didn't* want to. You'd got it all nicely planned so that you could take his place on the patrol. You've been aiming at something like this all the damned time?'

Von Arco looked back at the icy-faced skipper easily. 'I don't think it is very seemly to talk in this manner in front of a civilian, *Herr Kapitänleutnant*,' he said very formally. 'It is not in the best tradition of the German Navy.'

Christian rose to his feet angrily, eyes flashing fire. 'Fuck the best tradition of the German Navy!' he exploded and grabbed for his battered cap. 'Frenssen — *Obermaat* Frenssen,' he bellowed up the conning tower. 'Stand by with a vehicle at once.'

'At once, sir,' Frenssen's voice echoed back.

Von Arco's smirk changed to a sudden look of alarm. Even the bored Gestapo man seemed slightly impressed by Christian's sudden rage. 'What are you going to do, Jungblut?' he stuttered. 'Where are you going?'

'Where am I going?' Christian yelled, slapping the old white cap on his blond head. 'I'll tell you where I'm bloody well going — to Mürwik! I'm going to speak to the Big Lion personally and I'm going to tell him that *Herr Kapitänleutnant*' he sneered over von Arco's new rank, 'bloody von Arco is coming on the U-200 only over my dead body. *Morgen*!'

'*Morgen,*' the Gestapo man said automatically, as Christian started to clamber swiftly up the ladder of the conning tower. Then he turned to a frozen von Arco and said, 'Looks as if the wet fart has hit the side of the thunderbox, don't it, Haupsturm?'

Von Arco remained stonily silent…

The long white-painted train was just steaming into Danzig main station, as Christian, followed by a panting Frenssen, pushed his way through the barrier, ignoring the shouts of the chained dogs posted there and the moans of the ticket collector. Already the long lines of white-clad nurses and the middle-aged ladies of the *Frauenschaft* carrying huge jugs of coffee and trays of cigarettes were beginning to move forward to meet it. Further back, the fleet of ambulances, their doors already opened, were reversing into position; while the waiting doctors, instruments bulging from their pockets, stethoscopes hanging from their necks, were stubbing out their cigarettes in preparation for what was to come.

Now as the long train creaked to a halt, a panting Christian could already hear the cries, the moans, the calls like those of trapped animals, coming from the white-painted train with the great red crosses adorning its sides and roof. Next to him, Frenssen bit his lip and said, 'Sir, it is a hospital train … straight from the Russian front. They must be seriously wounded, urgent cases, or they wouldn't unload them in broad daylight so that the civvies can see what's happening to the poor old hairy-assed stubble-hoppers out there in the East.'

Christian swallowed, his rage suddenly forgotten. 'I suppose you're right, Frenssen,' he whispered.

Now all along the train the doors were beginning to swing open and almost at once the nostrils of those waiting on the icy platform were assailed by the nauseating fug that came from the train, a mixture of ether, faeces, and sheer, naked, human misery.

Christian stared aghast. This was not a hospital train like they sometimes showed in the newsreels on the *Deutsche Wochenschau*, all gleaming steel and white paint, complete with immaculate bunks and crisply uniformed nurses. Here the wounded lay groaning in dirty straw stained by bloody faeces, packed together like animals in a cage, tended to by haggard, ashen, wild-eyed nurses, their aprons dirty and covered with patches of rust-coloured blood, with here and there a soldier gasping hectically as if he were running some great race — a last race with death.

Hastily the nurses and doctors went into action. It was almost as if they were racing against time. '*Los … los!*' the doctors cried hastily at the sweating stretcher-bearers, as they sprang from case to case, feeling pulses, testing reflexes, pushing home hypodermics, throwing blankets over the faces of those they could help no more. All was controlled chaos, misery and sheer naked horror. And there seemed no end to the wounded. One fleet of ambulances, packed tight, left to be replaced immediately by yet another and still the terrible victims of the war in Russia kept on coming.

Now the whole length of the platform was littered with their broken, lice-ridden bodies, as the nurses went from one moaning man to another, slicing off the blood-stained paper bandages and rags. They were followed by elderly soldiers, with masks over their mouths, pumping great clouds of lice powder over their half-naked broken bodies to stop typhus.

'Poor — poor young bastards,' Frenssen whispered through gritted teeth, for even his customary high spirits were stilled by the sight of so much human misery. 'It brings it home to you, sir, don't it?' He shook his head in sorrow. 'Yer forget just how much those poor shits of infantrymen are suffering out there.'

Christian wrenched his gaze free from the tortured face of a boy, who tossed and turned on the platform, held by some private nightmare, two purple suppurating holes where his eyes had once been. 'Come on,' he said tonelessly. 'Let's get back.'

'Where sir? To the boat?'

Christian nodded numbly.

In silence, Frenssen followed him out into the bright clean morning, gulping in great, grateful gulps of fresh air after the fetid stench of the hospital train. Without a word they walked to where they had parked the Volkswagen jeep. Frenssen got behind the wheel and started up. In the driving mirror he cast a furtive glance at Christian, but the latter's pale young face revealed nothing. Yet as Frenssen began to drive away, he knew what his boss was thinking. What did all the von Arcos of this world matter, compared with the suffering of those broken young men? With or without von Arco on board the U-200, *Kapitänleutnant* Christian Jungblut wanted revenge for all those young Germans, soldier or civilian, who were suffering so much in this winter of 1944...

CHAPTER 9

'*SILENCE IN THE FRIGGING KNOCKING SHOP!*' *Obermaat* Frenssen's voice boomed from one end of the festively decorated shed to the other. At the long tables, groaning under the weight of mounds of cold chops, rings of salami, and case after case of beer and schnapps, the officers and crew of the U-200 waited expectantly for the 'piss-up' to commence.

Frenssen, his face flushed a brick-red with the half litre of potent firewater he had already consumed, looked around at their expectant faces and snorted, 'Well, you've heard the Big Lion telling yer what a bunch o' brave shits you are, ready to sacrifice yer stupid turnips for the Fatherland.'

Von Arco, awkward in his new navy uniform, sitting next to the myopic gunnery officer, frowned.

Frenssen ignored the frown. 'You've heard the skipper tell yer he don't want no dead heroes — just live sailors. If anybody wants to die a hero's death for his frigging country, let it be the frigging enemy sonavabitch! Yer've heard the Number One, too, tell yer he's gonna come down hard on any man who fucks up. Strict disciplinarian measures was his words. Now in my kind of German,' he poked a thumb against his enormous chest, 'that means like shit through a tin horn ... crap going through a goose, *get that you purple-pissing pansies!*'

Number One flushed with embarrassment and Christian grinned at his discomfiture. Frenssen was in fine fettle, running well and truly to form. Most of the men were virgins without doubt. This night, if Frenssen had his way, not only would they take aboard much strong water, but they would also be relieved of their virginity.

'Now you've heard the brass, full of the usual pious piss and vinegar. Now you reluctant heroes, wankers and piss pansies all, if I'm not mistaken!' He grinned hugely and made an obscene gesture with his cupped right hand. 'Hey, the old five-fingered widow, eh. Oh, look it just came off in me hand!' He guffawed hugely at his own humour, while some of the young sailors blushed and von Arco looked severe.

'Well then, you're gonna lose yer cherry this night, if I have my way. I'm not gonna have no wanking on board the U-200, I swear that by the Great Whore of Buxtehude, where the dogs shit through their ribs.'

He gasped for breath and then took a huge swallow from the water glass of *Schlichte* which stood before him on the table. 'Don't think that's water, shipmates,' he commented, wiping the back of his hairy paw across his lips. 'Never drink water, lads.' He winked knowingly and lowered his voice, 'Cos fishes fuck in water, that's why!'

They roared with laughter. Even the myopic gunnery lieutenant tittered.

'Now where was I?' Frenssen bellowed.

'Losing our cherry this night, *Obermaat!*' a handsome young sailor cried excitedly, as if he couldn't wait to be relieved of his virginity.

Frenssen looked at him sagely. 'Well, I don't know about you, handsome,' he simpered, hand on hip. 'But for these here normal lads, yes, it's gonna be cherry-picking time tonight.'

Again the shed rocked with laughter.

'Right, then, this is the ship's course. First, we're gonna fill our guts with good grub.' He indicated the huge plates of food. ''Cos from tomorrow onwards yer gonna be eating dog food outa cans — and it's no use asking dear old Petty Officer Frenssen, which can's got the gash in, *Obermaat?* 'Cos there ain't any.'

Once more the sally was greeted by laughter and Christian told himself the big bluff petty officer was really enjoying his role. Besides he, too, was letting off steam, relaxing from the tension which had been steadily building up these last weeks. Soon there would be tension enough, he reminded himself grimly. That exit from the Baltic would really be a bitch. Hastily he dismissed the thought from his mind and concentrated on Frenssen's virtuoso performance.

'After the grub comes the suds. Plenty of it!' Frenssen was roaring, tipping back another glass of the fiery colourless schnapps. 'Sauce and suds, that's the next stage of the course this crew is steering tonight, shipmates. So just to get in practice, *fill glasses*!' As one, both officers and ratings unscrewed the caps of the bottles of schnapps in front of them and filled their glasses to the brim. '*Two*!' Frenssen barked, as if he were on the parade ground, 'raise glasses!'

The whole crew raised their glasses to the level of their chests, forearm set rigidly at the forty-five degree angle regulations prescribed for such formal toasts.

Frenssen waited, then barked, '*Three*, get this inside yer Uncle Otto!'

With a flourish he drained the glass, as did the others, coughing and spluttering as the potent mixture struck the back of their throats. Next to Christian, the gunnery officer, his face purple and twisted to one side, as if he were being choked, gasped, 'Do you … always do this … before a combat patrol, *Kapitänleutnant*?' Christian laughed softly. 'Yes. It's a kind of drug. These youngsters won't know what's hit 'em for the next twenty-four hours. By the time they do, it will be too late. We'll be out to sea and …' His voice tailed away.

The gunnery officer suddenly looked very scared.

'And finally comrades, when you're all suitably pissed, there'll be the women. Fat 'uns and thin 'uns,' he modelled the shapes with his big eyes, rolling his eyes lasciviously, 'black 'uns and blonde 'uns. Great crap on the Christmas Tree, there's gonna be some parting of the old beaver tonight — *and it's all for free, courtesy of the German taxpayer!*'

There was a great roar, wild cheering, and clapping of hands. The gunnery officer swallowed hard and whispered to Christian, blinking behind the thick glasses. 'Does one really have to — er — indulge in these whores?' He cleared his throat with difficulty. 'I mean, *Kapitänleutnant*, one might — er — catch a certain — hm — disease.'

'*Herr Leutnant,*' Christian said cynically. 'According to the statistics, which they tell me do not lie, sooner or later all U-boat men catch a certain disease. They call it — *death!*'

The gunnery officer looked aghast.

Up at the head of the table Frenssen was bellowing, 'Did I ever tell you the joke about the two nuns practising *hymns* together in bed. Come on, you bunch o' piss pansies, laugh and give her ears a visit. *Hims*, don't yer frigging well get it…' The big 'piss-up' was under way…

Now the 'piss-up' was degenerating into a noisy drunken confusion of slurred voices, each trying to outbid the other in volume, with trestle tables littered with 'dead soldiers' and awash with spilled beer. In the corner the radio was going full blast, too, adding to the roar. But the red-faced intoxicated ratings did not notice; they were too concerned in putting across what they thought, in their drunken state, was some

90

witty point or a terribly funny joke.

'And the whore had tits of wood. I kid you not! 'Cos when he came to he found he had splinters in his lips.'... 'In the end I found out she didn't like the old salami. Can yer imagine that, not liking the salami?'... 'She was after women and playing around with candles and dicks made o' rubber.'... 'So the recruit pulled out this bit of horseshoe and sez to the kitchen bull, "But sarge, there's a bit of a horseshoe in my giddup soup." And the kitchen bull just laughs and sez, "Get it down yer, son. It'll put iron in yer!" '... 'So she sez to me, "Come on up here, sailor and I'll give yer summat new." ... and I sez to her, "Yer, *like leprosy, perhaps.*" '...

So it went on, a confused collection of stale old jokes that Christian had heard on such occasions a dozen times before; traditional sailors' songs and lores, complaints, snatches of dirty ditties, and beer, beer, beer, punctuated by shots of schnapps, schnapps, schnapps.

Watching them, with the gunnery lieutenant, snoring drunkenly, his face in a pool of stale beer on the table, at his side, Christian felt a kind of weary happiness and compassion for his young men. Some people, he told himself, would not have found them very pleasant at this particular moment. They were coarse and crude, here and there vomiting into the corners. There was one of them, stripped naked save for his boots, drunkenly attempting to urinate into a beer bottle for a bet, while his red-faced comrades cheered and laughed and slapped his skinny naked rump with their caps.

But for him they were simply naïve boys, enjoying this time out of war while there was still time. For, as he had told the drunken soldier snoring at his side, there was the Mark of Cain on them all. They would kill soon and be killed. If they survived this patrol, they might well die violently on the next.

The law of averages was against them. Sooner or later they were all doomed, doomed to die young.

A 'beer corpse' passed; six giggling drunken sailors bearing an absolutely stiff rating, his cap placed tenderly on his unconscious chest. As the 'cortege' passed the senior rating snapped '*Eyes right!*' Solemnly the six of them carried out the salute and the senior rating cried above the racket, 'Died in the line of duty, sir. Too much sauce. Gonna bury him in the thunderboxes.'

Wearily Christian touched his hand to his forehead in a kind of response and smiled but at the same time he felt an icy finger of fear trace its way down his spine. Was this mock funeral a symbol of what was soon to come?

Frenssen didn't give him a chance to answer that particular overwhelming question for now he came pushing and barging his way through the milling drunk crowd, shouting at the top of his voice, 'Make room for a frigging admiral, will ya, you ape turds. Make way for an admiral!'

Face beetroot-red, red eyes sparkling wickedly, he snapped to attention and threw Christian a tremendous parade ground salute. 'Permission to speak to the officer, *sir*?' he barked formally.

'Fuck off, you big-horned ox,' Christian said without rancour, not returning the salute. 'Don't try to pull my pisser, Frenssen.'

'Wouldn't dream of it, sir,' Frenssen answered, smiling hugely. 'Some of the ladies of the night, waiting outside could do a better job o' that kind than Frau Frenssen's handsome son. Besides I'm a virgin in that way.' He rolled his eyes in what he probably thought was a seductive manner.

'Piss or get off the pot,' Christian said. 'What is it?'

'Thought it might be about time for the officers and gents to leave, sir. There are ladies outside who have been detailed to take care of the officers' and gents' special pleasures.'

'You mean you want to wheel in the whores now?'

'Exactly, sir.' Frenssen grabbed the front of his bulging trousers dramatically and whispered huskily, 'Got so much ink in my fountain-pen, I don't know who to write to first! I imagine it'll start getting a little hairy once the ladies begin taking off their clothes. I doubt if it'll be a pleasant sight and I'd like to spare your delicate —'

'We're off,' Christian interrupted him, grabbing his cap. He looked down the table where von Arco sat gloomily among the rest of the drunken U-200 officers and nodded.

Von Arco returned the nod and called to the others. Like drunken puppies they began to follow him to the door, reeling a little as if their legs were unsteady, stepping awkwardly over the 'beer corpses' which were everywhere now.

Frenssen looked steadily at Christian for a moment or two longer, eyes suddenly full of compassion, almost love. How many times had they gone through piss-ups of this kind together! Now so many of the young men who had drunk and whored together with them on those occasions were long beneath the sea, dead. 'Sir,' he said with unusual softness for him. 'Why don't you knock yourself off a piece as well? Christ knows what's to come for the old U-200. Might as well have something to remind you of the old country. You never know, it might —'

Christian forced a laugh. 'You're getting sentimental in your old age, *Obermaat. Los*, get on with it, wheel on the ladies of the night and pray to God that you don't pick on one of those *Veronika Dankeschöns* — VD for short — who might leave you with something else to remind you of the old country, namely a dose of clap!'

Frenssen laughed uproariously and threw Christian another tremendous salute. 'Right you are, clear the decks for action!' He spun round, clapped together the heads of two ratings who were in the way so that they reeled apart as if they had each just received an uppercut, and yelled 'Open them frigging pearly gates,' he indicated the big doors at the other end of the shed, 'and bring on the frigging dancing girls, 'cos I've got me party frock on already!'

Next instant the doors flew open and a mass of clawing, shrieking, excited, drunken whores fell in, tearing off their clothes as they did so, as if they could not get into action soon enough to service these randy sailors.

Christian sighed. He had seen enough. Stepping carefully over the 'beer corpses', nodding in approval of the drunken rating fiddling with his flies with clumsy fingers before keeling over, out to the world, he too left.

Behind him a beery woman's voice cackled, 'What do you call that little sad worm, sailor boy? You'll have to do something better than *that*, if you're gonna make yer Auntie Gertie happy…'

Feeling a little drunk himself, as the cold night air struck him, Christian wandered aimlessly through the blacked-out streets of the port. Not a chink of light showed and the cobbled, winding, medieval alleys behind the naval docks seemed deserted. But behind the blackout curtains and shutters, there was warm exciting life, he knew. He could hear the muted chink of glasses, the sound of gramophone music, the odd high-pitched female laugh.

The sounds made him feel sad, cut off from this nice cosy,

civilian world. Tomorrow, just before dawn, he would pass out of their lives like the shadow he had always been since the war started, unknown, unremembered, unlamented. If he and the rest of his 'Lords' died, all the Homeland would know of them would be a laconic notice buried in the inside pages of the local paper, '*One of our U-boats is reported missing*'. Who would know of them — care? Inside his head a hard, cynical voice sneered, 'Come off it, Christian Jungblut, you'll be wanting frigging eggs in yer beer next! It's always been like that. The civvies send the young ones off to war, full of piss and vinegar, and they stay behind — to frigging well die — *in bed*!'

Christian smiled to himself and wandered on. He was being sentimental. Of course it had always been that way. 'And the mate at the wheel had a bloody good feel at the girl he left behind him.' He hummed the cynical old sailors' song to himself suddenly. It about summed it all up.

'You sound happy, Mr Officer.' A voice startled him suddenly out of the inky darkness.

He stopped short and turned round swiftly. Behind him in a doorway a tiny flashlight beamed. For an instant he caught a glimpse of a pretty white face, framed by a mass of blonde hair curled in the newest fashion — 'the all-clear roll'. Then the light went out again, and the husky voice said, 'Sorry, but I've got to save the battery. They're terribly hard to get. Say, have you a light?'

'Yes, of course.' He fumbled for his cigarette-lighter in the pocket of his greatcoat and clicked it on. Again he caught the face and the look of those blue eyes, a mixture of youthful innocence and professional eagerness. He realized he had been picked up by a whore. 'You should have come to the party,' he said.

She laughed softly and puffed at her cigarette. 'I don't think so. I like my parties to be private.' She hesitated and he waited. 'Would you like to come home with me? It wouldn't cost much — and I'll give you a good time.'

Christian thought of what was to come. What had he to lose, he told himself, even if she was a *Veronika Dankeschön*? 'Why not,' he said. 'I don't think —'

'Don't think,' she interrupted urgently, pressing her body against him, grinding her loins against his stomach, 'just *feel*. That's the way to survive in this damned war.' There was a momentary note of bitterness in her voice. Next moment it had vanished and she was saying, 'Now come, let's not waste time, *Herr Offizier*. We've got to make every minute count because of what you're going off to…' It was only long afterwards that the full implications of that remark struck him, but by then it was too late to do a damned thing about it…

CHAPTER 10

Silently he dressed in the red light of the naked bulb which she had covered with a piece of red silk cloth, 'So you know where you are — a private whorehouse,' she had joked, though somehow, slightly drunk as he was, he had felt her heart had not been really in it.

But he had not needed any stimulants of that kind, once he had been close to her. She had begun to kiss him, cunningly, expertly, and he had felt a sudden burning eagerness. His hands had followed the seam of her sheer black stockings, searching for the free white thigh above, smooth, firm, utterly enchanting.

Abruptly, consumed with passion, he had pushed her on to her back. Then he had been boring into her body and he had forgotten the harsh world of men, their violence, their machines of death, the cruel logic of kill or be killed.

Thereafter he had fallen into an exhausted sleep, his blond hair matted damply to his furrowed forehead, while unknown to him the whore had stroked the back of his head like an anxious mother trying to soothe some fevered child.

Now he pulled on his boots while she lay there, her eyes closed, apparently asleep, hurrying for it was already four in the morning. The tug was scheduled to tow them out of the docks into the Baltic before first light; they had to leave Danzig before dawn. The fewer prying eyes that saw the U-200 leave port, the better.

He was almost ready. Hastily he took out his wallet and pulled out a note. One hundred *Reichsmarks*. He thought again and took out the rest of his notes. She might as well have the lot. She had made him happy for a while and what use would money be to him where he was going? Gently he crossed the room to where she lay on the rumpled, sweat-stained sheet and placed the notes on the night table next to the garishly tinted picture of some saint or other, with a rosary dangling from one corner of the frame. Did that mean she was Catholic he wondered. If she were, then in all probability she was — in spite of her perfect German — a Pole. He laughed gently to himself. He had added yet another nationality to the long list of women of all races he had bedded since the war had started. 'Something to drool about when you're an old man,' that cynical little voice inside his head hissed. 'If you survive to grow old.'

On the bed the whore stirred uneasily. For a moment her eyes flickered open. They were deep black and clear in spite of the night. For an instant he could almost believe that she was unspoiled and innocent. 'You're going?' she whispered.

He nodded fumbling with his buttons. 'I've left you some money — thanks.'

'You can come again,' she said.

'I'll try.' He grabbed his cap. He was running late. He touched his hand to the brim in a kind of salute and then he was gone — she could hear him clattering down the steps outside two at a time, as if he were in a hurry to go to his death.

For what seemed an age, she simply lay there, listening to the night sounds outside, the muted hammering from the docks, a ship's siren out in the fjord, the rumble of some troop train carrying its freight of cannon fodder for the Russian front, her eyes pressed tightly closed like a child trying to blot out a nightmare. She lay there completely still, her breast barely moving as she breathed in and out. She might well have been dead.

Across the road the church clock began to chime the hour. One … two … three … four o'clock this cold November morning. As that last metallic stroke died away, booming hollowly, she made up her mind at last and threw back the bed-clothes. She slipped into the gaudy mules that, with the see-through black nightie and the frilly knickers, went with a trade that she detested, and crossed to the phone. Predictably, it was hidden by a cheap doll dressed in an eighteenth-century crinoline. She picked up the phone and dialled his number, the one he had given her for special cases like this. Most of her clients were drunken sailors and dockers who knew little in spite of their boasting. But this was the 'ace' with the Knight's Cross who had been spotted arriving at the main station two weeks ago. Now he was sailing this morning. The Home Army would be interested to know about him.

That cold voice that never showed any human emotion answered and rapidly she told him the details in Polish. At the end of her report, all she got for her pains was the click of the phone being hung up — not even a 'thank you.' Patriot she might be, but she was also a whore. Those papist moralists of the Home Army HQ could never forgive that.

She slumped on the bed, all energy drained from her suddenly, as if a tap had just been opened. She thought abruptly of his face as he had slept and slowly two great sad tears began to roll down her wan cheeks…

Two kilometres away, Christian watched as the steel hawser tightened, came quivering out of the dirty water of the harbour, and the U-200 started to move. Down below most of the crew had a 'free watch' and were snoring on their backs, out to the world. Now the U-200 was in the hands of a skeleton crew, with von Arco in nominal charge. All the same he wanted to see the boat into the Baltic himself.

Slowly they moved forward and Christian could feel the first fierce bite of the sea wind. He buried his face into his collar, as the routine orders passed back and forth. Behind them Danzig still lay wreathed in darkness, sunk into the blackout. No one had come to see them off, save the cordon of chained dogs, weapons at the ready, eyes suspicious. The whores who had given so many of his young men their first taste of sex would be fast asleep now or counting their money. The mess stewards would be in the littered shed where they had celebrated, cleaning up, stealing the food and drink left over to sell on the black market. And soon all would be clean and tidy once more, with no trace of their passing left. They might never have passed this way at all.

To their front the tug sounded its siren. A flock of gulls which had settled on the deck of the U-200, hoping for the usual scraps, rose in hoarse raucous protest. Next to Christian on the conning tower, von Arco barked to the deckmen, 'Prepare to cast off!' Bending his head to the tube, he rapped 'Ready to start motors!'

Christian thought he sounded very professional; he hadn't forgotten the old routines.

The tug signalled again. They were obviously way out in the channel. Now when the U-200's motors started, they would be too far away from Danzig to alert any watchers to their departure.

'Cast off forrard!' von Arco ordered.

Hastily the deckmen, muffled in their heavy leather coveralls, wrestled with the big hawser. A splash and it had disappeared over the side.

Von Arco bent to the tube, 'Start both!' he commanded.

There was an asthmatic grunt. A cough. A whir. Suddenly the diesels burst into life and there was that old cloying stench of oil flooding the cold pre-dawn air. From below came the satisfying throb of the engines, as the U-200 started to move forward under its own power.

On the bridge of the tug, now beginning to turn for home, the aldis lamp commenced. Christian read the tug skipper's message without benefit of signallers. He had experience enough, after all. 'Good luck and good hunting,' it read.

Christian smiled a little cynically. It all sounded like an exciting game from the safety of the port of Danzig — 'good hunting', indeed! But he waved all the same as the tug started to disappear into the darkness, to leave them alone in that vast seascape.

He took one last look around it. It would be the last he would see of Germany for — *'perhaps for ever'*, that insidious little inner voice that always plagued him hissed.

He ignored it and turning to von Arco, snapped, 'I'll take over now.'

'Sir!' the other officer snapped politely enough, though it was fortunate that Christian could not see his face. For it was a curious mixture of nervous apprehension and hectic excitement, as if the thought of what was to come both frightened and excited von Arco.

Christian bent over the tube. 'Prepare to flood tanks,' he ordered. 'Clear the decks!' he cried an instant later.

In a clatter of nailed boots the deck crew rushed up the ladder and dropped below from the conning tower. Water showered everywhere. Christian looked to left and right, as von Arco hastened below. All clear.

Below the petty officers on duty were barking, 'Foreship on diving station.'… 'Midship diving stations.'… 'After-ship on diving stations.'…

Christian waited no longer. This was it. In spite of the routine of having done this a myriad times before, he felt a sudden thrill, a moment of utter finality. There was no turning back now. He slid down the dripping wet clammy ladder and fell on to his haunches in the centre of the control room.

The hatch cover thudded home. Automatically he checked whether the exhaust valves were closed. They were. Behind him the electric motors sprang into action, taking over from the diesels. He could feel his ears pop with the change.

'Tanks ready!' the petty officer shouted.

'Flood!' he commanded.

Hurriedly four ratings knelt and wrenched at the air levers. A sudden hissing noise. Rapidly the air escaped from the boat and water started to gurgle noisily into the tanks. He flashed a glance at von Arco's face. It retained the same mixture of excitement and fear. Christian frowned and dismissed von Arco. The U-200 rocked gently forward, then backwards. An instant later it righted itself, no sound now save the gentle throb of the electric motors.

Lying on his bunk, fighting to waken, knowing already he was going to have the father and mother of a hangover, Frenssen watched through narrowed eyes, the motors beating like the thump-thump of his own heart. For a moment the skipper was alone in the eerie green glowing light of the control room. Under the cropped blond hair, his face was tough and determined, the blue eyes firm and purposeful in spite of the evening's boozing. The skipper radiated confidence and self-assurance. There was no mistaking the look of a fighter in his prime about him. Yet, Frenssen told himself, the decisions he had to make now were almost unbearable for a man of his age. Before the sixty-odd souls now locked up in this steel coffin lay a voyage into the unknown in which everything depended upon luck — and that young man standing there alone. It was a damned awesome responsibility! Frenssen breathed out hard and the next moment wished he hadn't. A sharp stabbing prong suddenly seemed to be attempting to take out his right eye.

But up there in the control room alone, Christian Jungblut was unconcerned about what was to come. In the long bitter years of the war at sea, he had long ago learned to take obstacles as they came. He would do the same this time. First there would be the exit from the Baltic. Once that problem was solved, it would be the crossing of the North Atlantic, with all its dangers. Once he reached the eastern seaboard of the United States, he would open his sealed orders, discover what his real target was and begin worrying about that particular obstacle only then. Step by step — that was the only sensible way to do it. Otherwise a U-boat skipper would go stark raving mad.

Leaning against the bulkhead, almost hidden in the shadows, von Arco watched Christian, too, his arrogant face set in a look of naked hatred. Now he knew what Jungblut had done to his brother. In that last secret briefing with the Big Lion, Dönitz had virtually admitted the truth about his brother's suicide. The handsome cocky young bastard standing there so confidently next to the periscope had been the direct cause of Kuno's death.

Now all Jungblut needed to do was to make the slightest mistake, one single wrong decision, and he would take over — he had Dönitz's written authority to do so. Then, by God, he'd make Jungblut pay for what he had done to Kuno. *Herr Kapitänleutnant Christian Jungblut would never return from 'Project N.Y.'*…

BOOK TWO: THE ATLANTIC CROSSING

CHAPTER 1

There was no mistaking the sound. By now all of London had come to know it. That familiar chug-chug like the sound of a sinister aerial two-stroke motor-bike.

Potts paused and looked at the grey sky above London. Yes, there it was. A sinister black shape, spurting scarlet flame. A doodle-bug, one of the thousands that had been launched at the Capital since the summer, charging across London; a ton of high explosive piloted by a gyro compass. There was something horrific, almost demonic about the damned German missile.

Suddenly — startlingly — the engine cut out. 'Start counting to seventy,' someone cried, 'then duck!'

'I've got to get me false teeth,' a woman shrieked. 'I've just put them in water!'

'What d' yer think old Hitler's dropping,' a man's voice sneered urgently, '*frigging sandwiches*!'

Routinely, Potts turned his head to the wall and unfurled his precious black umbrella, which together with the black jacket and striped pants marked him unmistakably as a civil servant. He began to count, as did the others crouching next to the protection of the wall. He had just reached the usual count of seventy when there was a tremendous explosion over by Charing Cross station. The ground trembled beneath like a live thing. A hot blast wave buffeted him about the face. Instantly his horned-rimmed spectacles fogged over. A woman screamed. A dog pelted down the centre of the road, tail between its hind legs. Somewhere the bell of an ambulance began to ring urgently. It was over till the next time.

Carefully Potts flicked the dust off his umbrella. At least it had saved his precious suit. He had no more coupons for another. This one would have to last him for the 'duration', as they had been calling the war for five years now.

Next to him the woman without the false teeth said, 'I blame frigging Churchill for it.' She made a vague gesture at the ruins which were central London. 'Labour wouldn't have allowed it if they'd been in. Frigging fat sod!'

Potts gave her his polite civil service smile. These days, it seemed, they blamed Churchill for everything. He shook his head. What an ungrateful people the British were!

Five minutes later he entered Frascati's, handed his bowler and umbrella to the waiter with the usual injunction, 'Guard them with your life, Luigi,' and walked into the splendid Edwardian dining room.

C was already waiting for him, seated on one of the plush chairs under a gilded Edwardian cherub, staring moodily out of the window, as grey as the day, looking as if he might well already be dead.

He saw Potts and nodded coldly. 'Let's get the ordering done with,' he snapped, voice heavy with power. 'Nothing on the bloody menu anyway but dried egg and something called "Woolton Pie".'

'Yessir,' Potts agreed tamely and took the menu C proffered him. Of course, C could have eaten a splendid pre-war meal if he had wanted to. A fiver to the head waiter and the problem would have been solved very discreetly. But C wasn't like that.

As C studied the menu, Potts watched him over the edge of his own. The head of the British Secret Service had an utterly conventional background — Eton, the Life Guards, intelligence work in the Old War, with the usual DSO, a rich marriage. But his eyes were totally out of character. They were

107

cold and calculating; the eyes of a man who used his fellow human beings like pawns, to be dealt with and dispensed with as he felt necessary. Potts of the civil service told himself C was not a man to be lightly crossed. Suddenly he wished he was back in his old department of the Home Office, where everything had been statistics and figures, not bothersome human beings.

When the waiter had taken their order, C opened the conversation. 'Plenty of space in here ... not packed in like sardines, eh... Of course, only the best people eat here ... No problem of security, what.' Potts nodded his agreement and waited for what was to come. How he hated this business of being a spy, betraying the secrets of his own department like this to C. 'Well, then,' C got round to it without any further ado, 'what have you from the *gentlemen*' — he emphasized the word with a sneer — 'of the SOE? What have you on this sub business?'

Potts told him, keeping one eye open for the approach of the wine waiter. If he tipped him half a crown in advance, they might get something drinkable and he could always use a drink after these sessions with C. It helped to soften his sense of guilt.

C mulled over the information for a few moments. Then he said, 'According to a pansy professor, a broken-down Polish countess, and a renegade Hun whore — what awfully common people get into espionage these days — the Hun sub has definitely taken these doodle-bug things on board?'

'Yessir.'

'So what do you conclude from that, Potts — or better what do your masters conclude?' C asked.

Potts knew, as always, that C was putting him down. But there was nothing he could do about it. The C's of this world had always run the country in their high-handed, arrogant, upper-class way and they always would. In British society it was a fact of life. 'I think they are about to attempt a missile attack, using a submarine, just as they recently did on the Norfolk area using missiles borne by aircraft, sir.'

'Exactly. But what do your people think the Hun target is going to be?'

'So far, sir, they have not come to any conclusion about that. Departmental thinking and rumour at the moment, sir, is that it won't be the Channel — too heavily guarded. Perhaps Hull in the North, sir?' he ventured.

'Rubbish!' C snorted. 'Why risk a precious sub just to launch a couple of missiles at that godforsaken place! The arsehole of the world — *Hull*.' He laughed coarsely, showing his ugly false teeth.

Potts flushed. He had always hated their upper-class coarseness, the way they used crudities in public, even in front of women; but then their own women cursed like troopers. 'No, isn't it obvious, man?'

'How do you mean, sir?'

But before C could answer, the wine waiter came and C began to fuss with the ordering. But he didn't tip the man and Potts told himself they'd get one of those vinegar wartime brews which he swore they made in some cellar down in Soho.

When the wine had arrived and been served, C continued. 'Of course, it's our cousins across the sea — they're the folk old Hun is after,' he boomed.

Potts looked at him aghast. 'Do you mean the United States, sir?'

'Of course,' C said happily, as if he almost enjoyed the prospect, which in truth he did. 'We've been on the receiving end for five years now, let the Yanks have a taste of war for a change.' He took a great sip of his wine and said, 'Not bad, not bad at all.'

'But sir,' Potts objected. 'The Yanks are totally unprepared. I mean we had months to prepare for the V-1 attack. General Pile redeployed his guns on the coast to knock them out of the sky over the sea. The RAF moved its fighters down to the south-east and Squadron-Commander Savage's squadron perfected their new technique for dealing with them. There was a massive barrage balloon network set up... Well, sir, you know better than I what we did last spring. But the Yanks have nothing, absolutely nothing.' A little helplessly he took a sip of the red wine and wished next moment he hadn't.

C was unimpressed. But his cold cunning eyes were beginning to look interested. Potts knew the look of old. He was at it again, hatching up one of his devious schemes. He brushed the end of his clipped military moustache thoughtfully and said, almost as if he were thinking out loud, 'I wonder how long it will take our U-boat Hun to reach the American eastern seaboard?'

'But sir, with the correct procedures initiated immediately, we could stop the U-boat at the exit to the Baltic,' Potts objected.

'Damn fool! Of course, we don't want it knocked out on this side of the ocean. We *want* it to reach American waters. Now what do you think?'

Potts gave in. 'Seven ... eight, perhaps nine days, sir, depending on the weather.'

C pursed his lips. 'Do you think Savage's Spitfires could be deployed to the other side of the Atlantic by then?'

Perfect civil servant that he was, always ready with the right information when the minister called for it, Potts said, 'It would take five days in a fast cruiser. They could be launched by catapult out at sea and fly their last five hundred miles themselves to land at one of the fields around New York.'

C absorbed the information. Somewhere, Potts told himself, they were cooking that dreadful new fish snoek, which was now appearing on the menu everywhere. His stomach turned; the smell was absolutely dreadful. C didn't notice. He said, 'I am sure you are well aware of our position *vis-a-vis* our cousins from across the sea, Potts? Since they entered the war in 'forty-one, it has changed considerably. Once we ran the show and they did as we told them. Now the boot's on the other foot.' He sighed faintly. 'God, after all, is always on the side of the big battalions — and they have the big battalions. For every man we can put in the firing line on the Continent, they can field three. So now they call the tune and we dance to it, much to Winnie's chagrin, I can tell you.'

Potts murmured a polite, 'I am sure, sir.' Of course, the head of the Secret Service was right, he told himself. The Yanks did dominate both military and political affairs these days, but what that had to do with this lone U-boat now loose in the Baltic was completely beyond him.

'You see, Potts,' C continued, talking almost as if he were really thinking aloud, 'the new power of the United States over us is allowing that kind of anti-colonial scum to surface over there who would take our empire away from us.' He frowned with distaste. 'There are enough parlour pinks here in London who would do the same, but they have no power, no means of doing so. But in Washington it is different. First they'd force an independent India on us. Then it would be Egypt and our mandates in the Middle East. Finally Africa would go. And what would happen?' He answered his own question. 'The empire market for our goods would vanish and we would be reduced to the status of a third-class power, while the United States played top dog.'

Potts was astonished by C's vision of Britain's future if the Americans had their way, but still he could not see for the life of him what all this high-level political thinking had to do with the German submarine. 'But I don't quite follow, sir,' he began a little helplessly.

C wasn't listening. His mind was too full of his own bitter forebodings. 'Now, Potts, anything — and I mean *anything* — we can do to impress official America with the strength and power of the Old Country is of use,' he said, a sudden determination in his voice, as far away to the east of London, the air-raid sirens sounded their dreaded warning yet again. More missiles were on their way.

'But how can we impress them in this affair, sir?'

'Like this, Potts,' C snapped, mind made up now. 'We assume this Hun sub is going to make a missile attack on the American eastern seaboard somewhere or other. We assume, too, that the Huns want to make a big propaganda thing of the attack. Goebbels has had precious little to crow about of

late. So their people must select an important target in order to achieve the maximum publicity.'

As always Potts was ready with information, 'Portland, Boston, perhaps the navy yards at Norfolk, Virginia, sir?'

'Yes something like that,' C said hastily. Now the thump-thump of the anti-aircraft guns in Hyde Park was quite audible. A flight of rocket shells went screeching by the window, trailing fiery red sparks behind them like a swarm of angry hornets. The waiters began to look apprehensive, heads cocked to one side listening — straining — for the first sound of a doodle-bug. But their upper-class clients kept stolidly on eating and drinking, maintaining that pose which was expected of them. Potts, in spite of his dislike of the type, was impressed.

'Now if Savage's Spitfires can reach America before the sub, they can be split up into flights and located at strategically organized spots so that they can be airborne within minutes of the Yankee radar picking up the sub. With only three or four missiles to contend with, I am sure they can do their usual spectacular stuff and bring them down just before the missiles reach their target. What a tremendous propaganda scoop for the Empire!' C's faded careful blue eyes suddenly blazed excitedly. 'Imagine it — British planes beat off first German attack on the Continental United States! Wouldn't that show our *cousins* that the old lion still has some pretty powerful teeth, eh Potts? Up in Washington they'd learn some new respect for us and by jingo, you'd know what they'd be forced to do?'

Potts shook his head, wondering if he dare voice his own apprehensions.

'Why they'd have to request more of our fighter squadrons to be sent over to defend their coastal cities. Imagine it, two centuries after they ran us out during the American Revolution, the redcoats are back in force, defending them. *Winnie would love it!*'

'But sir,' Potts objected desperately, as abruptly, as if in answer to an unspoken command, everyone ceased talking and eating in the restaurant. For now that sinister chug-chug of a doodle-bug was directly overhead, 'what if Savage's planes don't manage to intercept them…? What if the German V-ls manage to get through? Why, sir, when we could stop that German submarine at the exit to the Baltic this very night, we're virtually condemning a large number of innocent American civilians to a sure death!' He stared wildly at the head of the Secret Service. 'Surely, sir, you cannot allow that to happen, can you, sir?'

But before C could answer that overwhelming question, there was that sudden frightening silence as the doodle-bug's engine cut out. Everyone tensed, frozen there like characters at the end of some melodrama. Potts felt his mouth drop open foolishly like a village yokel. But there was nothing he could do about it. He was completely transfixed.

Abruptly it happened. There was a tremendous crash. The ground heaved beneath them. 'Damnation!' C shouted. Glass smashed. Diners went flying from suddenly overturned chairs. Women screamed. One of the foreign waiters began to have hysterics in a strange tongue. A hot stinging wave of blast came bursting through the door, followed by a searing flame like that of a gigantic blowtorch. Potts caught one last glimpse of his precious umbrella and bowler on the hat stand suddenly consumed and disappearing in flame, then everything went black. Above him, C cried, his voice a mixture of surprise and indignation, 'Damn it, they've gorn and killed the fellah on me...'

CHAPTER 2

'But surely, Captain, you should be reporting in by now?' Von Arco glanced at his watch. 'It is nearly twenty hundred hours now. Grand Admiral Dönitz told me personally that all his skippers report in to his HQ every evening, without fail.'

Christian looked at von Arco. 'You told me you are a trained naval officer, *Herr Kapitänleutnant*,' he snapped coldly, eyes hard. 'But something must have been overlooked in your training.'

'What?'

'That the skipper's word is law in a U-boat! He makes the decisions. And I am skipper on the U-200.'

'But Captain, it is imperative that Dönitz knows where we are every day.'

'Is it? Let me be best judge of that,' Christian said icily. 'But for your information, I am not so sure that the Tommies have not cracked the enigma code. If they have, they'll know where we are immediately — and we have problems enough on our hands. If disobeying the Big Lion's standing orders will ensure that we all live a little longer, then I shall do exactly that. Now get about your duties —'

'*Sir*,' a sudden cry of alarm cut into his words.

Christian spun round. Pushing through the startled army gunners, an anxious sweating young face peered at him through the torpedo hatch. 'What is it?'

'Sir, one of the tin fish has broken loose.'

Christian acted at once. 'Take over, von Arco,' he rapped. 'Frenssen — follow me!'

Pushing and shoving the gaping, suddenly pale-faced gunners to one side, the two old comrades ran forward, ducked through the hatch, and stopped short.

One of the reduced number of torpedoes the U-200 was now carrying had slipped from its tube and was sticking into the hatch. Two wide-eyed anxious ratings, their singlets black with sweat, were trying desperately to prevent it slipping any further. All that was needed now for disaster to strike was for the U-200 to move a degree or two and the fish would fall completely, ripping a great hole in the boat. Frenssen flung himself forward and added his tremendous weight, the brutal muscles of his back rippling and twisting like snakes underneath his shirt. But even as he thrust forward, he called through gritted teeth, 'Not gonna to be … able to hold her for long, sir… Sonofabitch weighs … frigging tons!'

'TRY!' Christian bellowed. He raced back to the controls and yelled frenzied instructions to the ratings manning the hydroplanes, praying as he did so that he and they were reacting correctly. If they didn't, the patrol would be over before it had really started and they would end up as fish bait at the bottom of the Baltic. But all of them were reacting correctly.

With maddening slowness the U-200 righted itself, while the beads of sweat stood out on Christian's forehead and his hands balled into tight, painful fists.

Up front there was a strangled cry of triumph from Frenssen as the fish slowly began to slide back into its tube. He sprang forward, gasping as if he had just run a great race and snapped the lock closed behind it, before leaning unsteadily against the bulkhead. 'I swear I've pissed myself,' he said weakly. 'The urine's trickling right down me frigging right leg!'

'Somebody else is going to have the piss squeezed right out of him,' Christian's voice cut in grimly, 'if there is any carelessness of that kind again.' He shot an angry look at the crestfallen torpedo ratings. 'Is that understood?' They lowered their eyes in shame and mumbled, 'Yessir.'

Frenssen glared at them and hissed, as Christian turned and went back to the control centre, 'Not only will the piss be strained, my friends,' he threatened, doubling up a fist like a ham, 'but the frigging eggs'll come off as well. I swear, I'll cut 'em off'n yer mesen — *with a blunt razor!*'

Back at the control centre, Christian looked coldly at von Arco. 'It is not only their responsibility, von Arco, but yours as well as armaments officer,' he said.

'But I can't be everywhere —' von Arco began.

'You'll be *everywhere* I say you should be, von Arco,' Christian cut him short. 'That is if you know what is good for you. Once and for all, *I* am the skipper and *I* make the rules.' He stared at the other man's arrogant face, now pale and angry. 'Remember this — for the duration of this patrol, I am the lord and master of this boat. You are a nothing, a complete nothing! Now I shall take her up…'

Five minutes later they surfaced, the conning tower empty save for Christian himself and Frenssen, the only man in the whole green crew Christian could trust to react swiftly and efficiently in an emergency.

Beyond the fringe of white spray at the bows, the darkening seascape was completely empty; they could well have been the last people alive on the earth. But Christian, swinging his big glasses from port to starboard systematically, knew that wasn't the case. Out there, just beyond the German-controlled narrows, the enemy submarine chasers waited. The low cloud, for all he knew, hid the feared Tommy Sunderlands and

Catalinas. Below him yet another new enemy minefield, as yet unmarked, might well be in position, ready to bring death and destruction to an unsuspecting submariner.

Frenssen rubbed his unshaven jaw and yawned, 'What's the drill, sir?' he asked, as if he were completely unaware of the lethal dangers that lurked all around him.

Christian frowned. 'I just don't know, Frenssen,' he answered slowly. 'Now, there is virtually nothing I can do about underwater mines. We're sunk if we run into a minefield in the narrows.''They could have sown them on the surface too,' Frenssen said casually.

'God, what a ray of sunshine you are!' Christian sighed. 'Now if we continue on the surface till we're through, we do chance the sub-chasers and the seaplanes, but we can see and fight them, if necessary —'

'Sir,' Frenssen cut in suddenly. 'To port... There's a craft!'

Christian swung his glasses round, bracing his legs against the swaying of the deck. Immediately they fogged up. He cursed, rubbed them clean and focused again. Now he had the object, a lean grey craft, low in the water, perhaps some five to six hundred metres away, proceeding westwards at a slow pace.

'What do you make of it, sir?' Frenssen asked urgently. 'A Tommy?'

Christian shook his head, hurriedly adjusting his glasses. 'No, by the look of it … one of our E-boats, setting off on a patrol in the North Sea probably.' Now Christian could make out the typical lean shape of a German motor torpedo boat, the kind of craft that the Big Lion could still afford to use in the waters off the English coast on account of its high speed. Hurtling in at forty knots, the E-boat skipper could launch his 'fish' and be off again before his target knew what had hit him.

'He's going damn slow, sir, for an E-boat,' Frenssen ventured.

Christian lowered his glasses for a moment and looked significantly at his old comrade. 'You can guess why, can't you, you big ox?'

Frenssen affected surprise. 'You mean mines?'

'I mean mines,' Christian echoed.

Frenssen whistled softly through his teeth. 'So the shitting buck-teethed Tommies have laid them near the surface, after all, sir?'

'Looks like it,' Christian agreed and bending close to the voice tube ordered the engineer officer to speed up.

Frenssen frowned. 'But why, sir?' he asked, as the U-200's speed began to pick up and they started to close with the E-boat which had still not spotted them.

'Why what?' Christian snapped, still busy with his binoculars.

'Why are we closing with the E-boat?'

'Because whoever is the skipper of that craft is going to see us through the minefield — it is as simple as that.'

Out of the corner of his eye, Frenssen looked at Christian's pale strained face and told himself the skipper had changed. A year ago, he wouldn't have announced so cold-bloodedly that he was going to use the unknown captain of the E-boat as a kind of guinea pig, letting him do the dirty job of navigating them through the minefield.

Christian seemed to sense what the big petty officer was thinking, for he snapped, 'Well, don't just stand there, waiting for the wet fart to hit the side of the thunderbox! Get the deck crew on watch. I want every spare hand up here looking for mines. Now move it, *Obermaat*!'

Frenssen 'moved it'.

Now the U-200 closed with the E-boat, which still was unaware that it was being trailed, while Christian peered anxiously to left and right for the first sign of those deadly metal eggs. Below, his deck crew poised on both bows, boathooks at the ready, gaze fixed on the green, heaving waves.

In front the E-boat slowed down even more. Now it was proceeding at a snail's pace. Christian guessed its skipper, probably one of those pasty-faced teenagers who commanded such craft, had spotted something. 'Look-outs, keep your eyes peeled!' he cried in warning.

'Ay ay, sir,' they called back, not taking their eyes off the surface of the sea for one moment. They daren't; their very lives depended on their vigilance.

The minutes ticked by leadenly as the two craft ploughed steadily through the water. Suddenly Christian held his breath. There was no mistaking that sinister, black-horned shape. *A mine*! Slowly a cold bead of sweat began to trickle down the small of his back.

'Look-out — to port,' he croaked, suddenly very dry in the throat. 'Mine!'

'Got it, sir!' the look-out called back.

Hastily, Frenssen, armed with a boathook now, strode across the wet deck to the man, ready to help in an emergency, as the U-200 began to rock slightly as she hit the turbulence of the E-boat's wake.

Suddenly, startlingly, it happened. The E-boat hit a mine. The grey sky was slashed abruptly by a knife of scarlet flame. In an instant, the E-boat's sharp prow had vanished to leave a huge gaping hole. Almost at once it began to sink, with sailors throwing floats and rafts overboard, shouting wildly, ripping off their shoes, tying themselves into life-belts with frantic fingers.

'Hold her steady!' Christian cried desperately through the voice pipe, as the U-200 yawped and swayed wildly with the force of the explosion, and the conning tower was struck by the blast. 'For God's sake get a grip of her, down below!'

'Shall we stand by, sir?' Frenssen called anxiously from the deck.

'Stand by — *for what?*'

'Why, sir,' Frenssen stammered, as if he were suddenly embarrassed, 'to pick up survivors…?'

Christian shook his head. 'No, *Obermaat.* We can't risk heaving to. We'd be a sitting duck out here in the narrows, if any Tommy seaplane came along.'

Frenssen gasped. 'But sir, you can't mean —'

'No more chat!' Christian cut in harshly, eyes blazing. 'The mission and the safety of the U-200 come first. Now get on with your damned job!'

'Ay ay, sir,' Frenssen said numbly, looking at Christian's thin taut face, as if he couldn't believe that this was the same skipper he had sailed with for the last four years.

Slowly the U-200 nosed its way through the flotsam from the sinking E-boat that was now almost gone. Floats, bottles, what looked like a joint of beef, charts, a dead man, suspended by a rubber life-belt, face upwards staring at an unfeeling grey sky with eyes that were sightless.

Then came the survivors, struggling in the garish red light cast by their craft. Drenched in oil and panic-stricken, they threshed the water trying to keep afloat, their faces black with the diesel oil, teeth startlingly white. 'Over here, comrade!' they choked when they saw the U-boat emerging from the grey gloom. 'Throw us a line, shipmate…!' 'Here am I!' One even began to sing a kind of doggerel, enthused by a sudden happiness at the thought of being rescued, 'Even the black men in Africa,' he croaked, 'sing Heil Hitler!' As the U-200 came parallel with him, he stretched up one arm, treading water as if he expected a rope to be thrown down to him the next instant. Then he saw the look on the deck crew's faces and the grin died an immediate death. 'What is it, comrades?' he called piteously. 'Aren't yer gonna help a shipmate?'

The drowning man saw Christian looking down from the conning tower and recognized the battered white cap which marked him as a U-boat skipper. 'Sir,' he cried desperately. 'Get them frigging lords o' yourn to throw me down a rope, please. Once the oil gets to yer lungs —' The plea turned to a yell of rage and despair, as the grey boat started to slide by. 'For God's sake, don't leave me — us — I've got a wife and four kids back at Bremerhaven…!'

Now the frantic pleas and cries started to go up from all sides, as the U-200 ploughed steadily on through the wreckage. 'Mateys, don't leave us to the fish…' 'Come on, comrades, I've a bride waiting for me in Hamburg…' 'You can't just let us drown … we're your comrades. Come on, have a heart … *have a heart, shipmates!*'

Someone screamed as the bow took him down, the only sign of his passing a sudden frothing of the water as his lungs expelled the last of their oxygen. Suddenly the surface turned a bright pink and Frenssen, his fists clenched desperately to prevent him from screaming, stared up at the bridge, his eyes like those of a madman. 'Sir, you can't just let 'em drown like this… Radio for help, if you can't stop the ship! But to let them drown —' His voice broke off. He was too overcome to say any more.

'Later, when we're through, I'll radio then. Up to that time they'll have to take their chance like the rest of us,' Christian replied stonily, trying not to see the brawny arm raised in a last plea, a name tattooed on it above a crimson heart. The unknown sailor would be another one who would never see his loved ones again. In this cold they couldn't last more than an hour, Christian knew that. But the mission came first. He bent to the tube. 'Number One,' he snapped, 'both engines full ahead. I think we're through now.'

For a moment he sensed the young officer below hesitating. Then the familiar repeat came back, 'Full ahead it is, sir.'

On the deck Frenssen howled like a trapped animal. He turned and banged his head against the conning tower. He could see no more.

So the U-200 disappeared into the grey gloom, pursued by those broken cries, '*Comrade ... comrade ... please comrade ...*' until finally they were gone...

CHAPTER 3

The flotilla of enemy sloops caught them half an hour later. The U-200 had just submerged to periscope depth when Christian spotted them. A line of tiny black shapes, their bows furled white. He turned up the intensifier. They were British all right, he could see that immediately. And they had already spotted the U-200 for they were surging forward in that typical British attack formation; three in line abreast with another three coming in behind.

'Periscope down!' he yelled urgently. 'Sound the alarm!' As the alarm bell shrilled its urgent warning, Christian began to rap out his orders, trying as he did so to outguess the Tommies. Had they set their depth charges so that they would explode at what they believed was an extreme diving depth for a U-boat, namely 180 metres? Or were they going to explode their deadly eggs at a medium level? He had to make up his mind — *and make it up immediately*!

'Take her down to eighty metres,' he ordered and said a quick prayer that he had made the right decision. '*Stand by for depth charge attack*!' he yelled. The operator tensed over his hydrophones, his young face glazed with sweat, as he listened to the threshing of the enemy propellers racing ever closer.

'Trim the boat for silent running,' Christian ordered, beads of sweat already hanging from his eyebrows like glistening pearls.

Von Arco looked at him. Christian looked back, realizing that von Arco was just as much a coward as his brother had been. There was fear written all over his face.

'Props at high speed, sir,' the operator sang out, hands tensed like claws over his earphones. 'Trying to pick us upon their Asdic, sir… *Here they come*!'

What seemed like a handful of gravel ran the length of the U-200's hull. It was the enemy Asdic. Christian tensed. Now they were for it. They had been spotted. Frenssen crossed himself with mock solemnity for the benefit of the white-faced ratings. 'For what we are about to receive,' he intoned, 'may the Good Lord make us truly grateful —'

A shattering blow rocked the boat crazily. Glass tinkled. The lights went out and came on again. Another crazy hammer blow. Christian caught a stanchion just in time as the U-200 plunged a good ten metres. Von Arco reacted too late and went flying.

'Prop noise aft!' the young hydrophone operator sang out bravely, voice near breaking point.

Christian reacted immediately. His first dodge had not worked out. They had been well and truly spotted. The sweat streaming down his face, he said calmly, 'Slow ahead — both engines… Start taking her down — *slowly*!'

Now as the sloops thundered back and forth up above, the U-200 began to dive, the control room crew's eyes fixed hypnotically on the depth gauge.

Another salvo of depth charges exploded close by. The U-boat rocked madly. Again the lights flickered off and on. Somewhere a jet of water erupted into the boat. In that tense silence, Christian could hear the water spurting through the leak quite clearly.

Now the Number One was calling out the depths in a tense hushed whisper, 'One hundred metres … one hundred and twenty … one hundred and thirty…'

'Oh my God,' von Arco croaked, eyes bulging from his head with unreasoning fear. 'We can't go much deeper… She'll crack wide open…!'

Christian looked at him icily. 'Please keep your opinion to yourself, *Herr Kapitänleutnant*,' he commanded softly.

'*Two hundred metres*!'

The young Number One looked at Christian. He nodded and said calmly, 'That should do it for the moment. Thank you, Number One.' He waited. They had reached their maximum diving depth, thirty metres deeper than the Tommies thought a U-boat could go. Now the question was not only whether the Tommies would continue depth charging them, but also whether the U-200 would hold together under that enormous pressure. Christian licked hard parched lips. 'Level off, Number One,' he ordered. 'Keep her trimmed at two hundred. Steer due north. Revolutions for three knots.' Deliberately Christian made a great show of yawning, as if this was awfully boring and very routine.

Frenssen shook his head in reluctant admiration. On this mission the skipper was proving to be an awful bastard, but he certainly had a lot of style and courage. One wrong move in a situation like this and the kind of green crew they had would panic and run wild immediately.

Now they waited, while 200 metres above them, their hunters churned back and forth desperately seeking their prey. Christian knew what they were doing, of course. They were doing test runs without depth charges, trying to estimate the submarine's depth. Once they had worked out that they were losing the Asdic echo at a range of 150 metres, they would realize their prey was deeper and set their depth charges accordingly. Now it was up to him to keep moving, changing his course all the time, trying to fool them. 'Set off SBTs,' he commanded, changing course once again. 'Perhaps we can trick the English gentlemen with them?'

The first of 'the submarine bubble targets' was released, a huge bubble fired from the torpedo tubes which gave off an Asdic ping similar to that of a submarine.

Around Christian the control room crew tensed, eyes fixed on the dripping bulkhead above them, young faces hollowed out by the eerie green-glowing light to burning-eyed skulls. Christian began to count off the seconds, estimating the time it would take for the SBT to reach the surface and hoping the Tommies would be fooled by it.

They weren't. In the very instant that he finished his count, the U-200 was rocked by two tremendous explosions directly over the submarine. Again the lights went out. There was the sound of rushing water. Someone shrieked. The Number One flashed on his torch. 'Depth gauge leaking, skipper,' he reported hurriedly, as the lights went on, and Christian could see the jet of water spurting down on to the floor of the control room.

'Yes, thank you, Number One,' Christian snapped. 'Riggers — up here at the double,' he whispered urgently. 'See what you can do with it *quickly*!'

Von Arco caught Christian's eye and looked away sharply. His fear was all too obvious. He knew just as well as Christian did that with the depth gauge out of action, they could no longer tell whether they were rising or sinking. Now they were groping about the bottom of the sea blindly, risking the craft at pressures which might well rip open her hull as if it were made of soft tin instead of Krupp steel, running, running, running until their batteries died on them and they were forced to surface.

Christian made his decision, knowing he simply couldn't chance remaining below any longer. 'All right,' he said softly, trying to keep his voice under control, 'this is what I am going to do. I'm going to take her up to periscope height. With a bit of luck I might get a hit before they spot us. If I do, then I'm hoping that the confusion will enable us to escape on the surface. Thereafter we can repair the depth gauge and submerge once more.' He looked round their worried faces and smiled, focusing on the obviously terrified *Wehrmacht* gunners who would man the missiles, if they ever reached America. 'Now for you army boys, this must all seem very horrific. But it is routine in the U-boat service. We know how to tackle the problem, so don't worry yourselves too much.'

Just behind the myopic gunnery lieutenant, Frenssen clasped his fingers to his nose and made a gesture, as if he were pulling a lavatory chain. Christian knew why. Frenssen thought his plan stank. Christian did, too, but there was no other way. At least this way they would go down fighting.

'All right, Number One,' he commanded, very brisk and businesslike now, 'let's see about taking the bitch up.'

The Number One gulped and said hastily, 'Yes, sir… Of course, sir.'

Slowly, very slowly, they began to raise the U-200, Christian using all his expertise to guess the depth as they inched their way upwards. His fingers tingled, itching to take the periscope and attempt to find out where exactly they were. For above all else, he could not risk popping right up to the surface and perhaps finding himself right in the midst of the whole damned English fleet.

Now all was tense anxious silence in the control room, save for the harsh breathing of the riggers as they tinkered with the depth gauge. All of them were sweating, fists clenched, chests heaving with the awesome tension of it all. For even the greenest of the young lords knew that in a few moments they might well be dead, if their skipper made the slightest wrong move. Their very lives hung on his next action.

By a sheer effort of naked will-power Christian kept himself calm, well aware of the tremendous responsibility resting upon him, spacing out his orders so that they broke that heavy brooding silence and relaxed the tension for a moment. 'Stand by the gun crew,' he commanded. A few moments later he followed it with, 'Torpedo mates stand by.' Frenssen rumbled something and headed with the greenhorns for the torpedoes. He was going to take care of his beloved 'tin fish' personally.

Now it was time. Quite deliberately Christian turned his cap so that the battered tarnished peak was to the rear. 'Up periscope,' he ordered.

Someone gasped. Von Arco bit his bottom lip in sudden apprehension. 'Oh, my God!' the bespectacled gunnery officer sighed. Christian affected not to notice. Instead he grasped the handles and slowly turned the instrument, surveying the green swaying surface of the sea, the top of the periscope a bare half metre above the waves. All around him the others waited in white-knuckled tension for his verdict.

Still Christian did not speak, taking his time, making absolutely sure, hardly daring to believe the evidence of his own eyes.

In the end von Arco could stand the silence and uncertainty no longer. 'For God's sake,' he cried in a strangled choked voice, eyes wild, '*what can you see?*'

Christian hesitated one more moment before replying, 'What can I see? I shall tell you.' He turned and faced them, cap still set comically back-to-front. 'Nothing save the rear of the Tommies' sloops.'

'*Rear?*' the gunnery officer quavered, bottom lip trembling, as if he might burst into tears at any moment.

'I don't understand,' von Arco said.

'Neither do I, quite frankly,' Christian agreed. 'But that is a fact. The Tommies have abandoned the chase.' His voice rose. 'All right, Number One, take her up to the surface — and we'll have a real look.'

Now the control room crew broke into excited chatter. The news swept down the long shell of the U-boat to the forward torpedo compartment. Frenssen popped his head round the hatchway. 'Did someone say the Tommies have gone and pissed into the wind?' he cried excitedly.

One of the gunners said, 'That's what the captain sez at least. Too good to be true, ain't it, mate?'

Frenssen was too elated even to be offended at the fact that a common soldier in the Army was addressing a chief petty officer as 'mate'. Instead he agreed, with new hope surging across his broad red face. 'You can frigging well say that again, my hairy-assed stubble-hopper. Christ, it'll be raining beer next!'

Moments later they had broken the surface. Immediately the hatch was opened, Christian clattered aloft, as always savouring the good sea air, cold as it was after the fetid, oil-tinged stench of the submarine. Bracing himself on the dripping metal deck, he flung up his glasses and stared around at the grey sullen sky. Nothing! Not a single Tommy seaplane in sight. He was safe from that quarter.

Hurriedly he focused the glasses and stared to port. The sloops he had spotted as they had come racing in to the attack, with a bone in their teeth, were departing as swiftly as they had arrived. There was no doubt about that. They hadn't left one of their number behind in an attempt to trap him. They were *all* scurrying westwards at top speed, as if they couldn't get away fast enough. But why?

Christian bit his bottom lip in bewildered frustration. Surely they knew they hadn't 'killed' the U-200? They had been receiving his 'ping' until the very last moment when they had broken off their attack. So why hadn't they waited in that stubborn dogged Royal Navy manner? They must have known that he would have to surface sooner or later, once his electric batteries were exhausted.

'It's very strange, sir, isn't it?' Number One's puzzled voice broke into Christian's reverie. 'Almost as if they were *ordered* to break off the attack?' The young lieutenant tugged at the end of his long nose, as if he might well be angry. 'But perhaps there are better pickings for the Tommy bastards elsewhere? That might be it, sir, don't you think?' He looked at Christian enquiringly.

Slowly Christian nodded his head, still not taking his gaze off the departing enemy vessels, not quite believing that they were really going. 'Yes, Number One, that might be it. But as far as I know there are no wolf packs operating in this part of the North Sea. It has been too dangerous to do so for years now. It's all very strange indeed. Oh well, let's forget it. Off you go and get on top of those riggers. I want that damned depth gauge patched up in the next half hour so we can dive with confidence again.'

The Number One touched his hand to his cap in salute and clattered down the ladder into the interior to carry out Christian's order, leaving the skipper to stare moodily at the rolling, billowing seascape.

There was something totally rotten about 'Project N. Y.' he told himself sombrely. First Skorzeny and those poor wretches in that underground concentration camp. Then von Arco's mysterious transformation into a naval officer assigned to his ship. Now this strange business of the English leaving the area so unexpectedly. What did it all mean?

But for the time being there seemed to be no answer to that overwhelming question and in the end the young skipper gave up and concentrated on the more important task of getting himself and his men through another day of total war…

CHAPTER 4

J. Edgar Hoover looked out of the window at the busy Washington street below, thronged with businessmen wearing overcoats, and women, most of them with umbrellas against the threatening skies. It was a typical December day in the capital and there was something careless about the way the civilians moved, which annoyed him. The small, square-faced head of the Federal Bureau of Investigation lived off his nerves and was so dynamic that he had little time for more relaxed people, even if they were only enjoying the midday break from their overcrowded war-time offices. Americans would have to be taught a lesson, he told himself grimly, and then concentrated on the briefing.

'Men!' he snapped suddenly, turning to the smoke-filled room, crammed with his assembled agents, 'let me have your attention, please.'

The effect was immediate. The talking stopped at once. Some of the special agents even stubbed out their cigars. For tough as these men were — back in the roaring 1920s some of the older men had even fought pitched battles with gangsters and bootleggers — all of them were afraid of their secretive, possessive, moody boss. Why, even the President was scared of Hoover and wasn't Hoover currently spying on Roosevelt's wife, who seemingly was having an affair with a young sergeant, a commie, at that! No, it took a brave man to cross J. Edgar Hoover.

''Kay, men,' he started briskly, 'we've got a problem on our hands. Those secret Limeys in New York have just informed me that we are to expect a Nazi attack on the Continental United States very soon!'

The announcement struck home like a bomb-shell. There was a burst of excited talk. Someone exclaimed, 'Well, I'll be goddamned!' Another whistled softly through his teeth in amazement and said, 'What in the name of Sam Hill will the Krauts do next?'

Hoover held up his pudgy, sickly white hands for silence, pleased with the effect of his opening words. 'Quiet, men, *please*! Now, you all know back in 'forty-two the Japs tried to fire-bomb us by floating flammable balloons across the Pacific, but nothing came of it except a few forest fires in Oregon. Strictly small time. But this new threat is to be taken much more seriously because, according to the Limeys, the Nazis are gonna launch missiles against our coast from a sub.' He frowned at their flushed, heavy faces seriously. 'Missiles bearing *one ton of high explosive* per warhead.'

'You mean, sir, like the ones they are currently firing at London, England?' someone asked.

'I do.'

They looked impressed, all save Chief Inspector Hart, a tall, middle-aged agent, with a hard tense face under a yellow crew-cut that was now beginning to turn grey. 'But if a Nazi sub can only carry half a dozen missiles, sir,' he objected, 'what real damage can they do? I mean, according to the newspaper reports from London, these V-ls average out by killing five to six civilians. It would be hard luck on the individuals concerned, but there would be only a score of deaths at the most.'

Hoover looked coldly at Hart, who was a typical New Englander, hard-headed, pragmatic, not easily impressed. Hart had been with the Bureau since the 1920s, when he started off by fighting the bootleggers running in hooch from Canada at the start of Prohibition. He had been twice wounded in the line of duty and had received numerous commendations. But efficient and brave as he was, Hoover didn't like him, for he suspected that Hart was not so impressed by his chief as most of the operatives were. Hoover liked his men to crawl and the slow-talking, hard-faced New Englander was no crawler.

'But what if the missile had a special target, Hart, what then? A target of some great significance that would make a great impact, irrespective of the number of people concerned?'

Hart stuck doggedly to his guns, while around him the agents seemed to draw back, as if they did not wish to be associated with this maverick who was daring to talk back to J. Edgar. 'I've been reading up a bit on these V-ls. My boy is over in Europe, you see, sir, with the ETO and I'm, well…' Hart hesitated. As a New Englander he hated to show emotion, '…concerned.'

'Get on with it, Hart!' Hoover snapped.

'Well, sir, these missiles would need some sort of fix, a prearranged signal, something of that sort, so that the guys who launch them could set their gyro-compasses accordingly. Or whatever they use to steer them. Without a fix there's no certainty they can hit a specific target, sir.'

'How do you know they won't be able to get that fix, Hart?' Hoover snapped icily.

This time even Hart was impressed. 'You mean, sir, they have an agent in place somewhere on the eastern seaboard?'

'That is *exactly* what I mean!'

Again the FBI agents were impressed and Hoover's pale fat face was crossed momentarily by a smirk of self-congratulation. For nearly a quarter of a century he had run the FBI like a private police force — some of his enemies called it a 'private Gestapo' — and he had always believed in running 'a tight ship' where every agent knew his place and jumped when he, J. Edgar Hoover, cracked his celebrated whip. Now they were jumping.

Hurriedly he continued. 'Now we don't know exactly who and where this lone Nazi agent is. But we *do* know that four Nazi agents were landed off Long Island at Amagansett four weeks ago. Strangely enough just as they were about to reach land their dinghy was illuminated by a star shell from their own sub. It was almost as if they had been deliberately

betrayed to the Coastguard. Within the hour they were in our custody.'

He paused and noted to his satisfaction that even Hart was absorbed by what he had just said. His old trick of knowing more secrets than any of his agents was paying off once more. He could always spring a surprise on even the most hard-nosed and cynical of his FBI men.

'Now we started working them over in Boston straight away.' He made a gesture with his pudgy white fist as if he were wielding a rubber hose and Hart frowned, as if he disliked the thought of the third degree being used, even on Krauts. 'They began to sing right off. They knew they faced the chair if they didn't squeal. They gave us their contacts in the States, where they had been trained, the fact that Nazi subs can operate at depths well beneath the killing range of the Navy, things like that. Army and Navy Intelligence were plenty surprised. As always it takes the FBI to get to the real truth of the matter, don't it, fellas?' He smirked at them and dutifully his cronies sang out, 'Yes, sir. Sure does, J. Edgar!'

Hart's frown deepened. All of them knew that Hoover was a power-crazed maniac. Why the hell did they flatter him like this? Hoover had already lost virtually all contact with reality.

One of these days he'd blow his top altogether and then it'd be the funny farm and the guys in white coats with the rubber hammers for J. Edgar Hoover.

'But none of these Kraut spies could figure out why the sub had betrayed them to the Coastguard like that. They were pretty damn bitter about it, you can be sure. So I began to think about it, just running it through my mind for a day or so while the agents continued to work the Krauts over. And fellas,' Hoover looked at his men with his faded eyes full of mock sincerity, 'do you know what I came up with?'

'What?… Come on, J. Edgar, spill it, sir?' the office-seekers egged him on, knowing their boss loved this kind of thing. 'Let's have it, sir!'

'The four Kraut saboteurs were a feint, a decoy to put us off the scent,' Hoover announced proudly. 'That's why the sub betrayed them to our people. Of course, the coastguard investigators were too dumb to figure that out.'

'Swell, J. Edgar!' they called enthusiastically. 'It takes a Hoover to figure out a lulu like that, sir!'

Hart pursed his lips and said, 'But Mr Hoover, who was this other spy and how did he get off the sub?'

Hoover glared at the New Englander. He hated to be interrupted when in full flow. 'Hart, I was just coming to that when you broke in,' he snapped, telling himself that he'd have a look at Hart's personal file after this briefing was over. His record in the past was good, but you couldn't coast on your past record. Perhaps it was time to put Hart out to pasture, bring in a younger man who knew who the boss was. 'After our people began to grill them for the second time, we started to get them to go over the crew, one by one, working from the captain downwards, trying to find someone who didn't really have a proper job in the sub. And we found him. Some guy in his mid-twenties who *seemed* to be a petty officer — at least, he wore a petty officer's uniform — yet who they never saw actually carrying out a duty. All four of the spies' testimonies agree on the fact that he was tall, blond, cocky and in his mid-twenties.'

Already here and there an agent was scribbling furiously in his notebook, obviously attempting to impress the boss with their keenness. Hart was not impressed. Taking his gaze off the 'eager-beaver' next to him, who was making a great show of his note-taking, he said, 'But did you find evidence, Mr Hoover, that a *fifth* person actually landed on Long Island at that time? After all, you'd be looking several days after the original landing. A lot of other craft could have landed during that period of time — fishing boats, locals out sailing and the like.'

Next to him the 'eager-beaver' whispered out of the side of his mouth, 'Brother, you're a real glutton for punishment!' Hart appeared not to notice.

'No, we did not find evidence of another craft landing, Inspector Hart,' Hoover answered, his voice surprisingly gentle, though his eyes shot fire. 'By then the trail was cold, as you say. Other craft had come ashore all over the place and so on. However, we know that a fifth man *did* come ashore that same morning. For the ticket clerk at Amagansett opened his window that morning to find a man unknown to him waiting for a ticket.'

'Well?' Hart grunted.

'He was blond and in his mid-twenties.'

Hart shrugged carelessly, unimpressed. 'Could fit the description of a lot o' guys,' he persisted.

Next to him the 'eager-beaver' crossed himself as if in final salute.

'Agreed. Could fit a couple of million other American men,' Hoover said with deceptive mildness. 'Save for one thing.' He fumbled in the pocket of his rumpled white linen jacket and brought out a note. 'You see this bill. Well, this is the bill with which the blond kid paid for his fare.' He held it up so that they could all see, gaze fixed on Hart's face, maliciously ready for the punch-line. 'Looks okay, guys, doesn't it? Well, it *ain't*!' he barked, iron in his voice abruptly. 'This type of bill went out of circulation *nine* years ago. Now what right-thinking New Englander who is careful with his dough would hang on to a bill that was totally, absolutely useless, not worth the paper it was printed on? No sir, only a German who didn't know this country or had been out of it a long time would be playing around with a bill like that.' He waved the note like a flag. 'This bill, I can say with one hundred per cent certainty, came from no other place but the German *Reichsbank* in Berlin — and was used to finance their spies in this country.'

Hart let his shoulders sink as if in defeat. Next to him the 'eager-beaver' chortled, 'The old fart really got your dong in the wringer that time, old buddy!' He grinned mischievously at Hart.

'Screw you,' Hart snarled.

'So assuming they have got their agent in place,' a triumphant Hoover went on, 'the one who will contact the missile-bearing sub in due course to give the Krauts the bearing of their objective, the question now raises itself as to what their target or targets are. Where can they do the maximum damage with the handful of weapons at their disposal?'

'Washington, sir?' the 'eager-beaver' suggested. 'The Pentagon, for example? There's plenty of top brass there to make a real hole in the war effort in Europe if they were taken out.'

'Good guess, Al,' Hoover answered. 'But Washington is beyond the range of these missiles, according to the experts.'

'Boston?' came the cry.

'Perhaps New York?' someone else suggested.

'What about Norfolk, Virginia, sir?' another called.

Hoover beamed at his agents, outbidding each other excitedly to gain his attention. He liked it, it was obvious. Grimly Hart told himself Hoover would die a thousand deaths if he ever fell out of the limelight. He loved being the centre of attention.

'But, gentlemen,' Hoover raised his pudgy pale hands for silence, 'all these are great cities with thousands, even millions of inhabitants. What difference would it make to the course of the war if certain individuals were killed there? Not much I would think. The President in Washington is safe. The Combined Chiefs of Staff — also in Washington — are safe, too.'

'*You* are, as well, sir, being located in Washington,' the 'eager-beaver' said hurriedly.

Hoover beamed at him and lowered his head modestly, 'Well, I'm not really *that* important.'

Hart groaned inside. What a creep the boss really was!

'So who is there left?' Hoover asked rhetorically. 'Who is worth risking a submarine for? What might make the most impact on the war if he were killed by these missiles? Now —'

Suddenly he broke off. Down below on the pavement, small boys draped in huge cloth caps were rushing from the offices of the *Washington Post* crying excitedly as they ran, '*Extra … extra … read all about it…*!'

'Open the window and damn the air-conditioning system,' Hoover commanded, as a dozen of his agents rose to open the windows and let the cries from below flood in with their alarming news. '*Extra … extra … read all about it… Great surprise Hun offensive in Belgium… Major enemy attack… US reeling back… Read all about it… American positions overrun…*'

Hart thought of his son Gary, a sergeant with the Fourth Infantry Division. The last time he had written his mother he had done so from 'somewhere in Belgium'. Was he one of those now whose positions had been 'overrun'?

Suddenly Hart was overcome by a great burning anger at Hoover, the unknown German agent who had brought them here to this stuffy, airless room, the whole goddamn war. Christ on a crutch, he raged within, when will the damned miserable business ever damn well end?

Up in the front of the room an energetic Hoover was now snapping out the names of his agents, hurriedly assigning them to areas of search. In an angry daze he heard his own name mentioned. 'Inspector Hart will take over downtown New York…' Minutes later he was out in the streets, dazed and angry, trying to hail a cab to take him back to the station, trying to figure out how he could apprehend one blond young German in a city of seven million inhabitants. And all the while the cheeky young newsvendors cried out their tale of woe. 'Ike' summons emergency conference in Paris… More troops being rushed to Europe… Read all about it… Extra… Extra… Great German counter-attack… *US positions overrun…*'

It was Saturday, 16 December 1944, and it had started…

Eisenhower, the Allied Supreme Commander.

CHAPTER 5

As the harsh brassy fanfare of trumpets ended the announcement, von Arco sprang proudly to attention and shot out his right hand, face flushed with excitement. 'To the victory of our comrades in Belgium,' he cried. '*Sieg Heil!*'

Obediently the young crew, cramped as they were in the crowded interior of the U-200, raised their hands and responded. '*Sieg Heil!*' they yelled.

'So comrades,' von Arco cried, carried away by excitement, 'now you know why we are at sea, because we are part of that same great striking force which is hitting back at the Anglo-American air gangsters. Germany marches. Victory — final victory — will be ours *yet!*'

Christian stared at his excited arrogant face and thought how like he was to his dead brother. He had the same ambitious drive to take over, too. Over the last few days, as they had ploughed through the dreary waste of the North Atlantic, well away from the usual allied shipping lanes, von Arco had begun to exert himself more and more with the young crew. Once Christian had caught him giving orders to the Number One, even though the Number One was his superior. As Frenssen had commented sourly, 'Just like his frigging unlamented brother, allus throwing his frigging weight about!'

Now, as he watched von Arco harangue the crew about the great new counter-offensive currently driving the Americans into headlong flight in Belgium, which had just been announced over the radio from Berlin, he wondered what exact role von Arco was to play on this patrol. Everything so far, since the day he had first met von Arco with Skorzeny, had been too neat, too pat, as if it had all been planned well in advance; as if the Big Lion himself had had a hand in planting von Arco, suddenly transformed into a lieutenant-commander with submarine experience, on the U-200. Why?

Abruptly he felt the need to urinate. Like most old hares in the U-boat service, his kidneys had been affected by the constant soakings and chills of the conning tower. He had to have a leak. He pushed his way through his excited young men, faces flushed at the great news from the Homeland, to the heads.

Balancing himself there, he enjoyed the flood of hot urine, eyes taking in the usual pencil drawings of men and women engaged in sexual intercourse that bored and sexually deprived sailors always scrawled in such places. Someone had written in red ink, 'This bloody roundhouse is no good at all. The seat's too high and the hole too small.'

Beneath the couplet another hand had printed, 'To which I must add the obnoxious retort, *Your arse is too large and your legs are too short!*'

As he started to pump out the urine with the hand pump, Christian could not prevent himself laughing.

Behind him Frenssen coughed and said, 'Don't like to disturb the Captain while he is commuting with nature —'

'*Communing,*' Christian corrected the big petty officer routinely. But as usual Frenssen never listened to even his captain when he had something important to say. 'It's about von Arco, sir,' he said in a whisper.

'*Kapitänleutnant* von Arco!'

'All right, frigging *Kapitänleutnant* von Arco!' Frenssen growled as Christian did up his flies and turned to face the big *Obermaat*.

'What about him?'

'There's a signal coming in for him over the radio. At the moment, he's too busy playing the great frigging orator to know about it, of course,' he nodded contemptuously up the boat to where von Arco still stood addressing the crew.

Christian frowned. Signals always went to the skipper of a U-boat, unless they were of a personal nature, the birth of a baby, the death of a parent, that kind of thing. 'Is it personal?'

'No, sir, it's from the Big Lion himself.'

'In code?'

'Yessir. All the operator knows is that it's from Dönitz.' Christian was too surprised even to correct Frenssen for having failed to use the Big Lions military rank. 'That's strange, Frenssen.'

'There's more, sir,' Frenssen went on, keeping his voice low. 'The operator sez he don't recognize the code. It's not the usual one.'

Christian looked at Frenssen's broad face sharply. 'You mean that von Arco is receiving a message in a private code?' he snapped.

'Well, it looks very much like that to Mrs Frenssen's handsome son, sir.'

Christian considered a moment what he should do. He knew he had every right to demand the message from von Arco, personal or not. A U-boat skipper had power of life and death over his crew, whatever their rank. But if the message was in a private code how could he force von Arco to decode it if he did not want to?

'You could threaten to shoot him, sir,' Frenssen suggested, obviously reading Christian's mind. 'I'd volunteer to hold the gun —'

Christian smiled coldly, his brain racing. 'No, Frenssen, I don't think we can do that exactly.' He pursed his lips, while the big petty officer waited eagerly for his decision.

'All right,' Christian said finally. 'This is what we'll do. Order the radio operator to accept no signals — no, *better*, order him to accept any signal that von Arco may give him, but not to send it. Somehow he must find an excuse not to send while von Arco is in the radio shack and then bring the message to me, *personally*.'

'That's the way, sir,' Frenssen said excitedly. 'Let him have a taste of his own shitting medicine. He spied on us back in Danzig, now we'll spy on him. But,' he stopped short, 'but what good is it gonna do us if you can't read the code, sir?'

Christian nodded, as up in the control room, von Arco ended his excited harangue.

Frenssen shook his head angrily. 'Holy strawsack, I'd just like to know what his frigging game is!'

'And so would I,' Christian agreed. Then he pushed by a bewildered, angry Frenssen, saying, 'Now come on, you big rogue. Let's get on with the war and stop playing cops and robbers…'

The next couple of days passed in the deadening, uneventful routine of a U-boat sailing away from the main shipping routes in the North Atlantic in mid-winter. Still-tired, unwashed bodies being forced from cramped bunks for yet another maddeningly long watch. Hour after hour of the sweating fetid atmosphere of the submarine's interior, the bulkhead running with liquid, the stench of diesel making the men vomit at times, the escaping gases occasionally making them pass out altogether. Or up on the deck, eyes narrowed to slits against the fierce wind and icy spray on look-out, boots slowly filling with seawater, extremities growing steadily more numb until finally the blessed relief of falling into a bunk, warm from its previous occupants, and the oblivion of sleep.

Already the fresh meat they had brought with them from Danzig was beginning to become stale and rancid, just as the precious milk had already become. So they lived from tins, forcing the tasteless mess down before savouring the two cans of ration beer which turned the evening watch into the best part of the day. Then came the pipe, a lazy tired chat, usually about women, a half-hearted game of *skat* without the customary table-slapping, and yet another long, boring, hard day at sea was over.

Already the strain of the patrol was beginning to tell. The young greenbeaks who served below deck were starting to turn very pale from the lack of fresh air. Dark shadows of weariness appeared beneath their eyes and ugly red spots, a sure sign of vitamin deficiency, were beginning to spring up on their cheeks. And they were becoming increasingly edgy,
ready to fight or find offence at the slightest matter. There were lice, too, passing from man to man with tremendous speed so that by the end of that first week everyone save Christian, who had his own cabin and own bunk, was infested by the loathsome, irritating creatures.

The first to be infested discovered the pests with cries and anger and loathing. But in the end they accepted the 'lodgers', as Frenssen called them, casually. Soon they could watch without revulsion as he squatted on his bunk of an evening, naked to the waist, running a lighted taper along the seams of his shirt, crying happily, 'Crack them arses, yer little bastards … 'cos Uncle Frenssen's flame-thrower's gonna get yer if yer don't!'

Surprisingly enough, in spite of the tension within the U-200, von Arco remained amazingly calm. He carried out his duties efficiently enough, though he tended to be a little too overbearing and strict with the crewmen if they weren't quick enough for him; but the fact that he had not received a reply to the message he had sent, presumably to acknowledge the receipt of the original signal, did not seem to worry him. Nor did he attempt to send any further signals to Dönitz.

For a while that fact had puzzled Christian, but in the end he concluded that Dönitz had passed on an order to von Arco that was final in itself; there was no need of any further communication apparently. But what that signal from the Big Lion had contained was beyond him. Several nights he had worked on the copy he had had made of it in the privacy of his own cramped little cabin, but without success. So in the end he gave up, telling himself that if it had anything to do with their final target, he would find out once he had opened his sealed orders off the American east coast.

Now that they were slowly approaching their destination, Christian occupied himself, in what little free time he had, in studying the very complicated temperature gradients of those waters. Like all experienced U-boat commanders he knew that a temperature difference of as little as three degrees Celsius could weaken the echo a submarine gave off in an enemy Asdic. If a U-boat skipper knew his waters, he could dive into or beneath a temperature gradient as some poor hairy-assed stubble-hopper might drop into his foxhole during an artillery bombardment. Thus he could pull the layer of cold or warm water over the boat like a blanket and the enemy Asdic operator could go and piss in the wind.

Night after night he laboured over his charts with his instruments, working from point to point to map out the best possible approach route. For he had no illusions about what lay waiting for him off the American coast. The US eastern seaboard was as well defended by aircraft and submarine-chasers as was the English North Sea coast. Once they had fired their missiles at whatever the target was going to be, all hell would be let loose. The whole might of the US Navy would be in on the chase. He would need all his cunning, his expertise, his knowledge of their coastal waters to escape their damned airborne radar. And even as he worked in that cramped evil-smelling cabin, listening to the lazy chatter of his ratings outside, and their regular farting (the sole green vegetables available now were dried green peas, which they ate in soups, and the peas had an unfortunate effect on the men's digestive systems), a plan of escape was beginning to form slowly in his mind.

Meanwhile he decided to conserve his electric batteries as far as was possible for submerged running during the hunt. He had the snorkel of course, but he knew he couldn't rely on it in an emergency. He had to have enough battery power to run below the surface for at least forty-eight hours, just in case the snorkel let him down. Thus it was, as they came ever closer to America and the weather became ever damper and foggier as was customary in these regions in midwinter, he began to run more and more on the surface during the daylight hours to conserve his batteries. As he told Frenssen, 'Their airborne radar might pick us up, but they'll be without visual contact in these wet mists. By the time they spot us with their flying-boats, we'll be safely at the bottom of the drink.'

Frenssen had not been impressed. He had shivered dramatically and growled, 'Don't use that phrase, sir, "*at the bottom of the drink*"!' And he had shuddered yet again.

Christian had laughed and said easily, 'You're letting your imagination run away with you, you big ox!' But in the event, Frenssen was right.

It was on the morning of 18 December, a Monday, just after the *Wehrmacht Report* had announced, after a bombastic fanfare of trumpets, yet another tremendous victory against the 'fleeing, demoralized Americans' in the Ardennes, that von Arco on the conning tower said excitedly through the voice tube. 'Aircraft noises, faint but distinct, north-north-east!'

Christian sprang into action at once. 'Prepare to dive,' he commanded. Grabbing his cap, he scrambled up the conning tower ladder to where the deck crew, muffled in dripping oilskins, surveyed the fog-bound sky.

Up top a typical pea-souper swirled around the U-boat, a cold wet grey fog, curling in and out of the sad slow breakers, muffling all sound save for the muted steady throb throb of the diesels.

Von Arco, face flushed and excited, pointed a gloved finger to the east and dutifully Christian cocked his head to one side. He strained his ears, feeling the dampness of the fog engulf his face. For a moment he heard nothing and was about to tell von Arco he was mistaken. Then there it was, the soft hum of an aircraft engine. He frowned.

'Anything wrong?' von Arco asked anxiously, lowering his glasses and poising his forefinger above the alarm button.

'No, not at the moment. But that engine … there's only *one* of them.'

Now it was von Arco's turn to frown. 'One?' he repeated slowly.

'Yes, we're a good eight hundred kilometres off the *Ami* coast, so what would a single-engined plane be doing patrolling so far out? Their Catalina flying-boats have two engines —'

'Starboard, sir!' the deck look-out's voice cut into his words dramatically. '*Aircraft*!'

Frantically Christian and von Arco flung up their glasses and focused them madly.

There it was, sliding through the grey rolling fog like a great black bird. There was no mistaking it. 'My God,' Christian gasped, recognizing the silhouette immediately, 'what in three devils' names is *that plane* doing out here?'

'What do you mean?' von Arco stammered, as the plane disappeared into the fog once more, vanishing almost as soon as it had appeared. 'I don't understand...'

'Why, what is a plane like that doing off the *Ami* coast ... *an English Spitfire?*'

'What —'

In that very same instant, the Catalina, its engines momentarily cut off, came sailing in, its deadly eggs already beginning to tumble from its evil blue belly. They hadn't a chance...

CHAPTER 6

'*AL … LARM…!*'

Sirens shrilled frantically. Officers bellowed out urgent orders. Already the diesels had been switched off and there was the great bubbling hissing as the tanks started to flood. On the conning tower, Frenssen manned the machine-gun, sending an angry stream of tracer towards the enemy seaplane.

Crump … crump … crump! The stick of bombs straddled the U-200. At that range, the Catalina could hardly miss. Christian was momentarily blinded by a sheet of bright light ringed in violet. The deck came up to meet him. Next to him, Frenssen was thrown from the gun and slammed against the steel plating. He howled with pain. Next moment he slipped to his knees, dark-red blood oozing from his nostrils and ears. Madly Christian grabbed his dead weight. With the last of his strength, deafened by the roar of the Catalina's engines as it skimmed in over the surface of the waves for the kill, he heaved the big petty officer down the hatch, crying frantically, '*Dive … dive … FOR GOD'S SAKE — DIVE!*'

A shattering noise. Christian gasped and choked as the air was torn cruelly from his lungs. A terrific explosion. He reeled down the hatch. Urgent hands grabbed him and pulled him clear as the hatch clanged shut in the same instant that the U-200 reeled and shook as if struck by a gigantic metal fist. A thunderclap struck the boat. Suddenly — startlingly — the submarine careered off at an impossible angle. The lights went out. Men yelled. Someone whimpered with fear. Tins and equipment went rolling everywhere, and then, in a cloud of cork particles and a thick choking dust shaken out from the bulkhead, the U-200 started to go down stern first, with the ice-cold seawater already beginning to flood the stricken vessel. Momentarily Christian blacked out, vaguely aware of that most ominous sign for a submariner, a dramatic, painful increase in the air pressure, which could only mean that the U-200 had shipped a vast amount of water…

'We've been badly damaged … aft, sir!' The words seemed to come from the remote distance.

Christian shook his head and Number One's anxious face came into focus. Christian winced at the pain in his ears, like a very severe ear-ache.

'We've taken a lot of water, sir!' the Number One continued, 'Don't know as yet how far forrard we're flooded, sir!'

Christian nodded his understanding and rose groggily to his feet, grabbing a stanchion to support himself. The crippled U-boat had now come to a stop, her engines silent, at a forty-five degree angle so that now the compartment loomed up in front of him like a steel cliff-side. 'We're watertight at least,' he commented, trying to give an air of normalcy to the disaster for the sake of the wide-eyed ratings.

'Like the Queen of the Fairies, never been done, tight as a drum!' a familiar voice just behind him roared joyously, as if he were having a really good time.

Christian turned awkwardly. It was, of course, Frenssen, face covered with blood but otherwise apparently all right, up to his knees in debris. He grinned and winked.

Christian winked back. 'Thank God for the Frenssens of this world,' a little voice within him said. Then aloud, 'All right, Number One, casualties?'

'Two stokers missing, sir.' He lowered his gaze as if ashamed. 'We had to close the watertight doors on them — if they were still alive. It was the only way to save the boat, sir.'

Christian looked gently at the younger officer. 'You did exactly the right thing, Number One. I would have done the same. Now come on, let's have a look at the damage.'

'Want me, too, sir?' Frenssen sung out, wiping the blood from his face.

'Yes, you too. You might not have much in your turnip, Frenssen, but you've got the muscle.' He looked across at von Arco, whose fear was obvious now. 'You take charge, von Arco,' he snapped, unable to conceal the distaste in his voice, 'while I go forrard.'

Without waiting for an answer, Christian and the two others began to work their way upwards, tugging and hauling themselves up the steep metal ascent with the aid of instruments and stanchions.

They came to the first watertight door. Christian hesitated. If the water was piled up behind it, to open the door invited disaster. With an effort of sheer naked will-power he forced himself to begin opening the clips, nerves tingling electrically, body tensed for the first onrush of escaping water.

Nothing happened. No water sloshed over the bottom sill to meet them. Beyond, as they flashed their torches into the confused mess, a jumble of cans, foods, hams, and shattered equipment, there was no sign of water. This particular compartment was dry.

Number One licked his parched lips. 'Will we go on, sir?' he asked a little anxiously.

'Of course, we'll go on, sir,' Frenssen said before Christian could speak. 'Shall I close the door behind us, sir?'

Christian shook his head in mock wonder. 'Look at what has become of the U-boat arm, Number One. Even hairy — assed petty officers give orders to their skipper these days. Yes, you big rogue, close the door behind us,' he added with more confidence than he felt. Now they were cutting themselves off from the rest of the boat and if the next compartment were flooded... He decided not to follow that particularly frightening thought to its end.

Silently the two officers waited until Frenssen had closed the hatch door behind them, then they groped their way forward to the next one, finding a path through the mess with their torches.

'Here we go again,' Christian said and stopped. 'Hold my torch, Frenssen, I'll do this one.'

'Right sir.'

Gingerly, with fingers that trembled with tension, Christian began to open the clips of the second chamber, hypnotized gaze fixed on the sill in the circle of cold light from the torch. Suddenly, frighteningly, as he opened the first clip, water started to seep through.

Number One gasped. Frenssen lunged forward, ready to throw his tremendous weight against the door to stem the flood of seawater. 'Gently does it,' Christian soothed them through gritted teeth. 'Gently —' He opened the next clip and the hatch gave way with the pressure of the water accumulated at the other side.

Suddenly he found himself flung off his feet, slithering across the deck, spluttering and gasping as the water flooded in at a furious rate. The lights went out and they found themselves fighting for their lives in the pitch darkness, pressed up against the bulkhead, the icy water mounting ever upwards by the instant.

As soon as it started, or so it seemed, the sudden flood was over. One moment they were fighting for their lives, the next they were in water to their waists, gasping for air, trying to keep their balance, while an anxious Frenssen had somehow recovered his torch and was crying, 'Are you all right, sir?' He pinned Christian to the bulkhead wall in the circle of bright light and said with relief, 'Great buckets of flying crap, I thought we'd had it just then!' He gave a huge sigh and added, 'Hang on, sir. Here comes Number One.' He reached under the surface of the waist-deep water and grunted. Up came Number One, bedraggled, soaked, gasping for air.

In spite of the tension, Christian grinned at the sight. Poor old Number One looked like a soaked poodle. Then he was business-like again. 'All right, it looks as if the water level is not too bad after all. We're going to try the final compartment. If it can be drained, perhaps we can right the boat somehow. Come on, this is the last one.'

A few moments later they had opened the pins to the last compartment and were wading through the ice-cold water, grasping for anchor-points as they tugged themselves upwards. Everywhere their torch beams showed a horrifying picture. Smashed benches, broken tables and a half hundred other objects bobbed and wallowed obscenely in the filthy black slimy water.

Christian frowned. It didn't look good. With this much water, even if he managed to right the U-200, it might well flood the electric motors. 'What do you guess, Frenssen?' he asked after a moment, the only sound the mournful drip-drip of seawater.

'My guess is that we've shipped — say — one hundred and thirty tons of water, sir,' Frenssen answered after a moment's consideration.

The Number One gasped and Christian said hastily, 'It's not all that bad, you know. We've still got three hundred and eighty tons in the main ballast tank. If we fully blow it, we should have more than sufficient positive buoyancy to lift the U-200 to the surface, even though she won't be able to float very high in the water once she gets there.'

'Let's worry about that when we get there, sir,' Frenssen suggested.

'Yes, of course, you're right. Come on, let's get back to the control room...'

Ten minutes later, after he had quickly briefed the crew and the ashen-faced *Wehrmacht* gunners about what he was going to do, Christian began the first attempt to raise the stricken boat. 'Stand by to surface!' he snapped, very brisk and business-like, as if this was just a routine procedure instead of a life-and-death rescue attempt.

'Surface it is, sir!' the Number One sang out and began to issue his instructions for blowing the various ballast tanks.

Barely able to conceal his impatience, Christian waited until the final tank was blown and they were ready. 'Half ahead, Group Up!' he ordered, hoping that by moving he would assist the lift of the compressed air.

'Half ahead... Group Up!' the Number One echoed.

The U-200 lurched. Christian and his crew braced themselves. There was an ugly metallic rending sound, a kind of ragged scratching. Christian clenched his fists and willed the damned boat to move. 'Come on, you bitch,' he hissed to himself, feeling the sweat break out all over his body, '*move*!'

Slowly, very slowly, as if reluctant to do so, the U-200 began to move. Christian breathed a sigh of relief. Everywhere the crew's pale faces lit up. The Number One smiled at Christian in relief. Christian smiled back. '*Grr*,' Frenssen growled and clutched the bulging front of his pants melodramatically, 'this is almost as good as dipping yer wick in the old honey pot!'

'Full ahead!' Christian snapped.

Now his gaze was concentrated exclusively on the depth gauge. He watched as the red needle started to quiver and move. *Fifty metres … forty-five metres … thirty …'*

Faces glistening with sweat, the young ratings watched the rising needle with hypnotic fascination, knowing that their very lives hung in the balance.

Now Christian knew it was time to attempt to right the boat. 'Blow forrard!' he cried… 'Blow everything left aft!'

A sudden lurch. The hiss of escaping air. The whole boat quivered violently, as if it might fall apart. Frantically the men grabbed for support. Here and there a plate buckled. There was the noise of water trickling in where a seam had burst. Christian cursed. The U-200 remained obstinately at the same steep angle!

'Twenty-five metres … twenty…'

'At least, the bitch is still rising,' Frenssen sang out, as the repairmen crawled by him and began attempting to stem the new leaks. 'Come on, now fucking well — *make it!*' He clenched his massive fists, jaw set pugnaciously.

'Fifteen metres!'

Abruptly the red needle stopped!

The number one gasped and then struck the gauge with his hand. Nothing happened. The needle remained obstinately stuck at fifteen metres. Christian wiped the sweat from his brow and willed himself to stay calm.

'Try again, Number One, please,' he ordered.

'Yessir.' Lips trembling and a warm sheen in his eyes, ready to burst into tears at any moment, the young officer tapped the gauge once more.

Nothing!

The damned red needle remained obstinately stuck at fifteen metres.

Christian swallowed hard. Abruptly he was aware that all of them were staring at him, their lives depending upon his next decision. But he knew that for the time being he had run out of options. There was nothing else he could do. Yet veteran that he was, he realized he could not allow his young sailors to see that. He had to appear active, in command. 'All right,' he snapped, 'let's conserve our juice. Stop engines … stop blowing!' he commanded.

Dutifully the Number One echoed his orders.

Abruptly there was heavy brooding silence, each man suddenly wrapped in a cocoon of his own thoughts and fears. For a long moment, the U-200 remained suspended, then in an awesome total silence, she began to sink gently…

CHAPTER 7

It was a typical pre-Christmas day in New York, Inspector Hart couldn't help thinking a little cynically, as he pushed his way through the happy shoppers in Fifth Avenue. The same old padded Santas, reeking of rye whisky, ringing their bells and rattling their money-boxes hopefully; the cheap tinsel and cotton wool masquerading as snow in the glittering store windows; the Salvation Army band at the street corner manfully trying to compete with the radios blasting out Crosby's latest hit, 'I'm Dreaming of a White Christmas'; and the ragged bums standing trembling in the slush, trying to cadge a dime or a quarter before one of the patrolling cops caught up with them. Apart from the servicemen everywhere, there was no sign that America was at war. Even the dim-out had been lifted for the Christmas period. Momentarily he thought of his son over there in the ETO and wondered what he would think of America this wartime Christmas. Not much, he suspected. It was two days now since he had arrived at Central Station to begin his search. The local FBI, the cops, Navy and Army Intelligence had all been very helpful. But almost immediately he had realized that it was like looking for a needle in a haystack. How in heaven's name did you find a blond German in his mid-twenties in a sprawling city with a population of over seven million?

On the first day he had hung around the bars and cafes of the Yorkville district, round East 85th Street, where before the war the headquarters of the Nazi German-American Bund had been located; and where there were still plenty of Germans who had emigrated to the States in the hungry 1920s. But he had been without luck. Nowadays no one wanted to be known as a German. In the bars they spoke only American, however badly, and there was the Old Glory hanging everywhere. Yorkville, he had told himself ruefully, was more American than a Rockwell front cover.

The following morning he had tried the Central Draft Board. A fit young man of the unknown German's age group ran the risk of being stopped by the MPs, or even civilian cops, and being arrested if he didn't possess a draft exemption card to show reason why he was not in the armed forces. Again he had drawn a blank. There were thousands of blond young men registered with such an exemption for Greater New York alone. There were even five hundred-odd from Yorkville, the old German district, mostly with German-sounding names, too. By lunchtime he was bleary-eyed from looking at mug-shots of earnest young men with blond hair. In the end he gave up and went back to his hotel room, drowning out the sugary sounds of the old groaner's dreams of a 'White Christmas' by turning up the radio full blast.

That afternoon he tried the New York Central Post Office. He knew from past experience when he had placed 'taps' on suspects that they had a secret listening service, to which a government man such as an FBI agent could obtain access if he pulled the right strings. He also suspected and was proved right that they listened for illegal transmitters. Ever since Pearl Harbor they had been on the look-out for enemy subjects operating a clandestine radio in the Greater New York area. After all, it was from the east coast that the great convoys sailed carrying equipment and troops for Europe.

Again he drew a blank — save for one thing. Any transmitter used to give a fix had to be pretty close to the target selected for the missile. 'You see, Inspector,' a pale-faced technician with baggy eyes explained, 'the V-l steering mechanism is a pretty crude device. Reports from London indicate that they hit the target simply because London is so huge.'

'You mean, they can't hit a selective target, some object picked in advance?' he had asked quickly, an idea beginning to form in his mind slowly.

'Exactly. It's all very hit-and-miss, if you'll forgive the pun? There is only one way that a V-l could take out a specific target, a key factory, strategic bridge — something like that.'

'And what is that?'

'A homing device on which the V-l has a fix. The Krauts, so they tell me, have already done it with their acoustic torpedo. It homes on the sound of a ship's engines. If a ship were to go round in circles, then the torpedo would follow it until it struck home. Get it?'

'I get it,' he had said slowly. 'So if you had a sort of transmitter close —'

'Probably *in*, not close,' the technician had interrupted.

''Kay, a transmitter *in* the target, the V-l would home in on it. Is that it?'

The technician had grinned at him, showing a mouthful of bad, stained teeth. 'Yes, well, that's it in theory. Find a low grade homing device in operation and you'll find your target.'

'But can't you do that?' he had asked. 'Pick up this transmitter?'

The technician had shaken his head. 'Sorry, no-can-do. One, this device will probably be battery-powered to conserve energy so they won't start operating until the day of the operation. Two, even when it does start up, we haven't got the equipment to pick up that type of signal. You've seen those Hollywood movies about the Resistance over there in Europe, you know, with Bergman and Tracy and all those stars?' He had grinned suddenly and said a little huskily, 'Gee, hasn't that Bergman got tits on her! I'd give a year's pay to get my hands on those two. *Huba … huba* —'

'Forget Bergman's tits, on which your hands will never fall, and get on with it,' he had barked impatiently.

'Well, you've seen those directional vans the Gestapo uses, the ones with the round direction finder antenna on top?'

'Yeah.'

The technician had grinned maliciously at him, enjoying the destruction of the FBI man's hopes. 'Well, we don't have 'em, see.'

It was as he emerged into the afternoon crowds of shoppers and tired dock workers returning home from the swing shift, dragging their empty luncheon pails as if they weighed a ton, that he remembered J. Edgar Hoover's words about the importance of the enemy target. It had to be someone — or something — of such importance that it warranted risking a submarine and its crew.

But what in the name of Sam Hill, he asked himself, could that be? All the one-ton missiles would not suffice to knock out New York's harbour system. Sure, three or four missiles would destroy the port authority which directed the convoys, but the Navy and Merchant Marine, he was confident, would have a temporary system working within days. With this new Kraut counter-attack in Belgium, men and equipment were needed urgently on the other side of the Atlantic. The convoys just had to keep on sailing!

'*But what if he isn't in New York at all?*' a cold little voice inside him had asked insidiously. 'Perhaps he's somewhere in Boston or Norfolk, some place like that?' The target could be anywhere along the eastern seaboard. But now as he strolled blindly through the happy, flushed, pre-Christmas crowds, with the snow beginning to drift down slowly once more, Hart experienced that old certainty that New York *was* the place. It was that old cop's feeling that had nothing to do with police science and criminology. It was simply an irrational hunch that he was right.

Perhaps it was the same hunch that made him turn off after St Patrick's Cathedral and begin making his way up towards Radio City. The ice-rink opposite was as busy as ever, in spite of the fact that this was a work-day. All the usual types were there; the giggling girl beginners in twos, invariably tumbling to the ice after a few hesitant steps to lie there in hysterical laughter. The middle-aged exhibitionists swirling round perfectly in time to the piped music, faces set in proud, secret smiles as they performed for the admiring crowds. And, of course, there were those beautiful, smart young New York girls, dressed for the occasion in their short swirling skirts and tight silk knickers, executing tremendous turns that revealed vast glimpses of thighs and tight, plump, silken bottoms.

For a moment Inspector Hart forgot his problem at the sight. He felt the old familiar urge. It had been a long time! Emily, back home in Vermont, middle-aged and wan, given to headaches and 'sickly bouts', had not allowed him to 'do it' for years. When the need had become too great he had gone to the whores and the B-girls who could be picked up in any bar these days. But it wasn't the same thing as doing it with someone you liked who didn't stretch out her hand for money afterwards. He licked suddenly dry lips and tried not to stare too hard at a cute little redhead, whose crotch was perfectly outlined by her black pants.

'Take it easy, pop,' an amused young voice said behind him. 'That kind's jailbait, old man. She can't be no more than sixteen.'

He turned round startled.

A young sailor was standing there, white cap set back jauntily on his crisp curly hair, hands dug deep into the pockets of his pea-jacket. He looked the typical cocky young gob straight out of boot camp, come on furlough to New York for a 'piece of the action', as he would invariably call it, before 'shipping out'.

'You talking to me, sailor?' Hart rasped.

Suddenly the young sailor was unsure of himself. The civvy might be old, but the jaw-line was firm and the eyes were hard. He looked plenty tough. 'Just making fun, sir,' the sailor said. 'Pretty nice bunch of girls, but I'm on my way to the USO. It's in the Taft Hotel and I don't know where the Taft is. You see,' he grinned winningly, 'I'm outa town. Just spending a few days in New York before shipping out overseas, sir.'

Hart's face softened. The sailor was only a kid. He couldn't be much more than eighteen. He thought of his own son and said, 'I know where it is, sailor. I'll take you there, if you like.'

'Would you, sir?' the boy's face lit up. 'You know what New Yorkers are like? They don't have no time for nobody. Hell, some of them wouldn't give a guy the directions if he wuz Jesus Christ trying to find a church!' He grinned, obviously thinking he had said something very witty.

Hart returned his grin. 'Yeah, New Yorkers are like that,' he agreed. 'Come on, kid, let's go.' Deliberately Hart didn't look at the twirling little skaters. He thought it would embarrass the kid. In the kid's eyes, old guys like him didn't even *think* of such things. It wasn't proper.

Letting the young sailor chatter away, he led him towards the towering white mass of the Taft, which had once been one of New York's tallest skyscrapers. Now it was overshadowed by newer buildings and looked distinctly seedy.

'Of course, I'm not going to the USO for the Java and doughnuts, sir. I want free tickets to a Broadway show. They say that afterwards us service guys can go backstage and talk to the stars, even *date* them. Wow, fancy me dating Betty Grable, for instance, with them pins!' He sighed ecstatically and Hart was forced to grin at his youthful innocence.

'It's over there,' he broke into the kid's excited chatter. 'Can you see it, with all the flags — and things?'

The kid's grin broadened as he saw the women parading up and down in front of the hotel entrance under the watchful, knowing gaze of the military policemen guarding the place. 'Not for me, sir,' he said. 'Those hookers are real poison. We've been warned about them back at camp. Wow, some of them VD movies they showed us —' He broke off and said, 'Me, sir, I'll stick to Betty Grable.'

Hart nodded his agreement and fumbled for his billfold. He took out a note and offered it to the kid, 'Here you are, sailor. Have a good time.' The kid whistled softly. 'Gee, a sawbuck!' he exclaimed. Then his face grew suspicious. 'They told us back at camp —'

'No,' Hart interrupted him firmly, 'I am *not* a faggot! So you can save it all for Betty Grable.'

The kid grinned again and took the banknote. 'Thank you very much, sir. Sure do appreciate it… And Merry Christmas, sir!'

'Why, yes,' Hart stuttered, caught by surprise. 'And Merry Christmas to you, too.'

Then the kid was gone, running excitedly towards the entrance, as if he couldn't get to Betty Grable quick enough…

Hart stood in the now softly falling snow, watching him go, plunging into the excitement of a young man's New York. For a moment he wished he was young again and could get excited like that. But in December 1944 you had to pay for your excitement and for being young — you got killed. He turned and was about to wander on, when he saw the gaudy big poster framed in the centre of the USO window. It bore the usual bright and breezy legend, picked out in a patriotic red, white and blue. '*Christmas Eve with stars. Come and join, all you service gals and guys invited. Free punch and apple pie, just like mom used to make…*' All around the poster were the usual stars' photographs framed in silver stars, Joe E. Louis, Maria Raye, 'The Schnozz', of course — all of them 'cheerfully', as they always said it in the publicity handouts, giving their services 'free for our brave fighting forces.'

But it wasn't the stars or the legend which caught Hart's gaze. It was the big central picture, depicting a leggy blonde in a slinky gown, with her hair tumbling over her face, sitting provocatively on a grand piano. She was Lauren Bacall, the new teenage wife of Bogart, displaying her excellent legs for the benefit of the boys who would come to see the Christmas Eve show.

Yet the diffident little man in the rimless spectacles who grinned up at the young actress from the keyboard was no movie star. He was a politician, soon to become (if all the rumours about FDR's precarious state of health were true) *the* most important one in the whole United States, though at the moment, Hart told himself, hardly an ordinary citizen knew who this ex-shopkeeper from Missouri was.

Hart whistled softly. Now he knew the U-boat's target. It had to be — *him*!

CHAPTER 8

Slowly Christian wiped the beads of sweat from his forehead. With fingers that trembled slightly, he felt his pulse. It was 144, twice its normal rate. It indicated just how hard his system was having to work to provide enough blood oxygenation simply to allow him to slump against the bulkhead doing nothing, but thinking hard.

All about him were his crew, their faces glazed with sweat, eyes anxious. The air was running out fast — *and with it, time, too*! He had to think of something to bring the U-200 to the surface before it was too late and the men began cracking up. Already the gunnery officer's dark eyes were beginning to bulge dangerously behind his thick spectacles and his body was twitching constantly, as though he had some kind of fever. It wouldn't be long before *he* went into hysterics.

The men had already exhausted themselves pumping the boat dry of seawater, with Frenssen working all out until he had dropped to his hands and knees, gasping for breath, shaking his head doggedly like a fighter refusing to go down for the count. But it hadn't worked. The U-200 had stubbornly refused to level out. Thereafter he had used up most of the remaining precious high-pressure air to blow main ballast. He had also used some of the same air to blow out the freshwater tanks midships and reduce the crippled ship's ballast. The U-200 had stirred and groaned eerily and for a wild moment Christian had hoped it had done the trick. But it hadn't. The U-200 obstinately remained where she was.

What was left to him to try?

Surprisingly enough it was von Arco who suggested the dangerous manoeuvre still left to him. Speaking slowly, constantly wetting his lips, as if he were finding it difficult to speak, he said, 'There is still the "drop keel", Jungblut,' he said huskily, 'if you're prepared to take the chance. I was in the old U-33 before the war with Prien. He chanced it when we were stuck at the bottom of the Kattegat after an accident. It worked.'

Christian sucked his teeth thoughtfully, while von Arco stared at him, his once arrogant face drained of all emotion, even fear.

To drop the 'heavy keel' was a most dramatic step, Christian knew. It was an eleven ton addition to the boat that could be released in an emergency, without affecting the rest of the boat.

'You know the drawback, von Arco?' Christian asked.

Slowly von Arco nodded. 'If you drop it and we surface, it is probable that we shall never be able to dive again.'

'Exactly.' Christian hesitated. 'That means,' he continued thoughtfully, '*If* we make it to the surface, our mission will be greatly at risk. Or if we carry out the firing of the missiles, then we take the stick coming to us *on the surface*!' He grated out the last words, looking hard at von Arco to ascertain his reaction.

Von Arco sweated even more. 'I have been thinking of that, too, Jungblut,' he answered, 'but with a bit of luck we *could* make it to Mexico.'

Christian shot him a swift glance of surprise. Was that what the coded personal message from Dönitz had been about?

'Yes,' von Arco said hurriedly, 'make it there, beach the boat and then let our authorities take care of us.' He bent his head, as if he was somehow ashamed. 'The Mexicans will help us. Like all South Americans they hate the *Amis* like poison.'

Christian pursed his lips and tried the next logical thought. 'We could, of course, surface … and surrender,' he said softly.

Von Arco did not react, though Christian noted the whitening of the knuckles of his right hand.

He dropped the ploy and thought hard. *If* they made it to the surface and *if* they managed to limp the remaining kilometres to the American eastern seaboard, and *if* they managed to launch their missiles under cover of darkness, there might just be a chance they'd get away and make the Gulf of Mexico before the *Amis* discovered them. After all, they would expect the submarine to dive immediately after launching the missiles and head for home — *eastwards* — not hug the US coast, proceeding *southwards*. But it was a damned big chance!

Von Arco opened his mouth to speak, but Christian beat him to it. 'All right, there is nothing else we can do. We'll drop it. *Stand by everybody*. We're going to release the drop keel!'

'The drop keel,' the gunnery officer quavered in terror, 'what is that, please?'

But no one had time for the bespectacled gunner. Now all was controlled chaos as the crew prepared to take this last measure, the most desperate one of all. Even the greenest among them knew that.

Christian tensed. The Number One looked at him significantly. He nodded. There was a whir of machinery. Suddenly, startlingly, the crippled boat shuddered. Immediately all their eyes flashed to the depth gauge. The red needle *dropped*!

The gunnery officer gasped and his hand flew to his trembling lips in near-hysteria. 'Oh, my God,' he whispered, 'we're still sinking!'

'Hold on there!' Christian snapped. 'Give it time, men!' With infinite slowness, the red needle moved again. To the left. They were going up!

Now they watched with hypnotized fascination the maddeningly slow movement of the red needle. There was not a sound in the whole length of the battered boat. No one dared to breathe, in case he upset the movement of that needle. *Eighty metres … seventy metres … sixty* … and the boat began levelling out on to an even keel … fifty … Christian could feel the sweat trickling unpleasantly down the small of his back and his underpants were soaked and clinging to his crotch. *Fifty metres…*

'Prepare to start motors,' Christian whispered hoarsely, breaking that tense, awesome silence.

The Number One seemed to tip-toe away to carry out the order, as though he dared not do anything that might end the blessed upwards movement.

'*Forty-five metres … forty…*'

'Start motors!'

There was a soft whir as the electric motors started. Enthralled and speechless, no one seemed to notice. All attention was concentrated on the flickering red needle. '*Thirty metres … twenty-five metres … twenty … fifteen …*' Christian was ready at the periscope. There was no mistaking the relief on the crew's sweat-lathered pale faces now. '*Ten metres…*' Next to Frenssen, the gunnery officer sobbed in a broken voice, 'Thank God … thank God, we're saved!'

'Up periscope!' Christian commanded as unemotionally as he could. There was a restrained cheer from the crew. Von Arco beamed, as the Number One said, 'Well, your idea worked after all, sir.'

'It just came to me from the old days, Number One,' he replied modestly.

Christian bent to the metal tube, grasping the handles. Expertly he swung the periscope round the whole three hundred and sixty degrees. The grey-green heaving sea was empty. He breathed a sigh of relief. They were still moving upwards and the sea was blessedly empty. He turned up the intensifier. Everything leaped into clearer and larger definition. Still nothing. He waited no longer. Clapping the handles together, he snapped, 'Down periscope… *Take her up!*'

Now there was nothing to restrain the crew. Exhausted and worn as they were through the shock of the sinking and lack of oxygen, they burst into wild cheering, slapping each other on the back in congratulation, babbling away excitedly, 'like a bunch of frigging crazy chimney-sweeps!' as Frenssen commented scornfully.

Five minutes later the hatch was opened and a stream of icy, but blessed, sea air flooded the boat, setting the men coughing, the tears of joy and happiness still streaming down their haggard, wan faces.

His legs like rubber, aware now for the first time just what effect the lack of oxygen had had on him, Christian clambered wearily up the conning tower ladder, followed by von Arco, gasping for breath under the strain like some ancient asthmatic. Behind them the Number One was vomiting uncontrollably.

In silence the two officers surveyed the Atlantic, while below at the base of the ladder, Number One retched miserably, still unable to climb it.

The winter sea was thankfully empty. Not even a smudge of smoke on the horizon anywhere. They might well have been the last ship afloat in the world. Christian nodded his approval and, turning to von Arco, said, 'From now on we have a double watch on the deck. If we are spotted and attacked, we'll just have to fight it out. We can dive no more.'

'I'll see the eighty-eight cannon and the *Vierling* is manned all the time, Jungblut,' von Arco replied dutifully, as Christian noted that one of those typical New England fogs was beginning to drift over the sea. It would give them the cover they needed for the rest of this long day.

'Now my estimate is that we are some five hundred kilometres from the enemy coast. I think it is time to break open the sealed orders.'

Von Arco's eyes gleamed suddenly and Christian told himself that the glory-hunter was already visualizing his triumphant reception at the Führer's HQ to receive the coveted Knight's Cross. 'Don't imagine that you are going to cure your throat-ache that easily, von Arco,' he snapped harshly. 'If our luck runs out, we might all end up with a

severe headache instead. Worse, if the *Amis* find us with their damned Catalinas, it could be the bottom of the ocean for the U-200. Now place your deck watch and report to my cabin with the rest of the officers in five minutes' time.'

Ten minutes later, as the artificers busied themselves down below, clearing up the mess and making provisional repairs to the U-200, the handful of officers crowded expectantly into Christian's tiny cabin, with Frenssen standing guard outside the drawn curtain as a security guard.

Deliberately Christian broke the seals, watched in rapt silence by his young officers. Even the myopic gunnery officer had ceased his usual nervous fiddling with his glasses. Christian opened the thick wad of papers and glanced briefly at the usual precis which explained the whole operation. Then he began to read it out to the officers.

' "It has been commanded by the Führer himself that a revenge attack will be launched on the evening of December 24th, 1944 on the American city of — New York." '

He paused for the usual comments or excitement. None came, even from von Arco, for they all knew what it meant to bombard America's greatest city. The *Amis'* revenge would be deliberate and terrible, if they managed to catch the U-200.

' "The target for the attack will be assigned to the commander of the U-200 on the morning of December 24th by means of a radio signal (see attached for further details).

' "Finally it must be emphasized that this is *not* simply a revenge attack. After some consideration, the Führer has decided that a major blow which could have a decisive effect on the future course of the war, must be struck at American political life.

' "In view of the delicate health of the US President, which is well known to our specialists (who are of the opinion that he will not survive to the spring of 1945), the liquidation of his potential successor could render the USA leaderless at a time when our forces are achieving victory in the West. It is the opinion of this headquarters that this would ensure very favourable terms for Germany at the subsequent peace negotiations." '

Christian whistled softly, although he only half understood what it was all about. *How did Berlin know Roosevelt was dying? Who was this successor they were going to 'liquidate'? Did he live in New York?* The questions flashed through Christian's mind with bewildering rapidity.

' "In the case of *Kapitänleutnant* Christian Jungblut being in any way incapacitated by enemy action or otherwise — " ' Christian stopped short and shot von Arco a hard look. The latter flushed and lowered his gaze so that Christian knew instantly that von Arco knew already what that last paragraph of the summary contained. He had known it all along. It was part and parcel of that special plan Dönitz and he had worked out together. Von Arco had been placed on the U-200 to keep an eye on him. All along Dönitz had not trusted him. If anything happened, if he wavered in any way, von Arco would step in, quoting the Big Lion's order as his authorization, and take control of the submarine.

The Number One cleared his throat as the others stared at Christian in some bewilderment, wondering why he was not continuing with this exciting information. For what seemed an age, Christian did not appear to notice, as his brain absorbed that most significant phrase of the final paragraph, 'incapacitated by enemy action *or otherwise*'. It would be up to von Arco to decide how to interpret that 'otherwise'.

Then he seemed to remember where he was and that they were listening. Quite casually, almost as if he were bored by the whole thing, he said, ' "In the case of *Kapitänleutnant* Jungblut being knocked out, then the command of the U-200 will be taken over forthwith by *Kapitänleutnant* von Arco..." '

Outside the curtain Frenssen groaned and said quite clearly, 'Shit — *no!*'

CHAPTER 9

The wind came straight from the east. It was a bitter wind, scudding in straight from the Arctic Circle. It howled about the lone submarine limping through the immense green seascape, covering it with hoar-frost.

Standing shivering on the conning tower, huddled in his leather coveralls, Christian thought the sparkling boat, hung with the glittering frost, looked a little like a Christmas card. But there was nothing festive about her guns or her mission this black Christmas of 1944.

He yawned and shivered at the same time. Another hour before Number One took over and he could fall gratefully into his bunk and blot out the war and thoughts of their desperate mission for a fleeting four hours. Another day of sailing and they would be in the target area; then there would be no sleep for him until they had reached the Gulf of Mexico — *if* they reached it. Before then he needed all the rest he could get.

But even on this grim December day in the middle of nowhere, those of the crew who were off duty and not asleep thought of their homeland and Christmas. For above the steady beat of the diesels and the howl of the bitter wind, there came floating up the strains of '*Stille Nacht, Heilige Nacht*', a little sad, a little defiant, as if the singers defied anyone to tell them 'to put a shitting sock in it!'

Christian laughed softly at the sound and said to von Arco, standing next to him on the freezing deck of the conning tower, 'Amazing, isn't it? Nearly five thousand kilometres from home in the middle of total war and those greenbeaks down there behave as if everything's quite normal and they're back in some family front parlour, singing carols and waiting for the presentation round the Christmas tree.'

Von Arco whipped the dewdrop from the end of his red nose. '*Sentimentality*!' he sneered, 'typical German sentimentality. Provincial and absurd. Not worthy of our nation's greatness. The Führer deserves better than that.'

Christian didn't take offence. Von Arco's opinions did not move him.

'Oh, I don't know, von Arco,' he said easily. 'There's nothing wrong in it, if it amuses them and keeps them happy. It's an old carol, something they remember from their childhood — happier times.' He smiled bleakly. 'Give 'em a few beers and some schnapps and they'd soon change over to the usual dirty ditties.'

Von Arco remembered those Christmases back in the hungry 1930s when he had first gone to sea as a cadet in sail-driven training ships. Christmas had just been another day of back-breaking work, starvation, rotten rations and brutal discipline, carried out by a bosun wielding a rope's end. But it had made them hard, lastingly hard, with no time for that weak sentimentality which turned German men into such hopeless fools.

'If we Germans are to survive this war and be victorious,' he barked, almost as if he were addressing a public meeting, 'we Germans have to be ruthless, motivated solely by cold logic, our sole aim the triumph of the Greater German Folk.'

Christian looked at his frozen, arrogant face out of the corner of his eyes and told himself that von Arco was on his soap-box once more. Idly he wondered how von Arco would react when the real shooting commenced. But he refrained from commenting. The von Arcos of this world could never be changed. They had been formed in their harsh bitter unreasoning mould many years before; only death could ever break that mould.

The U-200 ploughed on through the limitless sea...

It was a quarter of an hour later that the heavy brooding silence of the upper deck was broken by the look-out's cry of 'Object ahead, sir!'

'Where?' Christian yelled, suddenly very alert, nerve-ends tingling.

'Green-one-zero!'

As one the two officers on the conning tower flung up their glasses. For a moment they could see nothing. Then a high white object slid momentarily into the circles of calibrated glass, before disappearing once more into the grey rolling mist. Christian whistled softly, while von Arco stared at him expectantly. In the end, he could contain his curiosity no longer. 'Well, *Herr Kapitänleutnant*,' he demanded very formally, 'what are you going to do?'

Christian did not answer straight away. Instead he focused his glasses once more and waited. Again the great white ship emerged from the mist, bearing straight down upon them, and there was no mistaking the huge, illuminated red cross painted on its side. 'But it's a hospital ship,' he stuttered. 'An *Ami* hospital ship, von Arco.' He looked at the other officer his eyes suddenly wild. 'Do you understand that — *a hospital ship?*' There was a note of hysterical pleading in his voice now, as if he were afraid that von Arco would make him do that unspoken terrible thing.

'Yes, I can see that, Jungblut,' von Arco said icily, in no way moved. 'It is a hospital ship, but it is also an American vessel. And you know as well as I do what its skipper will do when he spots us, which he will do soon.'

'The Geneva Convention —' Christian began wildly.

'He will radio our position to the American authorities,' von Arco cut him off brutally. 'They will find us and destroy us even before we can start our vital mission, Jungblut.' He looked hard at Christian, his face set and stony. 'You know what you must do. You have no alternative.'

'But …' The protest died on Christian's lips. He knew that von Arco was right. There was no chance of their escaping undetected; and the unknown American skipper *would* radio their position to his people, believing himself secure that not even one of the feared 'grey wolves' would attack a hospital ship.

'We must knock out the radio mast first,' von Arco persisted relentlessly. 'Even before we attack the ship itself.'

'Perhaps we could knock out the mast and let her sail on?' Christian attempted miserably.

Von Arco sneered at him. 'Jungblut, with all due respect, but I think you must have birds that go tweet-tweet in your head! How long do you think it would take for their radiomen to rig up a temporary aerial and send a signal? Or the skipper could turn for port or contact another vessel and relay our position that way. No,' he said with an air of finality, as the hospital ship came closer and closer, 'there is no way out. She *must* be sunk!'

Christian gave in. He bent to the voice tube. 'Tubes one to four,' he commanded, his voice unsteady. 'Ready for surface fire.'

'Tubes one to four — ready for surface fire, sir!' the aft petty officer in charge of the tin fish called back.

Christian swallowed hard. 'Deck gun, prepare to fire. *Vierling* prepare to fire. Target — radio mast.'

'Target — radio mast!' the petty officers echoed his command.

Christian brought up his glasses. At his side, von Arco did the same, face set in a look of triumph.

Steadily the hospital ship ploughed through the sea towards them, majestically unaware of what lay waiting for her and almost hidden in the heaving waves. The ship's look-outs were obviously slack, but then they probably felt themselves completely secure. Who would attack a hospital ship in daylight when it was so clearly marked?

'Target green ninety,' the range-finder sang out, 'speed eighteen knots … range two thousand metres.'

Christian heard himself call out, 'Fire at one thousand. Radio mast…' It was as if he were listening to a total stranger.

'Torpedo room, prepare to fire at my specific command.'

The reply echoed up from below.

Now an uncanny silence hungover the deck, as the hospital ship grew larger and larger, sailing straight into the trap. It was empty of patients. They could all see that; she was too high in the water. She was probably sailing to Europe to pick up the casualties from the new battle in Belgium. But she'd be carrying a crew, doctors and medics — and nurses, Christian thought. *Women*, even if they were in uniform! How long were they going to survive in this terrible freezing Atlantic weather? It was a question that not one of the watchers dared to answer.

Now the still unsuspecting hospital ship was almost in range and for the first time Christian spotted a swift glint of glass from her upper deck, as if a look-out was hurriedly adjusting his binoculars.

'We've been seen!' von Arco rapped.

Christian hesitated no longer. '*Feuer Frei*!' he yelled urgently at the gunners.

'*Feuer*!' the two petty officers rapped as one.

With a tremendous burst of noise, the *Vierling* flak opened up. At the rate of a thousand rounds per minute, the deadly little white 20mm shells went streaming across the water towards the hospital ship. On the deck the 88mm boomed. Automatically Christian opened his mouth to prevent his eardrums from being burst, as the hot blast wave struck him across the face. The huge shell went screaming towards its target while the gunners reloaded frantically, ramming home another gleaming shell case into the smoking breech of the great gun.

Hurriedly the two officers flung up their binoculars.

The first tremendous concentration of fire hit the hospital ship just behind the bridge. The ship heeled visibly under the impact. Fist-sized, red-hot fragments of steel hissed lethally across the deck. A fuel tank burst into flames immediately. A great searing tongue of fire raced the length of the deck like a giant blow-torch. With a metallic rending and clatter, the radio mast tumbled to the deck, sending angry blue electric sparks running everywhere.

Abruptly the great white ship came to a stop. For a moment nothing happened. Christian cupped his hands to his mouth and cried urgently over the frenetic chatter of the *Vierling* flak. 'Cease fire... For God's sake, *cease fire*!'

The firing stopped, the two vessels idling on the waves like two spent opponents in a contest, each waiting for the other's next move. Suddenly the American ship's signal lamp began to flicker rapidly. 'Read him, signalman!' Christian commanded curtly.

'Sir!'

Swiftly the signalman clapped his binoculars to his eyes and started to read the signal. 'Master... SS *Smithsonia* to submarine commander... Are you mad?... Or are you blind?... Can't you see the red cross? — Demand you cease firing at once... This is a grave breach of international law.' The signalman dropped his binoculars to his chest and faced Christian.

'Damned Yankee impertinence!' von Arco snapped angrily, 'attempting to tell *us* what to do!'

'Be quiet!' Christian cried, 'I can't hear myself damn well think, with all your noise.'

Von Arco half-opened his mouth to protest then he thought better of it. The look on Jungblut's face boded no good.

'Signal Captain SS *Smithsonia* that I require him to abandon his ship within five minutes. I shall then give him a course for the nearest US port before sinking his ship.'

'Sir!' The signaller crouched over the Aldis lamp and began to send the message rapidly in the best kind of English he knew.

They didn't have long to wait for the American skipper's reaction. Angrily it came flashing back from the stationary hospital ship. 'Damn you, this is an outrage. You can't make me expose my crew and female nurses to the elements in this kind of weather —'

'*Fire*!' Christian did not give the signaller time to finish the message from the irate captain. 'Fire one across her port bow!'

Down on the deck, the 88mm burst into life. *Crump*! The huge hundred pound shell shot across the water. It burst in a great flurry of wild white water, feet in front of the hospital ship's bow, drenching its superstructure with tons of seawater.

That did the trick! Quite distinctly the waiting U-boat men could hear the bosun's whistles shrilling and see tiny black figures run along the littered deck to the boat stations. Almost immediately the upper deck was flooded with figures huddled in extra coats and blankets. Christian focused his glasses and groaned. In spite of the blankets he could recognize the figures all right. 'Women,' he moaned. 'They've got damned nurses aboard as I suspected.'

Beside him, von Arco said coolly, 'So? Why shouldn't those *Ami* whores have a taste of the kind of misery that our womenfolk suffer nightly at the hands of those Anglo-American air gangsters? They deserve it.'

Christian didn't respond. Instead, he spoke into the tube, voice miserable. 'Slow ahead,' he ordered. Then to the deck crew. 'Stand by with boathooks to repel boarders.'

'What are you going to do, Jungblut?' von Arco asked in sudden alarm.

'Just see that all the poor devils get off in time, collect them together and then give them a course for the US mainland.' He shrugged. 'After that I suppose I'll sink her …'

'Wait for the sisters!' the elderly captain was crying when the U-200 reached his lifeboat. 'For God's sake, don't let those boats with the sisters fall behind there!' Now he became aware of the submarine towering above his frail rocking craft and glared at it defiantly. Formally Christian saluted, but the American skipper didn't respond. Instead he snarled, 'I'll see you in hell before I salute you! Why man, you don't even know what civilized behaviour is.' He pointed a shaking hand at a lifeboat coming up now, filled with whimpering women, blankets wrapped around their heads, hanging on to each other pitifully. 'How the tarnation do you think they are going to last even a day in these weather conditions? Why, in God's name? *I* couldn't bear to look at myself in the mirror if I had what you've got on your conscience, man!' He shook violently; then he bent his white head and began to sob.

Christian pretended not to notice. 'This is your course to the nearest landfall, Captain,' he said in his careful English. 'The tides are in your favour, you should make it in twenty-four hours. Good luck!'

The captain did not look up as the U-200 passed on gently, the deck crew indicating with gestures and sign language to the occupants of the pathetic little boats that they should close up on the captain's craft.

Five minutes later they had gone, vanishing noiselessly into the freezing grey darkness like pathetic ghosts and the U-200 was in position to torpedo the deserted hospital ship.

Routinely Christian rapped out his orders to the torpedo crew…

The dying radio operator had just finished stringing up the makeshift aerial with clumsy fingers that felt like sausages, as the first torpedo struck the *Smithsonia* below the waterline. The ship heeled immediately. Dying as he was, he could still hear the water begin to rush in. He fell to his knees, the electric pain searing through his torn body. He had to get that fuckin' signal back to base… *He had to…!*

He pressed his finger to the morse key. It worked! He coughed thickly and blood began to trickle from the corner of his mouth. He started to transmit.

Another tremendous explosion. The ship reeled madly. Suddenly water was pouring through the bulkhead by the ton - *and it was boiling!* He screamed shrilly as it smashed into his body. He was slammed against the bulkhead and pinned there as the water boiled him alive. He began to scream…

CHAPTER 10

Mr Finkel, the manager of the Taft, was irate, harassed, and not a little afraid. 'But you must be joking, Inspector,' he said, fussing with his dark jacket, pulling at the carnation in his lapel. The sounds of the Andrews Sisters belting out 'I'll be with you in apple-blossom time' drifted up from the USO canteen.

'We've never had anything like that here at the Taft in its whole long history. We have always been a highly respectable place.' He puffed out his fat little chest like a pouter pigeon and Hart would have laughed at the sight if the situation had not been so serious.

'I can assure you, sir, that everything I have said to you is gospel truth,' Hart said. 'Someone — a German national who is already here in position in New York — is to direct a flying bomb attack on your hotel in order to kill a certain outstanding political personality whose name I am not at liberty to give you at this time.'

The harassed manager pulled out a large flowered handkerchief and patted the sweat from his forehead. 'But we don't have anyone of any real importance staying at the Taft at this moment. Just before Christmas —'

Hart held up his hand to stop the excited flow of words. 'I know he is not a guest, sir,' he said soothingly.

'Thank God for that!' the manager breathed. 'The Taft's first duty has always been to its guests.'

Outside the open door to his office, the black cleaners shuffled by, clutching great bundles of sheets, and the manager forgot his fears sufficiently to bark, 'Come on there, move yourselves there. I want every bed changed and made up by midday.' He sighed and said, 'These people! We'd never have employed them before the war. But with all our people being in the services or war industry, what can you do?'

'Yes, what can you do?' Hart echoed and persisted with his questions. 'Now, have you on your staff anyone answering to this description?' He gave the manager the description, poor as it was, of the suspected German agent. The manager hardly listened. Instead he shook his head and snorted, 'I'd never employ a German anyway. I'm Jewish, you see,' he added, lowering his voice and flashing a look at the open door.

Hart repressed his grin with difficulty. 'The fella we're looking for would hardly tell you he was Kraut, sir,' he said. 'Our guess is that he speaks perfect American.'

Down below in the canteen someone had changed the record. Now the Andrews Sisters were zapping into the 'Boogie-woogie Bugle-boy from Company B...' The swift electric music seemed to lend new urgency to Hart's questions. 'All right, sir, let me ask you this. Does your house dick check out the hotel every day? Is there any kind of routine check for suspicious objects?'

The portly little manager puffed himself up to his full five foot five and said, 'Our hotel *detective* has all his hands full, trying to prevent certain females of dubious antecedents from entering the lobby, or even the guests' bedrooms. Since the war began morality has been thrown out of the window, Inspector. If I told you some of the things that go on here —'

'So there is no check?' Hart interrupted him harshly.

'No, there isn't.'

Hart sucked his teeth thoughtfully and wondered where he would damn well start? On the roof perhaps? A low-power transmitter might operate more efficiently up there, above the stone jungle below. Or the basement? Down in that rabbit warren of storage rooms, junk, cleaning tackle, etc., there could be hundreds of places to hide a transmitter. He paused, while the manager watched him, wondering what was going through the head of this tall, harshly handsome man. But one thing was certain, the agent would have to appear somewhere along the line to start the transmitter working, wouldn't he? When he did, he, Hart, would nab him. He had to!

'Well?' the manager demanded finally. 'I am a very busy man, Inspector, what with Christmas and everything…'

'With your permission, I'd like to take up residence here in the Taft.'

He saw the look in the manager's eyes and snapped, 'Any room will do. As long as there's somewhere I can flop at night and a place to get a wash. Nothing fancy.'

'Of course, of course, anything for the Bureau, Inspector, I'll take care of it personally.' He gave Hart his professional smile, a mixture of caution, fake bonhomie, and greed. He pursed his lips. 'Now there's three zero —'

'Inspector Hart,' a tough snarling New York voice broke in.

The manager turned, startled. His professional smile turned to one of distaste as he saw the shabby fat man standing there, with the bulbous nose and seamed face of a drinker, derby hat tipped to the back of his cropped head. 'Oh, it's you,' he snapped. 'What do you want, Murphy?'

'*You*, I do not want,' Murphy said, talking out of the side of his mouth in the manner of all the New York policemen Hart had ever known. Perhaps they trained them to talk like that at the Police Academy, he thought idly, as the house detective said, 'I want to talk to the Inspector — *privately*!'

'Privately?' the manager cried in exasperation. 'But this is my office, my hotel.'

'Sure,' Murphy twisted the unlit cigar stub from one side of his mouth to the other easily, contemptuously. 'Sure it's your office, your hotel, Mr Finkel. But still I want to talk to the Inspector, *privately*. It's official business and you're not official, see.' He stared at the manager challengingly.

Hastily, Hart soothed the manager. 'Mr Finkel, I told my office to contact me through Mr Murphy, if anything urgent came up,' he smiled winningly. 'I would certainly appreciate it if I could talk to him privately in your office for a few moments. The Bureau would appreciate it, too.'

The mention of the 'Bureau' did the trick. The G-men movies of the 1930s had made their mark. The general public might not be impressed by their local cops, but they certainly were by Hoover's FBI. The manager gave him a fake professional smile, glared at an insolent Murphy and bowing slightly said, 'Please be my guest, Mr Hart. For as long as you like.' As he went out he snapped at Murphy, 'And don't you dare smoke that filthy cheap cigar in my office, do you hear?'

Murphy kicked the door closed behind the manager and snorted, 'Creep! Scared of his own shadow. If I wanted to blow the gaff about the nice little racket he's running here for special guests with the local B-girls, it would be goodbye, dear Mr Finkel!' He waved his heavy-knuckled fist, as if bidding a fond farewell to the manager. Then he was business-like. 'Inspector, there's an urgent message just come in from your office here, via Washington.'

'What is it?' Already half-aware of what it might be, Hart tensed expectantly.

'A Kraut sub. It's sunk an American hospital ship. The bastards torpedoed it two hundred miles off the coast in broad daylight!' Murphy glowered at Hart, as if making him personally responsible for the tragedy. 'Fifty people are still missing, including twelve nurses, *dames*!' Angrily he twisted his stump of cigar from one side of his tough mouth to the other. 'Say, Inspector, give me the low-down, what the fuck is this all about, eh?'

Hart, his brain racing with the latest news, briefed the tough cop swiftly, abandoning the FBI rules of secrecy. He knew he needed an ally — quickly — and Murphy was his man. He knew the hotel, he knew the staff, and he knew the shady types who always hung around such a big establishment — the whores, the con-men, the pick-pockets and the like.

'So this German U-boat is gonna fire a goddam rocket — like the ones they have been firing at London, England, all winter — at the Taft?'

'Yeah,' Hart answered somewhat miserably.

'And there is some German spy around who'll signal the sub on Christmas Eve?' Murphy persisted.

'Yeah. I know, it sounds completely nuts! But I've got it straight from Washington and they got it from London. And, Murphy, remember this, we've only got twenty-four hours to find this guy. Tomorrow it's Christmas Eve, you know.'

Hart's lips tightened. That little bastard's as stubborn as one of his own state's Missouri mules he thought. Even Hoover couldn't pressure him. He wouldn't chicken out. No sir!

'Okay,' Murphy snapped. 'Let's get on the stick, Inspector. First thing, let's have a look at the outside lot. Then we'll work our way right through the joint up to the roof. We'll find this German bastard before tomorrow night or my name ain't Joe Murphy!' The cop slapped one clenched fist into the horny palm of the other hand with a satisfying smacking sound like that of the rubber club he had wielded in the old days against some reluctant hood.

Murphy's enthusiasm was contagious. Hart was seized by new enthusiasm.

'Sure, Joe Murphy, let's get on the stick!' he echoed.

Together they clattered down the marble steps into the big echoing lobby, filled with noisy young servicemen sprawled in leather armchairs, drinking coffee and wolfing down doughnuts, trying to date the overworked Red Cross girls in their smart powder-blue uniforms, or simply staring into empty space like men condemned, waiting for Death to tap them on the shoulder. Murphy pushed and shoved his way to the swing doors. Outside the snow was beginning to fall heavily now in big solid dry flakes.

Murphy pulled up his collar and turned to the doorman, a tall skinny young man, who looked a little out of place in the Taft's over-elegant livery. 'Say, Mike, keep an eye peeled for weirdos, anyone out of place, you know the type.'

'Sure, Mr Murphy,' the tall doorman said eagerly, smiling and touching his hand to his cap in salute. 'I'll be on the lookout, sir.'

The two of them went out into the flying snow. 'Nice Irish kid from the Bronx,' Murphy commented. 'Four F.'

Something wrong with his lung. Eating his heart out 'cos he can't get in the service and kill the Krauts.' Then he dismissed the doorman. 'Let's go, Inspector. Let's have a look at the back lot before this frigging snow covers every goddam thing.'

Mike watched them go, narrowing his bright blue eyes against the whirling snow, his young face suddenly very thoughtful. Then a long olive Packard flying Old Glory on its hood drew up outside. He forgot his problem. It was the director of the USO arriving for work. He rushed forward with his umbrella at the ready. With his free hand he removed his cap smartly to reveal the golden thatch below. 'Morning, ma'am!' he said, a ready smile on his face.

'Morning, Mike…'

The scene was set, the actors were in place, the drama could commence…

BOOK THREE: THE NEW YORK ASSAULT

CHAPTER 1

Sunday 24 December 1944. It was Christmas Eve!

In Paris, Allied Headquarters issued a cheerful, uplifting message to the hard-pressed troops up at the front in Belgium. In the gushing prose of the nice, fat public relations men, it read; 'We are giving our country and our loved ones at home a worthy Christmas present, are being privileged to take part in this gallant feat of arms and are truly making for ourselves a merry Christmas!'

In the overcrowded barns and the shell-shattered houses just behind the front, waiting to be evacuated, with the heavy guns thundering ceaselessly outside, the wounded, wrapped in their blood-stained blankets and bits of parachute silk from the supply drops, listened silently to the carols of their comrades and wondered.

'Oh little town of Bethlehem,' they sang hoarsely, 'How still we see thee lie... Yet in thy dark streets shineth, The ever-lasting light; The hopes and fears of all the years, Are met in thee tonight...'

On the other side of the line, in Berlin, Adolf Hitler's harsh guttural voice thundered over the radio; 'Our people are resolved to fight the war to victory under any and all circumstances...!

'We are going to destroy everybody who does not take part in the common effort for the country or who makes himself a tool of the enemy... The world must know that this state will never capitulate... Germany will rise like a phoenix from its ruined cities and this will go down in history as the miracle of the twentieth century!

'We shall fulfil our duty faithfully and unshakeably in the firm belief that the hour will strike when victory will ultimately come to him who is most worthy of it. *The Greater German Reich*!'

And in New York, the tills rang, the drunken fat Santas rang their bells and the Andrews Sisters sang that sugar-sweet song of that year. 'Don't sit under the apple tree, With anyone else but me, Anyone else but me, Anyone else but me. No, no, no... Don't go walking down lover's lane, With anyone else but me... Till I come marching home...'

Total war in New York, 1944...

The U-200, maintaining absolute radio silence this Sunday, crept along the fog-shrouded coast of New England in a kind of limbo, cut off from the great events taking place in Europe and the trite sentimental tinsel of an American wartime Christmas. Now, twenty-four hours after they had sunk the American Red Cross transport, the crew lived from hour to hour, constantly scanning the sky, heads cocked to one side, alert for the first note of an aeroplane engine, knowing that soon the attackers must come. But so far the U-200 had been surprisingly lucky, in spite of the fact that they were now only kilometres from the coast. Once they had heard the steady putt-putt of what might have been a fishing boat, but it had died away even before the look-outs could make out what kind of craft it was. Once, too, someone had reported an aircraft engine, but by the time the bridge had been alerted, all that could be heard was the normal throb of the diesels and the soft rustle of the off-coast breeze. They might well have been all alone in the world.

An anxious Christian knew that this was not so. To the west beyond the billowing banks of damp cold fog, there was a great teeming city, its sprawling suburbs packed with pulsating life.

There were military air fields, too, and naval bases, full of the long, lean dangerous shapes of destroyers and torpedo-boats, all of them, planes and ships, ready and alert, prepared to scramble immediately the alarm sounded. No, now they were so close, he and his crew could not relax for one moment.

On the deck, trying to keep out of the way of the double look-outs (for Christian was taking no chances; two men per post were better than one), the myopic gunner *Oberleutnant* and his gunners were busy, too. With a crude winch they had managed to haul up their ugly missiles from the torpedo bays and were now assembling them, ready for the signal; while below the radiomen tensed over their sets, eager for the first fix. For as Christian had told the assembled crew at first watch that dawn, 'Comrades, the safety of the U-200 and of us all depends upon the high speed firing of the missiles and an instant get-away before the *Amis* can react. There must be no slip-ups! Everything must function like clockwork. Is that clear?'

They had rumbled back their understanding and Christian could see from their pale bearded faces that although they were a little afraid at what was to come, they were also highly excited, like schoolboys preparing for some adventure. 'Like a frigging lot of Hitler Youth!' Frenssen had grumbled afterwards. 'Christ, what has happened to us up to now is like a suck of sugar-titty in comparison with what is gonna happen. Frigging Hitler Youth!' And he had wandered off about his duties, shaking his head like a man sorely tried. But in spite of the danger of their position, idling on the surface only a few kilometres from the enemy coast, von Arco could not conceal his elation at what was to come. He strode about the dripping deck, getting in the way of the gunners and then missiles, the deck watches, full of nervous energy, stopping to peer at the mist as if he half expected New York to come into view at any moment. In the end, Christian, on the conning tower, snapped, 'For God's sake, come up here and get out of the way. You're like a damned cat on hot bricks!'

In no way offended, von Arco clambered up the wet, dripping ladder, saying, 'But don't you feel anything, Jungblut?' His eyes flashed excitedly. 'Here we are, just a handful of us, sixty or more German soldiers, five thousand kilometres from our beloved Homeland, taking the war to the American enemy for the very first time! Why, it's a historic moment! Undoubtedly we shall go down in history. The first Germans to fight on the American continent since those Hessian mercenaries fought for the perfidious English here back in the eighteenth century.'

Christian looked at him coldly, while below the gunners sweated at their task, and said, 'I have no intention of going down in history, thank you. *Dead* men enter the history books. I intend that I and my boys remain alive and unsung.'

Von Arco's arrogant face looked at him challengingly. '*Gott im Himmel!*' he swore. 'Are we worthy of our Führer, inferior people like us? Have you no feeling for the historic significance of our mission, what it means to our Führer, Adolf Hitler? Why, soon we are going to have greatness conferred upon us. *Greatness*, do you hear?' he declared fervently, fists clenched, chest heaving.

At the hatchway, Frenssen farted contemptuously. 'With the permission of the gentleman officer, I should like to make my humble report to the Captain,' he said with mock servility and winked knowingly behind von Arco's back.

Von Arco spun round, face suddenly flushed angrily. 'Did you break wind, *Obermaat*?' he demanded.

'Break wind, sir?' Frenssen said, all innocence. 'Me sir? Break wind in the presence of the gentleman officer, sir? Why, sir,' he added with an air of offence, 'how could you think that of me, sir? I would never dream of —'

'*Frenssen*!' Christian broke in firmly. 'Make your report and then go and piss in the wind. Where's the fire?'

Frenssen was business-like immediately. The look on Christian's face boded no good. 'It's the radioman, sir. He's picking up a signal.'

Von Arco forgot 'greatness' and 'the historic significance' of the mission. 'You mean from the shore?' he rapped.

'*Jawohl, Herr Kapitänleutnant*,' Frenssen answered.

Christian wasted no more time. He cupped his hands to his mouth and called urgently to the gunnery lieutenant. 'Up top, Lieutenant,' he cried. 'Your type is in urgent demand. *The fix is coming through…*'

The first of the entertainers for the Christmas Eve celebration had begun to arrive outside the Taft; black musicians in zoot suits and wide-brimmed hats, high on the drugs they had taken; stand-up comedians, middle-aged and shaky, hip flasks peeping out of their back pockets; bored chorus girls, still pale and tired from the previous night's party, clutching their purses, with the customary five dollars, spare pair of nylons and panties inside, plus a vaginal sponge, *just in case*; and the managers and agents, of course, sleek, wordy men smelling of expensive after-shave — and money.

Watching the noisy procession troop into the USO, Hart thought of his son fighting out there in the snowbound hills of far-away Belgium and shook his head. Next to him, Murphy rolled the cigar stump from one side of his mobile mouth to the other and rasped, 'Penny for them, Inspector?'

Hart shrugged. 'Oh, I don't know, Murphy. Kinda wondering what all this has got to do with the real shooting war.'

Murphy's craggy face cracked into a cynical grin. 'Nuthin! Just showbiz razzmatazz. Why the war's been a goddam godsend to them guys. A bunch o' pimps and pros with not a pot to piss in back in 'forty-one before Pearl Harbor. Now they're living high on the hog —' He stopped short, face suddenly suspicious. 'Who's them jerks?' He pointed with his cigar at a group of tall, hard-faced men, in hats and all wearing the same sort of beige trench-coat, who were now getting out of a big black official-looking sedan. 'Are they in on the party?'

Hart shot the new arrivals a look and then relaxed. 'They're okay. The biggest fellah is O'Connors from Washington — of the Secret Service.'

'Secret Service?' Murphy echoed. 'But what are they doing here in New York?'

'They'll check the joint out first and then they'll be on guard duty this evening,' Hart answered easily, as the bit men, each armed judging by the lumps under their left armpits, started to disperse, as if to some unspoken command.

'Guard who?' Murphy asked stupidly.

'Truman… Don't you know that Truman is going to play the piano tonight?'

Murphy stared up at him blankly. 'Truman who?' he demanded.

'Truman — the Vice-President of the United States.'

'Never heard of him,' Murphy snorted, watching the Secret Service men disappear into the Taft.

'Well, you will do, Murphy,' Hart said a little wearily, '*if he survives*! Now come on, let's get moving…'

A high silver moon hung in the winter sky, casting a cold spectral light on the still ocean. The wind had died to a soft breeze and now a cold swell lapped against the steel sides of the sinister silent shape of the U-200.

Christian shivered. With stiff fingers he pulled at his collar, and tried to heat his frozen nose with his breath. Time was running out. He must order the missile launch soon and then make a run for it. Within half an hour of the launch, so the gunnery lieutenant had warned him, he could expect an enemy attack. By that time, he had to be making full speed southwards for the Gulf of Mexico.

Standing watch next to him, Frenssen, his old comrade, seemed to be able to read his thoughts, for he broke the heavy silence. 'What do you think our chances are, sir?'

Christian sniffed. 'If we're unlucky we'll be celebrating Christmas 1944 by looking at the potatoes from beneath. With a bit of luck, however, we've got a chance of making neutral waters before they cotton on they've been tricked.'

Expertly Frenssen whipped a dewdrop off the end of his big nose and rumbled, 'What a frigging way to be spending Christmas Eve! If the world wasn't crazy, a poor old broken-down sailor man like me, should be up to his back collar stud with sauce and suds by now, with a nice pair o' juicy tits to warm his paws on.'

Christian laughed softly, a strange sound at this particular moment. 'Get on with you, you big-horned ox, you wouldn't miss this for all the pavement-pounders in the *Herbertstrasse*!'

'Pull the other one, sir,' Frenssen said gloomily, 'it's got frigging bells on it!'

Christian dismissed Frenssen and consulted the green glowing dial of his wrist-watch. It was nearly zero, eighteen hundred hours, American eastern seaboard time. Softly he called out to the myopic gunnery lieutenant standing by the stark silhouette of the launching ramp. 'Are you nearly ready, *Oberleutnant?*'

'Five more minutes, sir,' he replied, equally softly, as if he half-expected some listening American to pop out of the silver gloom at any moment and order their arrest. 'Just a little trouble with the homing device.'

'Well, move your hind legs,' Christian snapped impatiently. 'Every minute we are stationary out here…' He didn't finish the warning; he knew he didn't need to. All of them were keenly aware of how exposed their position was. Disaster could strike at any moment.

'Sound action stations,' he commanded.

'Action stations it is, sir!' Number One echoed loyally from below.

Beneath his feet, Christian heard the sound of his sailors running to their stations.

'Stand by the deck crew!' Christian ordered.

There was a clatter of heavy seaboots as the deck look-outs and gunners began to clamber up the conning tower ladder, weighed down in their oilskins and leather coveralls. Expertly, they removed the covers from the 88mm and the *Vierling* flak, swinging them round to the west, from which the enemy attack would come. Grimly, Christian told himself the attack *had* to come. Just over the horizon there was one of the world's greatest cities, with a population of seven million. The enemy would not allow an attack on it to go unavenged.

He gave a last glance around the deck. The gunners poised at their weapons, the army types still doing some last-minute tinkering to their long sinister weapon, the look-outs sweeping the horizon ceaselessly with their night glasses. Suddenly his heart began to thump with that old unreasoning excitement, the primeval thrill of the chase, a blood-tingling, heady sensation, a sudden lust to kill, which even overcame fear. He swallowed hard and tried to keep control of himself. 'This is about it, Frenssen,' he said thickly in a voice he hardly recognized as his own.

'Party dresses on, ready for the ball,' Frenssen agreed and his voice, too, seemed unreal, not its normal cynical self.

'Are you ready, *Herr Leutnant?*' Christian called to the gunnery officer.

'Ready, sir.'

'Then begin to count down.'

'Count-down, it is, sir,' the gunnery officer cried, voice suddenly shaky. *'Ten ... nine ... eight ... seven...'*

Stark black silhouettes against the silver ocean, the helmeted gunners tensed around the missile, its nose pointed to the night sky.

'Oh, my God!' von Arco breathed in awe, face hollowed out to a glowing death's head in that spectral gloom. 'Oh, my God!' Suddenly he let his binoculars fall to his heaving chest, overcome by tremendous emotion, and stiffened rigidly to attention.

'Six ... Five ... four ... three ...' the gunnery officer intoned as the first flame from the missile's engine stabbed the silver gloom in a spurt of bright scarlet.

Proudly, brutally, symbolizing that bold cruel military empire which he represented, von Arco flung up his right arm and bellowed at the night sky, as if challenging God himself to stop them now, *'Heil Hitler... SIEG HEIL....!'*

CHAPTER 2

'*Listen*!' the blonde with the black parting was saying to her companion, as they passed through the door of the USO, the helmeted MPs saluting the women as if they were top brass, 'You've got to do it, baby... 'Cos if you don't, they'll suspend you.'

'Suspend me ... what's that mean?'

'It means, baby, you don't get no pay...'

'But that movie is a heap o' crap! It's got the makings of a first-class stinker and they want to dye my hair blonde and fix my teeth again.'

'So what?' the blonde with the black parting said casually, flashing Hart and Murphy a capped, dazzling, professional smile. 'It's better than getting on ya knees in front of the casting couch, ain't it, baby?'

Hart bit his bottom lip in frustration. It was now only an hour before the Vice-President accompanied Humphrey Bogart's new wife on the piano for the entertainment of the troops this Christmas Eve, and he had still not achieved one damned thing. Why, he didn't even know whether he had found the right target! All he knew was that there was a Kraut submarine lurking off the New England coast somewhere — and the New England coast was a damned long place!

'But if you think this guy Truman is the Germantarget,' Murphy had objected that afternoon at the end of their long fruitless search of the Hotel Taft, 'why don't you get him to cancel? Hell, cancel the whole goddam wing-ding and have done with it!'

'Haven't I told you the little guy's as stubborn as one of his own Missouri mules? But I did try to get at him through the Secret Service — I mean, hell, they don't want anything to happen to a Vice-President. But no deal.' He had shaken his greying head ruefully. 'He wouldn't cancel out. He told the Secret Service guys there'd be a panic in New York City if it came out that he had cancelled his visit to the Christmas Eve show on account of a possible German threat.' Hart had sucked his teeth grimly, as he had visualized what might well happen in the great sprawling city. 'And the little jerk is right, of course, Murphy. Hell, you know what these New Yorkers are like? They panic easily. Gee, that's perhaps what they want. Even if Truman *isn't* their target, just one of those missiles hitting downtown New York and the biggest panic this century since the Chicago Fire could well break out!'

Murphy had looked solemn as the realization of what might happen struck home. 'But, Inspector,' he had snorted, 'we can't just sit here like a spare dildo in a convent, waiting for the shit to hit the fan, can we? We've gotta do something,' he had added fervently.

'We've secretly shipped in some Limey fighter boys,' Hart had explained. 'Apparently these guys have been fighting the missiles over London ever since June. They're expert at knocking them down. Now they're on a five minutes' alert, waiting in the ready rooms for the first warning of an attack. Naturally the Navy, Coastguard, Coastal Artillery have been alerted too.'

Murphy had not been impressed. 'Limeys!' he had snorted contemptuously, letting rein to the old Irish prejudices his parents had brought with them from the 'Old Country'. 'Hell, they couldn't fight their frigging way out of a wet paper bag! And as for those coastal artillery jerk-offs, what do you think they'll be doing this Christmas Eve? I'll tell ya.' He raised a horny hand to his lips, as if lifting a bottle. *'Hitting the frigging sauce!'*

Now as a helpless Hart watched the glittering stars enter to the accompaniment of the mock moans of unrequited passion and wolf whistles of the gawping teenage servicemen, the full impact of what might soon happen struck him.

New York would panic if one single missile hit the downtown area. In Europe, every major city from London toLeningrad had been attacked repeatedly ever since the war had started. Their citizens had become hardened and accustomed to death raining from the sky. But New York, like all other American cities, had never been attacked from the air. Its citizens had had a good war so far. They had become fat cats, moaning always, of course, about rationing and the lack of gasoline, but steadily growing more and more prosperous as the war developed and business and industry thrived. Now, however, even as he stood here impotently, not knowing what to do next, New York was threatened for the very first time since Pearl Harbor. A catastrophe of unprecedented proportions was in the making; and opposite him in the foyer, a famous movie star with painted lips and dyed hair, who usually played 'tough guy' roles, was simpering to his 'friend'. 'But I do so simply love those Marines, darling. All those muscles and sweaty armpits. Delightful, ducky!'

Squadron-Leader Savage rammed down the phone a little angrily and gave his assembled pilots in the ready room his cynical, twisted smile, the result of five years of aerial combat — and a fragment of German cannon shell which, back in 1942, had nearly torn the side of his jaw away. 'No joy, chaps,' he announced. 'Their HQ reports they had a blob on their coastal radar, which *could* have been a Hun sub, but they lost it.'

There was a burst of contemptuous cheering and 'Tubby' White pinched his nose with one gloved hand and made a pulling movement, as if pulling a lavatory chain. 'Typical Yank balls-up!' Taffy Jones cried. 'Everything they do, they prang it up. Should have been a piece of cake for them. Just one lone Jerry sub to find — with all the equipment they have!' He tugged at the end of his great affected handlebar moustache, which hid the immaturity of his 21-year-old face.

Savage held up his hands for silence. As was his face, they were both scarred with old wounds and the burns he had suffered when he had bailed out of a burning Hurricane over the Channel in 1940. 'All right, chaps, put a sock in it, *please!*'

The noise died down and he stared around at their young determined faces in the harsh light cast by the neon strip-light and was pleased with what he saw. There were few of the old sweats left with the top button of their blouses undone in the old 1940 fighter pilot tradition. But the young ones, too, the kids who had joined the squadron from flying training school just before D-Day, radiated the same type of confidence this Christmas Eve, so far away from home and their loved ones.

'What's the big picture, skipper?' Tubby asked quietly.

'This. The Yanks are not used to this sort of thing. We've been at it for quite a little while, so let's have some understanding of the problems they face. To put it bluntly we are going to have to rely on ourselves to tackle the Hun doodle-bugs. There'll be no searchlights, no effective radar, and no ack-ack.'

'Thank God for that, skipper!' somebody chortled. 'Back in the UK, I often wondered whether those ruddy ack-ack gunners were on our side — or Jerry's.' They laughed and Savage laughed with them. General Pile's boys always blazed away at any aircraft, German or otherwise. They'd all had near misses from their own ack-ack.

'So,' he continued, 'this is what we are going to do. We're going to scramble ourselves without orders from the Yanks. It's the only way. We'll keep one flight in the air and two on the ground. When and *if* the buggers cross the coast, some of us are already going to be airborne, ready and waiting, as the actress said to the bishop.'

'But skipper,' Taffy Jones objected. 'Won't we be spreading ourselves too thin that way? There's one hell of a lot of coastline to be covered.'

'I know … I know, Taffy,' Savage answered. 'But we've got to take that chance. If we wait for the Yanks to scramble us, we'll be too late.'

'But we're supposed to be under starter's orders from the Yanks,' Taffy objected. 'Do it by the book.'

Savage looked at him hard, and the plump Welshman quailed a little. He knew that look. It was the skipper's killer look, cruel, unrelenting, and utterly ruthless. It was the one his scarred face bore when he dived in for the kill. 'Quite frankly, Taffy,' Savage said very softly so that the rest had to strain a little to hear, 'I don't give a twopenny damn about the Yanks, and doing it by the book. Ever since the damned war started there have been too many chairborne Johnnies, sitting on their fat behinds in safe offices, telling us how to do the fighting!' He poked his thumb at his own chest. 'We'll do it my way or no way at all. All right, chaps, we'll scramble now. Tubby, you take Bimbo and Pete and push in the first patrol. Taffy here and myself will stand by with the remaining two flights ready for the next op or a "bandit" from you.'

'Roger,' the flight commander said urgently and grabbed for his flying helmet. 'We're on our way.' He paused at the door of the ready room, handsome young face under the flaxen hair suddenly a little embarrassed. 'Oh, I say, chaps, before I forget — Happy Christmas!'

Savage was too surprised by the greeting to react, but the others did, returning the words, 'Happy Christmas'. But there was no enthusiasm in their voices. It was almost as if they were wishing their comrades farewell for good. '*Happy Christmas...*'

'Listen, buster, I've just told ya — we want no coloured guys in here! And I don't give a goddam if you *are* a GI!' the angry Bronx voice of Mike, the doorman, caught Hart's attention, distracting him from the glittering pageant of movie folk who were still entering the USO Club. 'Now beat it!'

He and Murphy swung round. To the right of the door, Mike was facing up to a huge black man in combat boots, fatigue cap at the back of his head, his chest ablaze with campaign ribbons. The man had a mean look in his eyes and he was obviously very drunk, otherwise he would never have dared to attempt to enter the club. 'I've got back from Italy, man,' he said thickly, but standing his ground, the hip flask in the pocket of his Ike jacket visible now. He poked a thumb at his broad chest. 'I've been in the firing line, brother, and no chicken-shit civilian like you is gonna tell me what I can do, no siree!' He put out a hand like a steam-shovel and placed it on Mike's chest, as if to push him to one side. Mike looked at it, his face suddenly flushing scarlet. 'Take your goddam hand of'n me!' he snorted, a nerve ticking angrily at the side of his cheek. 'Do you hear me?'

'I's hearing you, brother,' he said calmly. 'Now get outa my fuckin' —'

The words died on his lips. As if by magic, a Police Special had suddenly appeared in Mike's gloved hand and its muzzle was pointing straight at the soldier's heart. 'Now, boy,' Mike grated, obviously enjoying the GI's sudden look of fear, 'are you gonna move your ass, or am I gonna have to blow a frigging big hole in ya heart?'

Still the man did not move. 'Sure, whitey, blow a hole in me. But I sure as hell am *not* leaving here —'

'Now what's all this fuss?' Finkel's prissy voice broke into the mans words.

Distracted Mike turned his head. The soldierdidn't wait to be invited. One — two! His left fist flashed a tremendous blow to Mike's stomach. He yelped with pain and doubled up, revolver almost falling from suddenly nerveless fingers in the same instant that the man swung a haymaker at his chin. He missed, but struck Mike a glancing blow at the side of his jaw. Doubled up with pain, he reeled against the billboard, smashing it against the wall. His uniformed cap tumbled to the ground and as he fell to his knees, moaning in agony, his coat opened enough to show that his back pocket was full of tools.

Hart saw them in the same moment that Murphy did. Their eyes met.

'*The blond!*' Hart yelled.

'*What's a doorman doing with electric tools?*' Murphy shouted.

'*IT'S HIM!*' they cried as one.

Hart darted forward. Even in his agony, the Beacon knew he had been spotted. While the drunken soldier stared at him aghast and an ashen-faced Mr Finkel cowered against the wall, he raised the Police Special and said thickly, the Bronx voice suddenly seeming more guttural and un-American, 'Back off, copper … *back off!*'

Hart came to a dead stop. Shielded by the FBI man, Murphy fumbled for his own revolver, with fingers that trembled violently.

Hart hesitated for a moment, as they froze there like actors at the end of the third act of a melodrama, the only sound their own harsh breathing and the tinkle of the piano from within the club. 'Now listen,' he said carefully, soothingly, 'I'm offering you a deal. Drop that revolver and I'll see that the authorities —'

'Give me the frigging chair!' The Beacon cut him off brutally. 'Now move it, copper. I'm getting out of here!' He waved the pistol menacingly and started to move.

The soldier stumbled back and Finkel pressed himself ever closer to the wall. Behind Hart, Murphy crouched and whispered hoarsely, 'I've got the bastard covered, Inspector.'

Hart thought of his wife with her sick headaches and the boy out in the Ardennes. What did it matter now what happened to him? He had no future in the Agency. Hoover would see to that. Suddenly he was overcome by a great wish — an almost sexual longing — to put an end to it all, the endless ennui of life. He took a step forward, hand outstretched. 'A deal, kid. You needn't die —'

He stopped short. He saw how the German's jaw was hardening. The knuckles of his right hand gripping the Police Special were whitening, as he took first pressure.

'Watch him, mister!' the man hissed. 'He gonna blast you, if you don't watch out.'

'The revolver, kid!' Hart hesitated no longer. He darted forward. The Beacon fired at the same instant. At that range, Hart was lifted off his feet as if by a blow from a giant fist. He yelled with pain as a great hole was ripped in his stomach, his white shirt flushing a sudden scarlet. Behind him, as he slumped to his knees, Murphy fired. The Beacon slammed against the wall, mouth open stupidly, eyes wild and wide with fear. Slowly, very slowly, he began to slide down the wall, leaving a trail of bright-red blood as he did so.

Abruptly all was chaos…

CHAPTER 3

'SCRAMBLE!'

As Tubby's first flight came howling down the tarmac, brakes screeching, rubber tyres howling in protest, the distorted voice yelled its urgent warning over the tannoy. '*BANDITS HEADING FOR NEW YORK … SCRAMBLE … SCRAMBLE … SCRAMBLE!*'

Savage, lounging against his aircraft, needed no urging. He flung away his cigarette. 'Crew chief!' he yelled and clambered on to the wing. The lights of the second runway flicked on suddenly. As they did so, Savage slipped into the cockpit, fumbling with his flying helmet.

Below, the crew chiefs and mechanics were racing from plane to plane, ripping out the chocs, giving the first turns to the Spitfires' propellers.

Savage flashed a look to left and right. His flight was in position. The crew chief yelled his instructions. Savage pressed the starter button. The Merlin engine coughed once, twice, three times in the icy air. Suddenly it burst into a full-throated roar.

Savage wasted no time. He eased the throttle forward. The Spitfire started to taxi forward. To left and right, the rest of his flight did the same, bumping and jolting over the rough runway, gathering speed by the instant.

In his cockpit, faced by the cathode tube of the A-I Detector, Savage absorbed the American flight controller's instructions and information. Swiftly he transmitted them to his own flight, as the excited American's voice died in the earphones. 'Tubby spotted them twenty miles to the southeast of the coast in the general direction of New York. He counted three before he had to break off to refuel. Hard luck on Tubby. Now it's up to us, chaps. Remember, don't get closer than one hundred and fifty *if* and *when* you open fire.

Tally-ho, chaps!' Savage's voice rose with excitement. 'Over and out!'

With a grunt, the squadron-leader jerked back the throttle. The Spitfire responded beautifully. A moment later he was airborne, his undercarriage retracted, gathering speed rapidly, the airfield's lights swiftly vanishing below him. The hunt was on. Now if anyone was going to save New York from the first attack made on the great city for over two centuries, it would be these six lone young British pilots.

Now, as the land vanished below him, as he rapidly gained height, gaze constantly switching from the sky ahead to the A-I radar, Savage thought out his tactics once he spotted the doodle-bugs.

When a Spitfire attacked a missile, the pilot was usually a couple of hundred yards off when he opened fire. But a lot of pilots forgot in the excitement of the chase, they were also travelling at 350 m.p.h.! As a result they'd race right through the debris of the exploding bomb. Over the east coast of England that had been no problem. If they had been hit by the bits and pieces of the bomb they had just destroyed, they could rely on the RAF's highly efficient Air-Sea rescue launches to save them. They always found a pilot forced to bail out over the drink, even at night. But there was nothing like that over here. The Yanks had no such system; they had had no need for one up to now. If he or any of his pilots were forced down by an exploding doodle-bug this night, they stood little chance of surviving in the freezing water.

As a result, Savage reasoned, they were not going to take any unnecessary risks. They would try to take the bombs out at a safe distance; and if they couldn't do that, there was only one other way they could deal with the flying bombs, a way that could be employed only by the most skilled pilots. Indeed, in the whole of the squadron, there was only one pilot he would trust to carry out the highly dangerous, potentially lethal manoeuvre — *himself*!

As the last hearty cheer of the deck crew died away and the *Wehrmacht* gunners set about their task of removing the ramp — for once it was cast overboard, Christian reasoned, it would allow the U-200 to speed up another couple of knots — Christian Jungblut set about steering a course for the south. He took his eyes off the tiny scarlet dots now winging their way steadily for New York, just over the horizon. For a moment he wondered how they would fare in the great American city; then he dismissed them. That part of the mission was already history. Now his first duty was to his crew and boat. Somehow he had to reach neutral waters off Mexico.

The U-200 picked up speed, stealing through the night like a furtive beast of prey, hunted on all sides, while below the sweating operators tensed at their instruments, waiting for the first suspicious blob on the radar screen or engine noise. For his part, Christian was back and forth across the conning tower, supervising the deck watch, his gaze flicking constantly to the dark horizon to west and east. It was now fifteen minutes since they had fired their first missile. By now American radar must have picked up the weapons flying into their air space. The *Amis* must have also realized that the only way that they could have reached the American coast was from a U-boat. So, he reasoned, they had to be scrambling their planes and submarine-chasers for the attack. Now it was up to him to outguess them for the rest of this night. If he could do so then with luck he would get well down the coast to the south, while they extended their search further and further eastwards, thinking it the most logical course for an escaping German submarine to steer. So it was that Christian took a calculated risk. He ordered the Number One to take the U-200 closer to the enemy coast while still steering a southerly course.

'I know, I know, Number One,' he snapped a little testily, as he caught a note of doubt in the young officer's voice as he repeated the command, 'But trust me, I *do* know what I am doing!'

'Yes,' that cynical little voice at the back of his mind had sneered maliciously, 'you're going to get the crew of the U-200 killed. That's what you are doing.'

With a great splash the metal ramp went over the side and into the water. The U-200 shook violently, as if relieved of an intolerable burden. Almost immediately her speed began to pick up. The line of sparkling white foam at her bow increased. Suddenly Christian felt a sense of new hope. His jaw clenched. By God, he was going to bring her and the crew home! Of course, he was! On the horizon the fiery-red dots had now disappeared...

'The Vice-President of the United States and Miss Lauren Bacall,' the elegant USO woman announced to the crowded room, as the two burly Secret Servicemen, both still wearing hats, moved to left and right of the entrance, hands stuck inside their bulging jackets.

Truman, small, neat, insignificant, came in tugging at his bow tie and grinning madly, the teenage actress on his right, towering above the Vice-President, all long legs and blonde hair tumbling down the side of her young face.

Politely the assembled movie stars clapped the little politician, but the servicemen sprang to their feet and exploded into shouts, catcalls, wolf whistles at the sight of the sexy young star. '*Sock to me, baby!*'… '*Take me, babe, I'm all yours*'… '*Whatya doin' tonight after the show, honey?*'… they yelled in delight.

Truman beamed at the red-faced, cheering servicemen nervously, tugged again at his bow tie and then, extending his hand in a display of old world courtesy, said, 'Miss Bacall, can I escort you to the piano?' He indicated the grand piano situated in the centre of the dance floor, now illuminated by a silver spotlight.

'Why, sure, Mr Truman,' the actress answered in that low, husky, sultry voice that was now so famous, ever since she had taken up with Bogart on the screen. 'I'd be delighted.' In a slow, sexy walk, she allowed herself to be escorted to the piano by the nervous little political leader, while the boys whistled frantically or simply gazed in teenage awe at those delightful buttocks, swaying seductively beneath the tight silk dress.

Murphy looked on cynically. He wondered if the little creep knew that upstairs Inspector Hart was dying for him? The medics had refused to move the FBI man. They said he'd die in the ambulance. Now Hart lay there in the little room off Finkel's office, awaiting death. 'Ensure, Murphy, that they smuggle the body out through the laundry room,' Finkel had admonished him severely. 'Nobody, but strictly *nobody*, ever dies in the Hotel Taft. It is bad for the place's reputation!'

Now Murphy chewed sourly on his dead cigar and in his mind reviewed the events of this amazing Christmas Eve. Mike, 'a nice Irish boy from the Bronx,' revealed as a spy, dying, cursing in German, screaming for 'my Führer'; Hart struggling bravely to get things done, alerting the military, wringing the position of the beacon out of the dying Mike, before the blood had come rushing up out of his mouth and he had collapsed at last, knowing he could do no more; and now somewhere in the night sky those deadly missiles winging their way towards the Taft... Unless those unknown Limeys could stop them. He grinned cynically. *Limeys!* Why, hadn't his grandmother back in the Old Country broken the very saucers in her own home from which English people had drunk, when they had been offered a 'dish o' tay?' Now his — and all their lives here this evening — depended upon those self-same hated Limeys!

Murphy reached into his hip pocket for the flask of Irish. Covering it with one hand, he took a deep satisfying swig. The raw liquor hit the back of his throat with a satisfying smack. He felt the burn immediately. He grinned again. Might as well get sauced-up, he told himself wryly. After all, it *was* Christmas Eve and for all he goddamn knew, it might be the *last* one he ever celebrated.

'Ladies and gentlemen,' the smiling Vice-President announced from the piano, running his hands along the keyboard to get the excited servicemen's attention, 'Boys and girls, can I have your attention for Miss Bacall?'

Again the room exploded into violent applause.

Languidly, the film actress raised one hand, clutching the long ivory cigarette holder she thought made her look older and more sophisticated. 'Waal, gals and guys, I'd like to sing a little song for you this Christmas Eve.' She heaved herself lazily on to the top of the grand piano, while Truman beamed at her. Her dress slid open to reveal a long stretch of perfect, silken leg.

The servicemen gasped collectively.

She nodded to the Vice-President. Obediently the man who would soon command the destinies of the greatest power in the world touched the keys. 'My song is for each and every one of you,' she whispered in that sexy husky voice of hers, lowering her eyes and fluttering her long artificial eyelashes, 'It is … "Counting the Days". Take it away, Mr Vice-President.'

Murphy pulled a face. He took out his flask. This time he didn't even bother to hide it. Who cared? He took a hefty swig. Upstairs, hidden in the little back room, Hart died.

'Hello, Red Leader One … hello, Red Leader One.' In spite of the metallic distortion of the radio link, Savage could hear the excitement in Taffy's voice. 'Do you read me, Red Leader One?'

Swiftly Savage pressed his throat mike and called, 'Yes, I read you, Blue Leader One. Over.'

'Red Leader One,' Taffy could hardly bring himself to observe standard radio procedure, he was that excited. 'I've spotted the buggers, I mean bandits, Red Leader One… They're heading due north-west on a heading of…' Swiftly he detailed the course the missiles were taking and then cried, 'Tally ho, we're going into the attack!'

'Don't get too close, Blue Leader —' Savage stopped short. The radio had gone dead.

The hum of the Merlin engine rose to a startling howl as Savage turned in a perfectly timed curve, followed by the rest of the flight. He gave her more power. The Spitfire raced through the night sky towards where the bold young Welshman had spotted the doodle-bugs. Now Savage's plane was hurtling towards New York at 400 m.p.h., his keen-eyed killer's gaze flashing from the sky ahead to the glowing green circle of the cathode tube. He was tensed for the first blip which would indicate the presence of the missiles.

There they were! Two green blobs on the radar. Savage swallowed. He felt his brain racing electrically. His heart pounded. The adrenalin poured fresh energy into his bloodstream. His nerves tingled. This was it!

He pushed the nose down and opened the throttle even more. Behind him, his flight did the same. Up ahead the dark shapes of Taffy's Spitfires came into view — and beyond was the first bomb, its sleek, shark-like sides gleaming in the light of the wavering plume of fiery-red flame it trailed behind it. Although the racket it kicked up was barely audible above the howl of the Spitfires' Merlins, there was something uncanny, awesome, and full of fiendish purpose about this robot killer. Once again Savage felt that same old sense of outrage. What kind of world was it where people could be slaughtered indiscriminately by this soulless, mindless thing?

Suddenly he spotted Taffy. The flight leader was hurtling ahead of his other pilots, straight into the fiery wake of the missile. In that blood-red, unreal glare, Savage could see his plane quite clearly, as it tossed and yawed in the missile's turbulence. Now Taffy closed for the kill. Savage caught his breath. '*Fire!*' he urged as the Welshman hurtled right into the fiery maw of the beastly thing. 'Fire for God's sake — *NOW!*'

In spite of the cold of the cockpit, Savage felt himself break out in a panicky sweat. If Taffy didn't fire soon, he would be too close. Hell's bells, why didn't he fire, *now*?

Suddenly Taffy's plane quivered violently. He was firing. But it was already too late. The missile exploded with a hellish roar. Immediately the sky was filled with burning red fragments, fanning out, heading straight for Taffy's plane like a wall of red flak.

'*DIVE!*' Savage shrieked desperately, as the jet of air from the ventilator close to his head blew hot and acrid.

Taffy responded to the command. He broke to the right. In that same instant, a great fragment of the bomb sheered straight through his propeller. His crippled plane veered wildly to the right, completely out of control. Madly his wingman tried to avoid him. To no avail! There was a great rending crash as Taffy's plane struck the wingman broadside on. Neither of them had a chance. Savage watched in naked horror and fear, as the two planes, locked together like lovers in one final embrace, fell out of the sky, whirling their way down to the dark sea below. No one got out…

CHAPTER 4

'So,' Frenssen was saying, as the off-duty watch listened intently, 'there was the poor shit with his eight fingers sawn off by the prop, with the old bone-mender bandaging up the wound. And the frigging bone-mender sez, "Now sailor, if you had thought to pick up your fingers, I might well have been able to have sewn them on agen."' Frenssen grinned hugely, 'And yer know what the sailor-boy sez back, and I swear on my mother's head that it's true. He sez to the frigging sawbones, "If I'd have been able to pick up the buggers in the first place, I wouldn't have been here, would I?"'

The ratings laughed a little wearily and Frenssen, in high good form now that they were heading south 'for rum, rogering, and randy romeos', as the *Obermaat* had phrased his concept of Mexico happily, was encouraged to cry, 'Did I ever tell yer the one about the pavement pounder with two sets of tits? Yer, I'm not kidding yer, shipmates. There really was one, with big lungs on her — like this.' He held out his paws, as if he were fondling a monstrous pair of breasts. 'And she had four o' 'em! Christ on a crutch, you could get yer head between them — and not hear a thing for a week o' Sundays. Well, I was just strolling down Dammtor, past the station, keeping my nose clean, natch,' — he winked hugely — 'eyeing up the talent, when up comes this pavement-pounder, expensive written all over her. I was only a leading hand in them days. Sudden like, she opens her coat and I nearly fell off me frigging bike. 'Cos there they were, all frigging *four* of 'em —'

'*Obermaat Frenssen*!' von Arco's voice cut into his tale icily, 'must we have any more of this disgusting pornographic twaddle? I have never heard so much piggery in all my life.'

Slowly, very slowly, Frenssen rose to his feet, while the off-duty watch moved away from him slightly, as if they suddenly didn't want to be seen associating with the giant petty officer. 'You said something, sir?' Frenssen asked with deceptive politeness.

Von Arco's pale arrogant face flushed angrily, 'You know damn well I just said something, you insolent swine! And in three devils' names, stand to attention, when you address a superior officer! You people in the submarine service think you can get away with murder. Discipline has gone all to pot.' He glared at Frenssen.

Without any rush, Frenssen came to the position of attention, hands touching the sides of his dirty fatigues, but there was no fear in his blue eyes, only contempt. 'Anything else, sir?' he asked. 'I'm off duty, you know. I would like to hit the hay now — get some sack-time in.'

Von Arco's face flushed even more. He knew, as well as the watching ratings, that his authority was being challenged by the big swine. It was a case of dumb insolence. 'You will go to your bunk when *I* say so, *Obermaat*,' he snapped. 'Now what do you say to that, man?' He smirked at the wooden-faced petty officer. 'It's about time that you Lords realized exactly what an officer is.'

Frenssen said nothing. He remained standing there, staring at the bulkhead beyond von Arco's right shoulder.

It irritated the officer beyond all measure! 'When I speak to you, you insolent swine, you *will* answer,' he cried, face purple, thrusting up his hand and rapping Frenssen's chest with his forefinger. '*Do you hear me?*'

Frenssen remained obstinately silent, though now his gaze fell and fixed itself on the finger rapping at his chest. There was murder suddenly in his blue eyes.

'*Well?*' von Arco demanded, not noticing the look.

Still Frenssen did not react.

Von Arco jabbed him again. The ratings gasped. They all knew it was against naval regulations for an officer to even *touch* a rating or NCO.

'I asked you a question?' von Arco rasped in a strangled, choked voice, a vein ticking urgently at his temple. 'I demand an answer!'

Frenssen's right fist began to clench. The ratings watching pulled back even more. The tension was electric. There was going to be trouble.

'Did you hear me?' von Arco bored his finger into Frenssen's chest even harder.

Frenssen's knuckles were bright white now. His chest had begun to heave. He would strike von Arco, his tormentor, in another instant.

'Well?' von Arco demanded, lulled into a false sense of security by the big petty officer's silence, thinking that he had the situation well under control and that Frenssen was afraid of him. 'Well, what have you to say for yourself, you mutinous swine?'

'*This* —' Frenssen began, face glowing with rage, drawing back his ham-like fist.

'*Obermaat Frenssen!*' Christian's cool voice cut in and stopped the torrent of abuse about to erupt from the enraged petty officer. '*Kapitänleutnant* von Arco.'

Both of them spun round, startled. Christian stood there at the bottom of the ladder which led up to the conning tower, the spray dripping from his leather suit, his face calm, cool, and very authoritative.

Frenssen dropped his fist. Von Arco flushed even more. 'Did you see, Jungblut, what this insolent swine was about —'

Christian didn't seem to hear. Instead, he said, 'You off-duty men get to your bunks. That means you, too, Frenssen. *Kapitänleutnant* von Arco, may I have a word with you?'

Speedily enough the others turned, even Frenssen, and pushed their way to the bunks. Reluctantly, feeling somehow cheated of his fair rights at this moment when he had had full control over the big ox of a stubborn petty officer, von Arco came over to where Christian waited. At their instruments the operators pretended not to notice that von Arco had been foiled at the last moment, but their ears were pricked to hear what the skipper had to say to a suddenly crestfallen von Arco.

But Christian did not give them an opportunity to listen in. Instead, he commanded, 'Follow me, we'll go topside.'

Wordlessly he turned and began to clamber up the conning tower ladder, not even waiting to see if von Arco would comply. Reluctantly, sulkily, von Arco followed.

On the conning tower, its surface glistening in the silver light of the spectral moon, Christian wasted no further time. 'Von Arco,' he snapped, breath fogging in the icy night air, 'what you think of the discipline in this boat does not interest me one bit! I am skipper of this boat, as I have told you before. I am solely responsible for what goes on in her. So damn well keep your nose out of things, do you hear that?' He glared at the other man.

'But, Jungblut,' von Arco protested, 'the swine was being one hundred per cent insubordinate. Surely, as an officer yourself, you can't tolerate him behaving towards a fellow officer in the way he did? The officer corps must stick together. We want no second nineteen eighteen in the *Kriegsmarine*. Only the strictest discipline, even in the U-boat arm, will suffice.'

Christian looked at von Arco in that eerie silver light, as if seeing him for the very first time. 'Quite frankly, von Arco,' he said softly, but there was iron in his voice all the same, 'I don't like you. I have not wanted you on my boat from the very start. For me, you are just so much supercargo. In my book, *one* Frenssen is worth *ten* von Arcos, and just you remember that!'

Von Arco stared at him open-mouthed like a stranded fish, taken aback by the vehemence of Christian's attack, 'I — I — I —' he stuttered. 'I've never been talked to like that,' he blustered. 'You simply can't talk to me like that. I have the same rank as you... I have the confidence of the Grand Admiral himself. Why, in case anything happened to you, as you know, I was — am — to take over command of the U-200. It is a —'

The hollow boom of the explosion to the west drowned the rest of his impassioned outburst. Christian reeled back, feeling the blast slap him across the face. Next to him von Arco cried, perhaps in fear, 'What the devil is that?'

Shaken, Christian looked to the direction of the tremendous explosion. A flaming red ball was falling out of the night sky, the horizon beyond suddenly aflame, tongues of fire leaping upwards. He licked abruptly dry lips, trying to figure it out, before saying lamely, all passion spent now, 'Either our mission is succeeding, or —' He didn't finish the words. There was no time, for already he could hear, above the steady throb-throb of the diesels, the roar of high-speed engines approaching fast. Cupping his hands to his mouth, he yelled urgently to those below. 'Close up the gun crews! At the double now. Close up the gun crews... *Los, los!*... Here they come...!'

Like a sudden blotch on the silver sky, there it was, a small reddish cloud, half a mile ahead and below. One moment there was nothing; the next, in a flash, it was there, complete, ugly, and menacing. Savage pulled back the throttle. He hurtled forward, followed by his wingman, staring at the smoky, spark-laced trail of the missile, the smoky tendrils spreading out from its billowing maw.

'*Diving*!' he yelled over the radio.

'With you, skipper!' his wingman yelled back, R/T procedure thrown to the winds in his excitement.

Savage put the Spitfire into a dive. The missile grew ever larger. It seemed to fill the whole world; a long sinister metal monster, jetting scarlet flame. 'Don't get so close!' he cried urgently over the radio.

'But you're too close yourself, skipper!' his wingman protested with a gasp.

Savage laughed uproariously, carried away now by the thrill of the chase and lined the missile up in his sights. 'Here's to the next man to die!' he cried and began to hum that little mindless ditty that had become his talisman, his good luck charm, at such moments, 'Fee, fie, foe, fum … I smell the blood of — *an Englishman*!' He pressed the firing button.

The Spitfire jolted. The cannon blasted away. Glowing white tracer hurtled towards the doodle-bug. His cockpit filled with the acrid stench of burned cordite.

'Look out, skipper —' the wingman yelled in alarm.

Next instant the missile exploded. The Spitfire rocked alarmingly. Instinctively, Savage, veteran that he was, closed his eyes for a moment. When he opened them, he was hurtling through assorted ironmongery. With only the thin perspex cockpit cover to protect him, he flew on, watching with horrified fascination as pieces of glowing casing, cylinders, gear wheels, nuts and bolts whizzed past like some sort of strange and deadly flak.

The Spitfire shuddered. Savage held his breath. Was this it? Was he for the chop? Had he bought it *at last*? But the Merlin engine continued to sing sweetly and with a shudder, like a dog shaking itself after coming out of water, the plane flew on. He had done it!

'Skipper, sir!' the young wingman's urgent shout alerted him to the new danger. 'To port, skipper... There's the last of the bastards!'

Savage flashed a glance in the direction indicated. Yes, there it was; the same sinister flame as the killer robot headed for New York. He touched his mike. 'Got it,' he said and opened up the throttle. The Spitfire shot forward. 'We'll dive in from the quarter. Be ready to switch on your navigation lights, just in case Taffy is stooging around up here somewhere. We don't want any accidents.'

'Wilco, skipper,' his wingman cried excitedly.

The hum of the Merlin engine rose to a snarling howl, as he turned in a perfectly timed curve. Now he began to dive, face set and tense, animated by a primeval blood-lust. Lower and lower he hurtled. Now he could see the missile quite clearly.

More! Beyond it lay the twinkling lights of an un-blacked-out New York, spread out along the coastline like a string of glittering pearls. He whistled softly. 'Christ, I didn't realize that we were *so* close!' he said, talking to himself in the manner of all lonely men.

Now he was a bare three hundred yards astern of the flying bomb. Just the right distance. With his right hand he groped for the navigation lights switch, just in case, and flicked them on. To his right, his wingman did the same. He gritted his teeth, zooming in for the kill now. Nerves jingling, brain racing, he reached for the firing button.

'Tally ho, skipper!' his wingman yelled exuberantly.

He didn't hear. His whole being was totally concentrated on that ugly metal flying bomb in front. Now it filled his whole sights. In the blood-red glare of the engine flame, he could see every detail, even the rivets. He couldn't miss. *He dare not miss*! New York, wide-open and vulnerable, was only a matter of miles away. He had to knock the evil bastard out of the sky.

Calming himself by sheer naked will-power, breathing as slowly as he could, the cold sweat trickling down the small of his back, he pressed the button. *Nothing happened…*!

CHAPTER 5

The roar of the torpedo-boat's engines was tremendous. Its sharp nose high in the air, a huge white wave spurting high on both sides, it came racing in for the kill at 40 m.p.h. Suddenly it shuddered. Once … twice. The torpedoes slid neatly from their tubes, gleaming momentarily in the light before they hit the sea. Now twin arrows of destruction raced straight for the German submarine wallowing low in the waves. Laughing crazily, the American skipper flung his craft round in a tremendous burst of white, boiling water, in the same instant that enemy quadruple flak opened up, sending a solid wall of glowing white shells towards the torpedo-boat.

Christian flung up his glasses. There they were. A silver gleam of racing bubbles on the water, heading straight for the U-200. '*Torpedoes!*' he yelled frantically, above the mad chatter of the *Vierling* flak. 'Engine room — *hard to port!*'

Slowly, terribly slowly, the U-200 began to swing round. Now the torpedoes were almost upon them, as the American torpedo-boat, dodging the barrage of shells raced round in a triumphant curve, came in for the second attack.

'The bugger's missed!' Frenssen cried frantically, as the first torpedo hissed harmlessly by the U-200's bow. '*Now* —' His words were drowned by the smack of the second one ramming into the U-200's hull with a tremendous boom of metal striking metal, followed by the sound of steel being rent and torn apart.

On the bridge, Christian tensed. This was it! But as the enemy torpedo-boat came hurtling in once more, *nothing happened!* The torpedo had failed to explode! He ducked instinctively, as a burst of 20mm shell fire ran the length of the submarine. At the 88mm gun, one of the crew threw up his hands dramatically and fell over the side. Suddenly the air was full of the metallic stench of explosive and the paint on the U-200's hull began to hiss and bubble, puffing out in great obscene blobs like the symptoms of some loathsome skin disease.

Confident of its victory now, as the U-200 started to lose speed, the torpedo-boat surged in for the kill, bow cleaving the water at a tremendous speed, guns chattering. But the unknown American skipper had not reckoned with *Obermaat* Frenssen. Angrily, the big petty officer elbowed the sweating rating from behind the *Vierling* flak gun. 'Get yer yeller arse from that seat, sailor!' he cried above the roar of the enemy engines and the crazy thump-thump of the pom-poms. 'Let me take the bastards out!'

He sprang into the seat and swung the four long, air-cooled barrels round. Hardly seeming to aim, he pressed the foot pedal. The cannon erupted with fire. A solid wall of flak rushed to meet the attacker. Like great glowing golf balls, hundreds of them, the 20mm shells hurtled towards the American torpedo-boat. Frenssen could not miss. His shells raked the whole forward superstructure of the enemy craft. Masts and wireless rigging came tumbling down madly. The bridge disappeared, crumbling away visibly. The torpedo-boat staggered as if it had run into an invisible wall.

Startlingly, a white gout of glowing incandescent flame erupted from behind the shattered bridge. '*The gas tanks!*' Christian cried joyfully. 'You've hit the gas tanks, you big rogue!'

What followed Christian would never forget. Like a great blowtorch the flame seared right across the suddenly crippled, helpless, drifting craft. In an instant *Ami* sailors were afire everywhere. Insane human torches, thrashing at their burning uniforms with hands that were aflame themselves. Flames ripping, tearing at the soft human flesh, turning it into a black bubbling pulp, through which what looked like the rich red juice of overripe figs seeped.

Desperately some of the enemy sailors leapt overboard in an attempt to save themselves. But the water all around was on fire, too. Some tried frantically to swim for safety but in the end the burning petrol, spreading rapidly across the surface of the sea, caught up with them. They disappeared, their faces, tortured and tormented beyond belief, burning furiously.

Others simply succumbed, lying on the deck, with tracer ammunition exploding all around them in a kind of lunatic firework display, their flesh charring and shrinking by the instant, their spines arched like taut bows, skeleton arms, all gleaming ivory bone, flung upwards in a convulsive crucifixion.

Mercifully the great explosion came. One instant the torpedo-boat was drifting helplessly on the sea, burning from bow to stern; the next she had vanished, the only sign of her passing heaving white water and obscene bubbles of trapped air exploding on the surface — and the blackened ball which had once been a man's head bobbing up and down in the waves...

'Right, Ellis,' Savage snapped over the radio, 'it's up to you now, old chap.'

'Right ho, skipper,' his young wingman replied cheerfully. 'Will it get me a gong, sir?'

'A whole trayful, if you pull it off,' Savage said, with more confidence than he felt, as to their front the lights of New York seemed to fill the whole horizon and the damned doodle-bug plodded on stolidly towards its target. 'Off you go — and good hunting!'

'Thanks, skipper,' Ellis yelled excitedly. 'Over and out!'

Gently Savage throttled back as the dark shape of Ellis's Spitfire hissed by him in the silver gloom, heading straight for the remaining missile.

In a flash he had tightened up his turn and found himself almost vertically above the flying bomb, swinging from side to side to keep it in sight.

Savage tensed. Ahead of him, Ellis prepared to make his dive at the monster dragging its fiery tail behind it, as it came lower and lower over the water, heading for its unknown target. He bit his lip. If Ellis overshot and didn't pull out in time, he'd go straight into the drink. But that prospect didn't seem to worry the young pilot. Suddenly he jerked the nose of the Spitfire downwards sharply. At 400 m.p.h., he fell out of the night sky, roaring down towards the flying bomb until their collision seemed imminent.

Savage bit his bottom lip anxiously. Why didn't the young fool open up? Why was he taking such a risk? Carried away by the nerve-racking tension, he called helplessly, 'For God's sake, Ellis, open fire, man... Open fire now —'

Flame rippled the length of the Spitfire's wing. Angry violent flashes. Like a swarm of enraged red hornets, red tracer zipped towards the bomb. The fire never seemed to end. Ellis, Savage told himself grimly, had forgotten to take his finger of the button. Like all novices, he was concentrating on the kill and forgetting his own safety and the need to conserve ammunition. 'That's enough!' he cried. 'Pull out now, man. *Pull out* —'

Too late! Ellis was roaring down past the still undamaged missile, heading straight for the waters of the Atlantic.

'You're going into the drink… *ELLIS*…!' Savage's desperate cry turned into a moan as the Spitfire hit the crest of the waves, with Ellis frantically attempting to level out. To no avail. The whirling propeller beat the water into a frothy foam and carried the plane ever deeper. The tail-plane jerked upwards. An instant later it had gone altogether, disappearing beneath the freezing water, together with a trapped Ellis, leaving Savage alone with that sinister robot bomb… For what seemed an age, Savage simply flew his plane, too shocked to act, not even aware of the approaching city. How often had he seen a comrade go down like that, unable to recover because he was dying over his shattered controls or trapped by a jammed canopy, the plane which moments before had been his trusty friend, now his coffin?

But this time it seemed different. It was as if his system had suddenly at last revolted against the repeated exposure to risk of death which had gone on now year after year ever since 1940 and the Battle of Britain. It had always been inside of him — inside all of them — the secret enemy within. It was as if each fighter pilot had been granted a certain capital, a sum of fortitude, which he spent sooner or later. But when it was gone, life became a torment, with the spirit flogging a frightened, bankrupt body.

Abruptly his spirit felt drained. He seemed unable to confront the problem facing him so urgently and to take that overwhelming risk he knew he must take. His cannon wouldn't fire. He had excuse enough. Why carry on and chance his life? How often had he done that over England! Could anyone expect him to again in a foreign land, for people who were alien to him. *Hadn't he done enough?*

Now the awesome, jagged outline of New York was quite clear. If he had wished to do so, he could have picked out the various well-known skyscrapers individually, but as they came ever closer, he still wrestled with his problem. In a matter of minutes it would be too late to act.

What made him act then, no one ever learned for he was soon to die, body swept out to sea, never recovered, another victim of the war, fated to rot away beneath the surface of the Atlantic. Indeed, the only witnesses to what Squadron-Leader Savage, DSO DFC, did that Christmas Eve, 1944 were two sex-starved teenagers parked on the beach, grappling with each other's immature bodies in the backseat of an old jalopy, the girl fighting to keep the boy's hand from up her skirt, the boy desperately trying to find relief for the erection that tormented his loins…

Savage took the Spitfire down until he was flying parallel with the doodle-bug, both of them flying at about 300 m.p.h. just over the sea. Now he began to edge the plane ever closer to the missile, the sweat trickling down his face with the effort, as New York filled the horizon. Closer and closer. The tip of his own wing was almost touching the missile's stubby little right wing. He lowered his own slightly so that it was just under that of the missile. One mistake now and he would crash straight into the doodle-bug. He drew a deep breath, knowing it had to be now. He couldn't keep up this type of flying for much longer. Gingerly, very gingerly, he started to ease his own wing upwards. The sweat poured down his furrowed forehead. There was a slight jolt. He had touched the missile's stubby wing. Now the two planes were skimming across the surface of the bay, one pilotless, the other flown by a man at the end of his nervous tether, locked together in a lethal embrace.

Twice Savage prepared to execute the manoeuvre and twice his nerves simply wouldn't let him do so. Now he knew he would either have to carry it out or break away. Below he could dimly see the white breakers of the shore. In another moment it would be too late. There was a harsh grating. He felt the flying bomb resist. He exerted a little more pressure, doing so as delicately as he could. He knew just how volatile these damned flying bombs were. One wrong move and…

Suddenly the V-l began to turn. He felt his knees turn to water, all energy draining out of his body abruptly, as if someone had opened an invisible tap. *The bugger was turning round…! It was starting to head out to sea once again… He had done it—*

Startlingly, frighteningly, his Spitfire struck the side of the turning monster. He heard the wing crumple. The plane lurched violently to one side. In an instant, it was totally out of control. Savage fought to keep calm. He ripped back the canopy and felt the icy wind buffet him full-force in the face. Fighting the terrific G-force, he inched himself painfully upwards, ready to jump into the darkness. He still had height enough, and the shore was close. He *could* do it!

Tears streaming down his frozen cheeks, breath coming in hectic gasps, he clawed his way out of the canopy, engine dead now and propeller feathering, the only sound the hiss of the wind. He had nearly done it. In a moment he'd let himself fall out of the cockpit. Once clear of the dying aircraft, he could pull open the 'chute. 'Come on,' he urged himself. 'Come on, you old bugger! You're not for the chop just yet.'

Hadn't he done it before? In 1940 over the Channel. And again two years later over Occupied France and he had still escaped to tell the tale. Now he was going to pull it off over America. This would be a story to tell the chaps in the mess. It would be the granddaddy of all line-shooters. 'There I was chaps at six hundred, right over the ruddy coast of the US of A, when —'

The missile reared up in front of him. It filled the whole world. Sleek, sinister, shark-like, it hurtled towards him, as if it had an intelligence of its own and was determined to wipe out this mere mortal that had dared to challenge it.

'NO!' Savage screamed in terror, standing bolt upright in the cockpit, hands raised in front of his face, trying to blot out the monster with its fiery-red tail.

To no avail. The impact was awesome. Savage caught one last horrifying glimpse of the monster racing straight into his nose and then the world disappeared in a great, rending, red sheet of flame that seemed to go on for ever and ever…

Below the flaxen-haired boy gawped at the spectacle, the flame in the sky colouring the windscreen a blood-red. Next to him, the girl had frozen into shocked silence, mouth open like a stranded fish. He seized his chance. His cunning fingers slid up and under the elastic to find that delightful secret place he had been looking for all his young life. She did not even notice.

And three miles away, in the Hotel Taft, as the cheap bells tolled and the organist pulled out all the stops, the man who would soon control the destinies of the greatest power on earth rose from his piano stool and said, eyes gleaming behind the rimless spectacles, 'Boys and girls, I am now gonna ask Miss Bacall to sing that song which means so much to all us loyal Americans, especially on this Christmas Eve when so many of our boys are over there, in the Pacific and Europe, fighting for us far away from the ones they love.' He ran his fingers across the keys. 'Please join in with us — in — "God Bless America"!'

'Sweet Jesus,' the blonde with the dark parting whispered cynically to her friend. 'It'll be goddam hearts and flowers next…'

CHAPTER 6

Dawn!

A cold grey fog drifted in billowing damp clouds along the coast, clinging to the crippled submarine, muffling the sound its diesels made, dampening and muting everything in dreary sadness.

On the dripping cold deck, the men laid out the dead, placing them down like logs of wood. Numbly a waiting Christian stared at them, the victims of that surprise attack. Five young men, including the Number One, dead this Christmas Day, 1944 — for what? Solemnly Frenssen touched his hand to his woolly cap. 'We're ready, sir,' he said softly.

'Have you got the other bits and pieces, Frenssen?'

'Yes sir. I made levy on the crew. We've got enough of their duds to make it look as if the *Amis* did for us —' He stopped short and looked at the dead staring at the grey sky with sightless eyes (Christian had forbidden him to close them). 'But it doesn't seem right,' he faltered, 'that they should be tossed in the water, just like this, without even a word being said over 'em.'

On the shell-pocked bridge, the new Number One, von Arco, looked down at the big petty officer scornfully. As always he considered such statements as an expression of cloying German sentimentality.

Christian ignored von Arco, 'I know, old comrade,' he said a little wearily, not taking his gaze off the rolling fog bank. 'But perhaps in death they will help to save us all. All right, Frenssen, move — Oh, well, you know what to do.'

Frenssen nodded. He nodded to the nearest rating. 'All right, son, gimme a hand, will yer.'

Together they lifted the dead Number One and staggering under his weight trundled him to the side. With a grunt they heaved him into the water. A soft muted splash and up he came again, bobbing up and down in his life-jacket like some absurd human puppet. One by one the others followed. Then came the bits and pieces of uniform and personal possessions culled from the crew.

Christian looked up at von Arco. 'All right, Number One,' he said tonelessly. 'Now the bubble.'

Von Arco bent his head to the tube and rapped out the order. At the bow, the rusty paint now gleaming silver here and there where the enemy shells had struck it, there was an obscene belch and a moment later a huge bubble of compressed air and waste fuel oil exploded on the surface. Rapidly the oil started to spread outwards on the gentle waves, embracing the five dead men bobbing up and down in their life-jackets. Slowly, very slowly, Christian raised his hands to the brim of his battered cap in salute. Behind them, as the submarine limped on through the fog, the corpses rode the wake as if they might well do so for eternity.

Five minutes later Christian addressed the crew in the shambles of the interior, his words punctuated by the sound of hammering as the riggers attempted to patch up the damage made by the second torpedo. 'Let us be quite clear about our situation, comrades,' he announced. 'It is every man's hand against us now until we reach the Gulf of Mexico. At the moment luck is on our side. The fog is providing us with the cover we so desperately need. But it won't last for ever. The closer we get to the south, the more likely it will disappear and expose us. Our only hope is that by that time the *Amis* will have given up the search for us.' He paused and looked around their pale solemn faces and realized suddenly that his greenbeaks had aged overnight. Their faces were now those of grown men, worn and worried — men who had been through hell. 'I will say only this one last thing to you,' he added carefully. 'We have carried out our mission to the best of our ability. I think the Fatherland can expect no more from us. If the situation arises where it is either be sunk or — er — surrender,' he glanced around their faces in the dim green-glowing light, 'then I shall surrender the U-200. That is all. Dismiss.'

Frenssen shot von Arco a swift look. His face had suddenly set in a look of absolute evil as he stared at Christian. Frenssen read that look as if it were an open book. Von Arco would not surrender. He wanted to return home to 'cure his throatache' and receive the homage and acclaim that his arrogant vanity demanded. Now he would sooner see Christian dead than surrender. Frenssen licked suddenly dry lips. There was murder in the Number One's eyes at this moment...

So the crippled U-boat limped down the American coast, hugging the many bays and inlets, protected day after day by that beautiful wet thick fog. Time and time again the anxious, red-eyed look-outs reported aircraft droning above them, but the fog always saved them and in the end the planes invariably vanished, cheated of their prey. Once, too, a frightened look-out had reported ship's engines to the west. Hastily they had manned the guns, every man tense and afraid, waiting for the first crash of cannon that would open the U-200's final battle. But again the fog had saved them and after an agony of waiting, the sound of engines had died away, leaving them drained and exhausted.

In this strange limbo, cut off from the world, for Christian had ordered the strictest radio silence, the U-200 sailed down the eastern seaboard of the United States, progressing at a steady eight knots an hour. New York State gave way to Virginia, and in its turn, Virginia with its many naval bases, slipped to stern and they were crawling down the coast of the Carolinas, with the weather improving dangerously all the time. In the end, just before they reached Charleston, the fog disappeared altogether, burned away by the southern sun.

They found a secluded cove and while those off duty lounged on the deck, their bodies naked, soaking up the hot sunshine, the duty men worked with canvas and wood to transform the battered U-200 into what might appear as a coastal tramp steamer to anyone, as Frenssen commented sarcastically, 'who's blind in one eye and has never seen a ship in his whole shitting life!'

With the canvas rigged the length of the hull and with a dummy wooden funnel stuck in the blocked-off conning tower — they had even rigged up a stove to produce smoke from it, if necessary — they limped on steadily, ever southwards. Christian, hollow-eyed and weary beyond description by now, for he had slept less than six hours in the last three days, could not believe their luck. Here, with presumably the whole of the US Atlantic Fleet searching for them, plus the massed squadrons of the US Navy, his battered old boat seemed to be making it, within hailing distance of the enemy shore.

'Nobody should have such luck, Frenssen,' he commented, as the two of them, hidden by the canvas now enclosing the conning tower, enjoyed the hot Georgia sunshine, the breeze wafting in from the shore bringing with it the warm rich smell of tropical vegetation. 'We've been sailing off the coast of

America now for five days and still have not been spotted.' He laughed in a hollow, shaky way.

Frenssen grinned and rubbed his stubbled chin. 'Weeds never die, sir,' he said happily. 'That fellow up there, sitting on the cloud, playing his frigging harp —' he poked a dirty thumb at the cloudless tropical sky — 'is saving this poor old sailor man for them señoritas.' He sighed. 'D' yer know, sir. It's been so long, I don't know whether as not I'll be able to find it agen — the gash, I mean.'

Christian shook his head in mock wonder. 'That'll be the day, Frenssen, that'll be the day...'

On New Year's Eve, 1944, the U-200 crept through the Florida Strait between the Bahamas and Miami, steering due south of Key West, fringing Cuba and into the Gulf of Mexico. It was Christian's intention to take the shortest route across the Gulf, aiming at the Yucatan Strait, and the port of Merida. He reasoned that although Mexico was neutral, the United States, her powerful neighbour, might put pressure on the Republic to return the U-200 to the States if he docked her further north at Tampico or Monterrey, closer to the American frontier. Yucatan Province, he knew, was suitably remote and backward, far from Mexico City. Whatever happened to the U-200 later, the German Embassy might be able to spirit her crew out of the place and ensure their return to the Reich before the American authorities were aware that they were even there.

That evening, while just to port Key West celebrated the last day of the old year, the U-200 began to creep around the place. Trimmed right down to show the minimum of silhouette, the crippled U-boat edged its way around the dark smudge of land. Christian ordered the electric motors on to avoid noise and wash. So at five knots they began to creep into the Gulf of Mexico.

Christian had ordered the strictest sound control. Talking was to be kept to only the most necessary orders and those of the crew who had to be on deck wore plimsolls to make no sound on the steel casing. Nervously the crew went about their duties, while on the conning tower Christian and von Arco, constantly searching the soft velvet horizon with their night glasses, listened to the sound of dogs barking on the land and the occasional roar of a car engine, all carried out to sea by the off-shore breeze.

Time passed leadenly. Even the greenest of the crew knew just how vulnerable they were. It took only one lone tuna fisherman to spot them, or the rays of the lighthouse there on the point to sweep across the poorly camouflaged U-200 and all hell would be let loose. Here in the narrows they wouldn't have a chance in hell. They couldn't dive and they couldn't make a run for it. It would be either fight it out to the end, or surrender.

Now it was midnight. Over the land fireworks started to zoom into the night sky to explode in a profusion of bright multi-coloured stars. The Spanish-speaking population were celebrating the advent of 1945 in their own way. Now and again they caught snatches of drunken singing, too, as if the locals had staggered out from their bars and cafes to toast the New Year with songs.

'What a people!' von Arco snorted softly. 'How can such a nation command greatness or even respect? Pity our poorGermany if it were ever conquered by such decadent peasants!'

'Perhaps they are just happy,' Christian commented equally softly, suddenly feeling very lonely and envious.

Von Arco did not seem to hear. 'Such people do not deserve victory,' he hissed fervently. 'Why, their war is being fought in bars and brothels and not on the battlefield.'

Christian grinned to himself and imagined what Frenssen's reaction would have been to that particular statement. *He* would have dearly loved to have fought *his* war in those self-same places.

The minutes ticked by tensely. Now the sound of fireworks and singing was beginning to fall behind them. With them the land started to disappear, too, vanishing into the warm silken darkness of the tropical night. Christian began to feel a little easier. They were almost into the Gulf and he reasoned that the Americans wouldn't overly patrol this stretch of almost inland water. Any German U-boat venturing into it, they would think, would have a devil of a job getting out again, so why bother?

Lulled into a false sense of security, perhaps fuelled by the weariness of having been at sea now for over a month, Christian day-dreamed a little, wondering what Mexico might be like. His concept of South America was based on the old pre-war UFA movies, set in that never-never land, full of dashing *caballeros* and dark-eyed willing señoritas, who carried roses between their pearl-like teeth. He sighed. How good it would be to get away from the war even only temporarily! God, what he wouldn't give for a hot bath, a change of underclothes, and a soft, soft bed, where he could sleep for days, weeks? He yawned lazily. Beside him von Arco frowned, feeling that cold flame of hatred inside him flicker once again. How easy Jungblut's conscience must be! Always in this long war, the young handsome swine had come out of all the tight spots he had been in smelling of roses. Now, it seemed, he was going to do it again. Another twelve hours or so and they would be in the safety of neutral waters. Then the official embassy machine would take over. The U-200 would have to be impounded, of course, but Jungblut and his crew would be quietly smuggled back to Europe in due course. Once again he would have escaped the just retribution for what he had done to Kuno, his brother, back in 1941. Why, soon the war could end with a German victory and Jungblut would go on to be a respected hero, an idol of the recreated post-war German Navy, while he and his dead brother would disappear into obscurity. It wasn't fair. Was the swine going to escape after all? *Was he?*

Christian stared at the starry vault of the tropical sky and drew in yet another great draught of good clean air. After the oil-laden stench of their underwater prison, fresh air seemed the most precious gift of all. He thought of his poor sailors for a moment. All of them were lousy, of course, and suffering from skin diseases, their cheeks a greenish yellow, with dark circles under their eyes, so that they looked, young and fit as they were, as if they were in the last stages of consumption. What sufferings they had undergone since they had left Danzig in what seemed another age now. They richly deserved the landfall soon to come and what modest pleasures the obscure provincial Mexican town could offer them before the war took them over once more.

Thus it was, with the two of them wrapped up in a cocoon of their own thoughts, the one in hatred, the other in anticipation of the good things to come, that they did not hear the sudden burst of engine power until it was too late. Then the tracer shells were streaming towards the U-200, creeping along the surface at a snail's pace, like glowing angry golf balls, and the battered submarine was reeling under that first fearsome impact…

CHAPTER 7

'*Alarm … alarm … ALARM!*' Christian shrieked desperately, as the U-200 reeled under the impact of another salvo of tracer shells.

Abruptly all was controlled chaos in the U-boat. Whistles shrilled. Petty officers bellowed orders. The gun crews scrambled for their weapons, as their attacker came racing in, cannon chattering crazily.

At Christian's side, von Arco brought the boat round, bellowing out his orders furiously. He was trying to present the smallest possible target for the attacker racing towards them on a collision course.

'She's going to ram us!' Christian yelled wildly above the sudden burst of fire from the *Vierling*. 'Destroyer … ramming. For God's sake, hard to port… Do you hear me, Number One… *HARD TO PORT!*'

A burst of furious fire swept the length of the deck. The 88mm gun crew were wiped over the side as if swatted by some gigantic hand, shrieking and crying out in their sudden agony. Fist-sized, red-hot shrapnel hissed everywhere. Just in time Christian ducked behind the conning tower. The shards of steel struck it like tropical rain on a tin roof.

Next instant he was up again, as the U-200 swung round painfully slowly. Now the enemy destroyer was almost upon them. A white bone in her teeth, her sharp prow sliced the water with savage fury. In a moment more, that steel beak would crunch right into the U-boat.

Another salvo of shells hit the U-200. She reeled alarmingly. From below there came shrieks of agony. 'Medics … medics!'

someone yelled piteously. 'Oh, my frigging leg … *medics*!' On the deck a look-out, his chest ripped open, his ribcage gleaming like polished ivory against a scarlet background, clawed the air with his frantic hands, as if he were climbing an invisible ladder. A moment later he went over the side. Now the deck of the U-200 was occupied solely by the dead and dying.

Desperately, Christian, feeling utterly impotent, waited for the collision to come. They couldn't escape this time. *They couldn't!* But Christian had not reckoned with the resourcefulness of Frau Frenssen's handsome son. Down below in the forward torpedo room, already ankle-deep in water, shutting his ears to the moans and cries of the wounded, Frenssen worked feverishly at tubes one and two. Single-handed he prepared them for firing, without orders.

'Forward torpedoes — to Captain!' he gasped over the tube, still making final adjustments to the great lethal 'fish', hands bloody and covered in grease, 'Tubes one and two ready for firing, sir.'

'But you are unauthorized —' von Arco began.

Christian pushed him to one side. Swiftly he rapped out a bearing. The enemy destroyer was less than six hundred metres away. They had only a matter of seconds left. The torpedoes were their last chance of staving off doom. He waited impatiently as Frenssen made his adjustments. The destroyer was coming in for the kill now, forward cannon chattering frantically. He could wait no longer. '*Fire one … fire two!*' he yelled desperately.

The U-200 shuddered. There was a hiss of compressed air. A second time. A flurry of bubbles at the bow. And then the two deadly fish, both bearing one and a half tons of high explosive, went hurtling through the tropical sea towards the destroyer.

The racing destroyer grew to fill the whole world as Christian counted off the seconds, shells exploding all around him, making the U-200 reel with the impact time and time again.

Suddenly the American destroyer swerved. They had spotted the torpedoes! It heeled hard to starboard. For an instant, its superstructure seemed to touch the water, as the skipper flung the craft round in a mad turn to avoid the fish.

The first one hissed by her harmlessly. Christian swallowed hard and prayed like he had never prayed in his whole life before. The U-200 was badly damaged. He knew that instinctively. Perhaps she was already sinking. If they didn't stop the *Ami* this time, they would get no second chance. That second torpedo *had* to stop her!

Crump! There was a rending, a tearing, a ripping of metal, followed by a loud echoing boom that seemed to go on for ever. A great ball of evil yellow flame exploded towards the stern of the destroyer. The solid steel folded like soft tin. For a moment, an awed, gaping Christian could see her screws quite plainly, raised out of the water by that tremendous blow, thrashing the air purposelessly. With a thump they struck the sea once more and the destroyer came to a stop, water rushing into the hole torn by the torpedo by the ton.

'We've hit her!' von Arco shrieked hysterically, his cap gone, bright red blood trickling down the side of his fanatical face from a wound in his temple. '*We've hit the bastard*!'

Christian slumped back against the battered conning tower, hardly daring to believe the evidence of his own eyes. The American destroyer, her stern already deep in the water, had come to a stop, dark smoke spurting from her funnels, as though her boilers might have been damaged too. Faintly he could hear the cries of alarm and pain floating from her, as she wallowed there, suddenly weak and impotent.

Von Arco swung round on Christian, as from below came the whimpering of some grievously wounded man, punctuated by the sobbing of someone in quiet hysteria, 'Jungblut,' he gasped, as if he were running a race, 'we've got her! It'll be our final triumph before we make Mexico!'

Christian raised himself and looked momentarily at the bloody shambles of the U-200's deck, a mess of fallen cables and the 88mm gun twisted in a grotesque shape, its barrel shorn off, a gleaming silver. 'What did you say?' he asked dully, his voice seeming to come from far, far away.

'I said, we've got her!' von Arco yelled, as if he were talking to a deaf man. 'All she needs is the *coup de grâce* and we'll sink the *Ami* swine!' His eyes glittered like those of a man demented.

Christian shook his head weakly, eyes puzzled, as if he simply could not take in what von Arco was shouting. Below one of the crewmen was beginning to whimper, 'Mama, don't let me die!... *Mutti, ich will nicht sterben*!' Tears welled up in Christian's eyes at that piteous cry. 'Oh, my God,' he whispered huskily, letting his head fall in utter despair, 'what have I done to the poor young things...?'

Von Arco looked at him slumped there, head hanging, contemptuously. 'Well, damn you, Jungblut!' he said venomously, his full hatred of the man who had killed his brother finding its expression at last. 'Are you going to act? Or am I going to have to act for you?' He drew himself up to his full height, as over at the crippled destroyer, tiny figures began to throw carley floats into the sea and there was the rattle of winches as lifeboats were hurriedly lowered. 'Your day is over, Jungblut,' he declared proudly. 'You've had your run. Now it's the turn of someone else.' He posed there heroically, hand clasped to the pistol at his waist.

Christian, crouched there, stared at him numbly, the horror of what was happening dulling his brain, seemingly unable to comprehend what the other man was saying to him. 'How … what?' he stuttered, as on the sinking destroyer the ship's sirens started to sound 'abandon ship'.

'I'm taking over command of the U-200, Jungblut!' von Arco snapped. 'Do you hear that? You are totally incompetent to command. *Kapitänleutnant* Jungblut,' he said very formally, 'you are herewith relieved. Now get off my bridge — and out of my damned sight!'

Again that blind rage burned through his posturing and in that instant he almost jerked the pistol out. He calmed himself the next moment, hastily, for he knew he would have killed the handsome swine facing him blankly if he had not. But he must not let that act of revenge spoil his plans. '*Do you hear me?*' he demanded, face set in an arrogant sneer, as he took in just how broken Jungblut was at this moment. 'Get off my bridge, I am in command of the U-200 now!' He bent to the tube. 'Aft torpedo room,' he commanded, 'prepare to fire three and four tubes. At the double now!'

'Tubes three and four,' the distorted voice of the petty officer below came floating up, 'readying, sir.'

Proudly, von Arco flung up his glasses. Now he was every inch a U-boat commander, his head full of wild dreams of glory, as he stared at the dying ship, the sea around her already full of bobbing heads and floats. Steam was escaping with a roar from her ruptured boilers and on the bridge, dark figures ran back and forth, as she tilted at a crazy angle to port.

'Get away,' Christian croaked, slowly breaking out of this strange reverie which was imprisoning him. 'Make steam, while we've still time… They'll be radioing for help soon…'

Von Arco did not seem to hear. Instead he lowered his glasses and snapped into the tube, 'Are you ready, petty officer?'

'Ready — three and four,' came the reply.

Von Arco rapped out the bearing and cried, 'Prepare to fire.'

'*Von Arco* —' Christian cried desperately in the same instant that a heavy machine-gun on the sinking destroyer opened up. Von Arco screamed shrilly as the smoking tracer bullets ran the length of his body. Suddenly scarlet blood was jetting from a myriad wounds and his face had been transformed into a horrifying red jelly.

'*Von Arco*!' Christian cried again and put out his hand to help the dying man.

Savagely von Arco knocked away his hand. 'Get away from me, you bastard!' he snarled in a strange bubbling voice, pink foam mixed with blood flecking what was left of his mouth. He reached up with his shattered stump and tried to wipe the blood away from his wrecked face. But he couldn't. The stump wouldn't function. He staggered against the side of the conning tower and suddenly a horrified Christian realized that the last burst had blinded him. 'Point me in the right direction, Jungblut,' he gasped. 'In the right direction. Must sink her now…'

Aghast Christian stared at von Arco's face, which looked as if it had been first flayed with a whip and then roasted on a kitchen spit, as the former staggered from bulkhead to bulkhead, desperately fighting to find the voice tube. '*Tube*,' he croaked. '*Got to find the tube…*!'

Six hundred metres away, the stricken American destroyer heeled even more. Now her shattered radio mast and wires were trailing in the water. On the bridge, all activity had ceased. She was sinking fast. 'There's no need, von Arco,' Christian said gently, 'she's going under already.' Again he put out his hand to restrain the dying man.

Savagely von Arco thrust away his hand with the stump, thick red blood arcing from it in a stream. 'Got to sink her … *Just got to sink her* —' He sank to his knees, still fighting death to the very last, whimpering in a kind of trapped animal despair. '*Got … to … sink …*'

Now the US destroyer was going under fast. There were cries and shouts. Steam escaped with an explosive hiss like an express train racing through a station. All around her the sea heaved and boiled, as if greedy to receive her. Someone was singing crazily. But Christian only half-heard the dread sounds of a ship sinking. Now he knew what he had to do. He stared down at the mutilated horror crouched there on the blood-soaked littered deck, moaning and muttering in a crazy unintelligible babble. Slowly, very slowly, his hand fell to his pistol. There was no other way out for *Kapitänleutnant* von Arco.

As if mesmerized, acting on the instructions of some higher being, Christian drew out the pistol and cocked it. At his feet von Arco swayed back and forth, spilling great gobs of blood on the deck, muttering to himself crazily. Christian brought up the pistol and took aim. Six hundred metres away, the US destroyer slid under the surface of the sea in a sudden flurry of wild water, disappearing in a flash; and abruptly there was silence broken only by the faint cries of the survivors.

Christian didn't hear. His whole being concentrated on the dying man kneeling in front of him, as if in submission. Indirectly he had killed Kuno von Arco. Now he was fated to do the same to Johann. He felt neither pity nor anger. He was an empty shell, drained of all emotion. The von Arcos of this world mattered no longer. Quite casually almost, Christian pressed the trigger. The pistol jerked upwards, but he couldn't miss at that range. Von Arco uttered a soft little moan, afterwards Christian often fancied it was one of relief. Slowly, very slowly, he sank back against the bulkhead and died...

Thus it was that Frenssen found them. The red-topped horror leaned against the bulkhead looking almost as if it had simply dozed off, and Christian, pistol hanging from nerveless fingers, staring at the man he had just killed, with two glistening tears trickling slowly down his exhausted face.

He looked at the sea. It was empty now. The Americans had drifted away or were sailing and rowing for the shore of Key West, a faint smudge on that velvet horizon. Calm and peace had returned to the tropical night, the sky studded with a myriad silver stars. From the land a warm gentle breeze wafted the scent of some exotic flower or other. The horror had passed at last.

'Skipper,' Frenssen said with surprising gentleness for him, quietly releasing the pistol from Christian's nerveless fingers, 'I think ... it's time to ... go home...'

ENVOI

Relentlessly the midday sun beat down on the shabby waterfront street, with scrawny chickens scratching away in the dust and skinny-ribbed dogs lounging in the shadows, panting and long-tongued. Even the two bare-foot Mexican soldiers guarding the wreck of the U-200 leaned against the conning tower, grateful for the shade, rifles slung carelessly, eyes closed, seemingly asleep like the rest of this shabby provincial town. For it was siesta time and the Mexicans had fled the heat.

Not the survivors of the U-200. They lay naked in the hot rays, their skinny pale bodies covered with sores and lice-bites, rapidly turning lobster red; or they dashed in and out of the bright blue water, capped by the brilliant white rollers, shouting excitedly diving into the sea time and time again as if they could not get enough of it.

'Like frigging schoolkids let out for their holidays,' Frenssen commented, as he and Christian relaxed under the straw umbrella, sipping their weak Mexican beer.

Christian smiled lazily, feeling the beautiful heat even through the straw, telling himself he had never felt so at ease since 1939. As long as you had a few pesos, life in Mexico was easy, too easy. One could grow accustomed to it. 'That's what they are, aren't they, Frenssen?' Christian answered slowly, taking another drink of his ice-cold *cerveza*. 'Look at them. Not one of them is older than twenty.'

Frenssen nodded, telling himself the skipper was right. These last few days in Mexico had done wonders. The deep lines of suffering that had been etched in their faces during that long horrific combat patrol had vanished. They had softened out.

The tension had vanished from their eyes. Once more they *did* look like overgrown schoolboys.

Across the plaza, there was the rattle of wooden shutters being drawn up. The siesta was slowly ending. 'Sounds like the knocking shop's opening up for business agen,' Frenssen said, feeling with his free hand to check whether he still had any money left. For five pesos, the price of a packet of *Juno Eckstein* cigarettes back in the Reich, he could have one of the full breasted teenage whores from the interior. Ten would buy him a girl for the night — and a bottle of *tequila* thrown in for free.

'Haven't you had enough?' Christian queried, looking at the rusting, shell-battered wreck of the U-200, telling himself she would never sail again. She'd probably end up in some Mexican scrap yard. 'You've been at it like a damned fiddler's elbow ever since we got here, Frenssen!'

'Don't begrudge a poor old sailor man his simple pleasures, sir,' Frenssen said in a mock whine. 'Precious little he gets out of life, 'cept his pipe o' baccy, glass of suds now and again, and a bit o' the old pearly gates once a year.' He looked craftily at Christian.

Christian grinned and clicked his fingers at the unshaven waiter behind the bar, dozing among the flies and *bocadillos*, and said, '*Dos cervezas mas, por favor, camerero.*'

'*Sí señor*,' the sleepy waiter took the toothpick from between his teeth, flicked weakly at the flies with his dirty cloth, and reached in the ice bucket for two more beers.

'You're getting to speak the lingo all right, sir,' Frenssen said a little cagily, and drained the last of the beer.

'You're doing all right yourself, you big rogue. Beer, food, and women, you can find them all right.'

'The language of love is international, sir,' Frenssen said airily, but his look still remained cagey.

Christian knew the hulking petty officer of old, so as the waiter banged down the dripping bottles of ice-cold, fizzy beer, with a routine '*a su servicio, señores,*' he said, 'Come on … spit it out!'

'I was just thinking, sir,' Frenssen appeared to be reluctant.

'Well, think out loud!'

'It's pretty nice here, sir. Even on the poor pay that Grand Admiral Dönitz, in his infinite wisdom, deigns to give his Lords, just enough to whet their appetite, but not enough to spoil 'em —'

'You're getting as long-winded as the Mexes,' Christian cut him short, 'pee or get off the pot, you big-horned ox!'

'Well, sir, it's not a bad life here, is it?'

Christian nodded, face suddenly turning sombre and thoughtful, as if he already half-knew what Frenssen was going to say.

'The living's good, better than most of us have had in many a day.'

Again Christian nodded, but remained silent.

'So, sir, what's the hurry?'

'You mean, to get back to the Reich?' Christian snapped, looking at him sharply.

'Yessir. We all know that Germany is on her last legs. We've lost the battle in the west and we're about to lose it in the east. The Anglo-Americans and the Ivans have got us with our dong in the wringer and all the wonder weapons in the world won't save us now.' He looked hard at Christian. 'Why not just sit it out here in Mexico till the shit stops flying, then we can think of going back to the Homeland?'

Christian pursed his lips and Frenssen, his old comrade, could see that his mind was racing, as he considered the suggestion. The skipper knew that the Mexicans wouldn't and couldn't force them to go back to Germany. Nor could those warm brothers of the embassy in Mexico City. All they could do was advise. Of course, some of their relatives back in the Reich might suffer, but by the time it came to that, the war would be over and the Gestapo would be running for cover or making noises as if they were washed in holy water. Their situation was perfect. They were free men, able to come and go and do as they wish without any compulsion from above, or anywhere else for that matter.

'I know, what you mean, Frenssen,' Christian said slowly, as if he were considering each word he spoke very carefully. 'Germany is about finished and nothing short of a miracle can save us now — and I, for one, don't believe in miracles. It would be, therefore, the easiest thing in the world to sit out the rest of the war here, with sun, suds, and señoritas, as you might put it.' He gave an attentive Frenssen a brief wintry smile. 'But I don't think we should.'

'Why not, sir?'

Christian didn't reply at once. Over at the brothel, they had wound up their ancient gramophone and now 'La Paloma' wafted seductively over the still hot air. He thought of the young armaments officer — what was his name now? — languishing in a Gestapo jail, perhaps even dead; the two lesbians, again dead; and all the rest of them who had been killed in this crazy, bitter war, even von Arco, blind and hideous, and in the end a pathetic figure of compassion. What was it all about? Shouldn't a sane man simply drop out and leave the madmen to continue their purposeless, senseless destruction? But then, he realized suddenly with a sense of resignation, that he, too, belonged to the madmen.

'You know the old saying, Frenssen?' he said wearily. '*Mitgegangen, mitgefangen, mitgehangen.*' ('*Gone with, caught with, hanged with*')

Frenssen smiled a little. 'So we're going back?'

Christian nodded. 'Yes, we're going back. We're Germans. For better or for worse, we've got to take what's coming to our poor people, too. There's no escape…' He looked across that limitless expanse of glittering blue sea, as if he could see that crazy wasteland beyond, with its death and destruction.

Over at the brothel that sad seductive song had become stronger. Frenssen felt in his pocket again. There was only five pesos, he realized, left.

'No escape, sir?'

'No.'

Frenssen downed the beer in one swift gulp, mind made up. 'I've only got five pesos left, sir. Can you lend me another five?'

Christian shook his head, as if he were trying to wake from a deep sleep. 'Another five?' he asked a little stupidly.

Frenssen grinned at him and rose to his feet. 'For a poor old beaten-up sailor man, there is *one* escape, sir,' he said.

Christian grinned. 'Of course.' He took the cheap little coin from his pocket and flipped it to the big petty officer. Frenssen caught it neatly and with a mumbled, 'See you tomorrow, sir,' he was gone.

Lazily, Christian clicked his fingers at the sleepy waiter for another beer and settled back. There was still time…

A NOTE TO THE READER

Dear Reader,

If you have enjoyed this novel enough to leave a review on **Amazon** and **Goodreads**, then we would be truly grateful.

Sapere Books

Sapere Books is an exciting new publisher of brilliant fiction and popular history.

To find out more about our latest releases and our monthly bargain books visit our website:
saperebooks.com

Printed in Great Britain
by Amazon